Oh to Grace

OH TO GRACE
Copyright © 2013 by Abby Rosser

Published by VisionQuest, an imprint of DemmeHouse, Inc.
All Rights Reserved.

No part of this book may be reproduced or transmitted in any form or by any means, electronic, or mechanical, including photocopying, recording, or by any information storage or retrieval system without permission in writing from the publisher.

This book is a work of fiction. All characters, places, and incidents, except for references to public figures, are the product of the author's imagination and are fictitiously used. Any resemblance to actual persons, events, or locations are entirely coincidental.

ISBN: 978-0-9835246-1-8
Library of Congress Control Number: 2012950247

Printed in the United States of America

ALL SCRIPTTURE QUOTATIONS UNLESS OTHERWISE INDICATED ARE TAKEN FROM THE KING JAMES VERSION AT WWW.BIBLEGATEWAY.COM.

For more info, visit http://www.demmehouse.com.

COVER IMAGE CREDIT
Virginia Moss

BOOK DESIGN
Inline Graphics

AUTHOR PHOTO
Cogknitive Images

Oh to Grace

ABBY ROSSER

VisionQuest

For Evelyn Rosser

Thank you for welcoming me as your granddaughter-in-law
and sharing a lifetime of stories.

Acknowledgments:

When I originally wrote OH TO GRACE, it was seventy-five pages devoted to a story told to me by my husband's grandmother. Over several years it transformed into this novel. This transformation would have been impossible without the encouragement and support of so many friends and family.

I am grateful to a number of dear friends who read it for me—in some cases, more than once. To reduce the risk of leaving someone off my list, I will create an amalgamation of their names: Thank you Melvarabonathinawnstillemarizee! If you read my manuscript find a portion of your name and know how grateful I am to you!

I am *always* grateful for my sisters, Carrie and Becky. Your humor and love continues to shape me into an author who strives to write about why these relationships make us quintessentially human and exceedingly interesting. Extra thanks to Becky who faithfully reads the entire newspaper—even the obituaries—every day. If not for this diligence, I would have never known about the open call for new authors that brought me to DemmeHouse publishing.

Thank you to Bre Jackson of DemmeHouse for giving this stay-at-home mom a chance to live out a dream come true. I'm also indebted to you for introducing me to Jan Ackerson whose editing expertise refined OH TO GRACE and whose encouragement made me feel like I could do anything.

Thank you to Brent, my husband and best friend. I am the luckiest girl in the world! I still can't believe I get to fall asleep every night holding your hand. In your trademark matter-of-fact way, you've said "why not?" every time I've doubted myself before taking a new step. Thank you for being a great dad to Ella, Lucy, Knox, and Ezra. You're their hero and mine!

I am so grateful to be a part of a family who loves to tell stories. Listening to my husband's four grandparents relive their early lives in small towns in Kentucky and Tennessee has opened my eyes (and ears!) to the realization that everyone has a story.

I am blessed to think that the Creator of the universe and His Son, "the author and perfecter of our faith," both love a good story, too. For this reason and due to the fact that I can accomplish nothing good apart from my Lord, I am most grateful for a Savior who daily saves me with His never-ending supply of grace.

Prologue

Amelia hadn't seen another car on the two-lane country highway for fifteen minutes. She did see a tractor coming from the opposite direction, but the driver had turned down a rough road before she had reached him. Never one to enjoy visiting elderly relatives, she had known about this assignment for weeks but she had put it off. Now that she had a Saturday with no plans and no excuses, she made the drive to the nursing home.

As she turned into the parking lot, Amelia thought about seeing her Grandma Genny that last time. She had spent her final years in a nursing home much like this one. Remembering the smells of antiseptics and wet beds still made Amelia's stomach turn. She also remembered how confused her grandmother had been and Amelia wondered if she would be able to get the information she needed today.

She pulled into a parking spot and cut off the engine. After rummaging in her backpack in the front seat, she found and removed her tape recorder. She pressed RECORD and spoke into the microphone:

Testing. Testing. It's November 3, 2012 at 9:30 a.m. I'm sitting in the parking lot outside of the Dogwood Meadows Nursing Home. I've come here to interview my Great-Great Aunt Frankie. My mom told me that Aunt Frankie is a big talker so I've brought a recorder. This one has ... two hundred hours of recording space—I hope that'll be enough. The assignment from my creative writing teacher is to find an elderly relative and ask him or her questions about growing up. Then we're supposed to compile all of our information into an essay that shows (sound of rustling papers)—and I quote—"a common thread throughout the narrative." I've got a list of questions here but to start with I'm going to ask her if there's a memory from her childhood that she thinks about every day. Then we'll see where that takes us. Okay, I've got my coffee and my notebook. I've got to get this done before Thanksgiving break so…I'm going in. (click)

Chapter 1

Nobody in town could re-sole shoes like my daddy. Many a time I remember him comin' home late of an evenin' on account of that sweaty pile of shoes and boots in the back of his shop. Daddy always said that Nadine Henderson could make a pair of shoes last longer than what you'd think was humanly possible. She did wear a ladies' 11 ½ extra wide, so you could hardly blame her for keepin' 'em a good while. Why, she had to drive clear down to Nashville to get them big shoes! Anyhow, Daddy was workin' at pryin' up her cracked outsole when Little Jack came tearin' in. He banged open the door so hard he knocked off the little brass bell that hung just above the header and it skittered across the floor like it were scared, too. I jumped off the barrel where I was sittin' and pullin' tacks off some old work boots. I scattered them bent tacks all over the shop, he scared me so. Daddy hollered at him and told him to speak up, but Little Jack could only stand and breathe hard. I still remember his big white eyes and his ribs pokin' out the sides of his overalls. We was stuck to the floor, waitin' for him to talk and then the words he spoke were like a bucket of ice water in my face. He said, "Mister Frank... he dead... yor boy... is dead."

Oh to Grace

MORGAN'S HAT, TENNESSEE
OCTOBER 10, 1936

Matt had pitched hay since he was first able to walk. Left hand gripped above the right. Dig deep, swing high. He knew the rhythm of the motions like an experienced swimmer knows his strokes. He was a hard worker, but his mind wandered easily. He would allow his natural grace and athleticism to direct his pitchfork so he could think about the girl in town with the upturned nose and curly brown hair or the truck he was fixing or any other ideas that floated into his mind.

Lining the outside wall of the barn, there were tidy bundles of hay made during the hot, dry months of late summer, and Matt's job today was to move the last of the old hay from the loft to make room for the new. With one final scoop, he heaved a forkful down just as the barn door opened and a shadowed figure entered.

Matt heard an unfamiliar cry of bewildered irritation. This was not one of his seven younger brothers or sisters who he had just cloaked in dry straw. This was a woman's voice—young, most definitely annoyed. Matt slid down the ladder, his bare feet clutching the smooth sidepieces. In an instant, he was brushing hay off a young woman's shoulders. She was in her early twenties, wearing a pale yellow dress dotted with yellow and green flowers. The dress had stylish puffed sleeves nearly as high as her chin and a nipped-in waist, flattering to her petite figure. Perched on her head was a lime green hat, bowl-shaped and perfectly suited for catching each tiny twig of hay. Matt couldn't help but think she looked like some sort of autumnal queen with her golden crown. She noticed his amused expression as he regarded her hat, so she quickly took it off and slapped it against her leg. Her red hair spilled out of its hair pins, leaving unruly curls all about her forehead. One curl danced in front of her right eye. Matt was so struck by the force of her beauty and the afternoon sun streaming through her burnished curls that it took every bit of willpower for him to stay his desire to touch that red coil.

The young woman blushed, her cheeks coloring nearly the same degree of red as her hair. "I'm Anna, Ernest's wife," the young woman declared as she held out a small, white hand by way of introducing herself. "You must be Matt."

Matt was struck dumb by her words. Sunlit dust swirled around them both. Was he standing in the eye of a tornado or still on the bleached pine floor of his father's barn?

"Ernest has told me so much about you," Anna said politely, with her best city manners. Matt stared at the small piece of straw glued to her red lips for what seemed like an eternity until he collected himself enough to speak.

"We didn't 'spect ya'll 'til tomorrow," he said slowly. "I'm awful sorry 'bout mussin' up your clothes…Anna."

Matt hadn't intended to say her name just then, but with a pause, two syllables, and a warm rush, his words for this redheaded stranger held more meaning and emotion than all the conversations he'd had with the girls in town in his entire life.

"I told Ernest that I wanted to walk a little," Anna mumbled, two hairpins between her teeth as she attempted to fix her tousled hair. "Maybe I should get on back to the house. Your mother said if I saw you I should tell you to come in and wash up for supper."

"Yes'm," was all that Matt could say. As they began to walk toward the house together, Anna introduced several awkward topics for conversation.

"Do you like working on the farm?"

"Yes'm."

"Ernest said he mostly worked with your father fixing shoes growing up. Do you ever do any shoe repairs up at the shop?"

"No, ma'am."

"Ernest seems to like his job. He said you're the one who got his truck running. Do you like fixing trucks?"

"Yes'm."
"What's that growing on the far side of the garden?"
"Pumpkins."
"They're awfully big. Are they hard to grow?"
"No, ma'am."

Their awkward, lopsided conversation continued in this manner all the way to the house, consisting mostly of Anna asking questions that Matt would answer with a shy, brief reply. As they approached the back porch, Ernest swung open the screen door to meet them. He advanced on Matt with a firm handshake and an arm proudly gripped around Anna's waist.

As they stood facing each other, any observer would see two brothers with different physiques and tastes in fashion. Ernest wore a thin moustache perfectly resting on his upper lip. His hair was oiled to a fine sheen that complemented his dark eyes and lashes. He was several inches shorter than Matt, with a slighter build. His charcoal suit pants were neatly tailored to show off his trim lines. Looking at his brother, Matt realized that Ernest had made a calculated effort to impress his family, and as his mother beamed at Ernest, he realized that the effect was working.

"Good to see ya, Ernie," Matt said as he pushed his way through the group to enter the house. As he passed his mother, she nodded in the direction of the wooden stand just inside the door, where he saw a pitcher of water and a faded blue towel. His grimy appearance must have seemed more obvious than usual, compared to this prodigal in his Chicago clothes.

With his long legs, Matt took quick strides to reach the room he shared with his four brothers. He splashed cold well water on his face and dried it on the towel, which was now more brown than blue. Then he used the towel to wipe down his chest and arms. He ran a wet comb through the golden hair on top of his head and used his fingers, then his palms, to smooth down the browner sides. He put on a shirt and his other pair of pants, and suddenly wished he had a mirror. If he had seen his reflection, he would have noticed a muscular man of almost thirty, tanned from spending the summer in the fields. He would have paused to notice how different his eyes were from those of his brother Ernest—his pale blue to Ernest's deep brown.

With no other reason to stay indoors, Matt finally re-emerged from the house to join his family. Even before he reached the door, he could hear the laughter that always accompanied one of Ernest's visits.

"No, Anna, he's not dangerous. He's just…"

"Dumb as a bucket of rocks," George, age twelve, piped in.

"George, you hesh up. You know that Rufus Haskell can't hep how he is," said Momma.

"He just spends most of his days mowing the medians down by the square," Ernest continued. "It'd be helpful to the city if his push mower had a blade in it!"

Ernest's southern drawl was still evident, but five years in Chicago had cleaned up some of the country words and phrases from his vocabulary, like the basket in a percolator sifts through the coffee and leaves behind the grounds. Matt imagined all the *y'alls* and *reckons* sitting there at the back of Ernest's throat, waiting to be used, when he realized that Ernest was addressing him.

"Matt, tell the one about Rufus and Miss Bennie Lee," said Ernest. "Anna, you'll get a kick out of this one."

"Nah, Anna doesn't wanna hear that…" Matt mumbled.

Shy as he was in public, in his family circle, Matt was known as the entertainer. He had a natural musical ability and he was an excellent storyteller. He could amuse his younger brothers and sisters, especially George, Frankie Jane, and Della Mae, for hours with tales both true and fictional. Though unaccustomed to having a stranger present during story time, Matt eventually cleared his throat and began the story.

"Well, it seems ole Rufus was pushin' his mower down by Vine Street, when he saw he'd gone off 'thout his belt. He kep a-pullin' his trousers up and pushin' that dang mower and stoppin' to pull his trousers up again. He'd put on his daddy's ole trousers that morning and everybody knows that Big Daddy Rue was so big it was easier to go over him than go 'round him. Anyhow, Rufus walked over to the school to see 'bout getting some rope to tie up his britches. That just happened to be Miss Bennie Lee Waddle's first day of teaching. She grew up in Alabama and had never been, well... formally intr'duced to Rufus Haskell. He walked up to the window closest to the teacher's desk and pounded his fist on the glass. Miss Bennie Lee was scared nigh out of her stockins by this rough-looking bag of bones. She yelled to him, 'What d'ya want?' thinking he was a-comin' for her pocketbook. Rufus yelled back, 'I's needin' some rope—'bout dis long.' Right then, Rufus held up his hands to show the length of rope he was a-wantin' and he dropped them britches down to his toes. Poor Miss Bennie Lee fainted clear away and hit her elbow on the side of her desk on the way down. When the children came in for school that morning, they found their new teacher a-sittin' on the floor and cryin' like a newborn baby."

Though most of them had heard the tale many times, by the close of Matt's story they were all wiping their eyes and holding their sides from laughing. Only Anna retained her composure. She was unacquainted with this folksy kind of humor and considered certain parts of the story to be inappropriate.

"That poor woman," she said, as much to herself as to anyone listening.

"Miss Bennie Lee?" said Momma, "Oh, she got over it mighty quick. We've got some real char'cters in Morgan's Hat." She affectionately patted Anna's hand. "Gad night a-livin'! I'm out here a-jawin' with you younguns and your daddy's gonna be home and hungry 'nuff to eat the south end of a northbound skunk."

The screen door slammed behind her. Frankie Jane, not quite

nine years old, used the change in subjects to begin her interrogation of Anna. She liked to tell stories just like her oldest brother Matt, but there was a definite difference in how they collected their material. Matt would sit back and silently watch people to form his stories, and Frankie Jane liked to interview them, often to the point of intrusion.

"Anna, Della Mae and me wanna know 'bout you. We heard you and Ernest met up in Chicago, but is that your home? I mean, where did you hail from?"

Oh to Grace

Chapter 2

Chicago
1923 & 1929

Anna was like a big sister to me and Della. Not at first, mind you...at first she was a little uppity. Momma and Daddy took to her just like white on rice, though. I reckon she made Momma think of her Clara. In fact Anna and Clara had the 'xact same birthday. They would-a been the same age if Clara had made it past three. You know what? I hadn't thought about Anna's first visit to Morgan's Hat in years. She just changed so much. When we met her—they was just newlyweds—she seemed to love Ernest so pow'rfully...but, you know, he could make a dead woman blush. He was what we used to call a tomcat. He knew how to treat the womenfolk. It didn't hurt none that he looked just like a movie actor. But there was somethin' between him and Anna that wasn't your ordinary married love—it was like she was holdin' on to him for dear life, and he petted her like a prize puppy. Anna's face would just start a-glowin' when she looked up at him. Reminds me of a paintin' I once seen in Memphis of a man named Tom

Lee. He saved a bunch o' people from drownin' when their steamboat sank. He couldn't swim but he kept a-rowin' back to get more people. The painting was of a girl lookin' up at Tom Lee as he pulled her into his rowboat. That's the look I sometimes saw on Anna's face. It made me feel a mite strange to see it—like we never got the full story 'bout her.

SISTERS OF SAINT REGINA HOME FOR GIRLS, CHICAGO
SEPTEMBER 21, 1923

Anna sat in the front row of the silent classroom while Sister Jeanne-Marie perched behind her desk, facing the girls. The Sister was unusually tall and thin, with a narrow, beak-like nose that began its descent down her face between her eyebrows. Anna secretly imagined Sister Jeanne-Marie spreading out her long arms with the draping sleeves of her habit hanging at her sides, making her look every bit like a somber black stork. This was one of the many daydreams that crept into her head unbidden during the quiet times of the school day. She never shared these thoughts with a soul. If Anna had been braver, she might have kept a diary, but she was afraid of who might get hold of any incriminating evidence. How this would be incriminating, Anna was never quite sure, but she tiptoed around the Sisters of Saint Regina for fear of breaking any unknown rules.

There was a scratching of pencils as the girls completed their geography tests. The map at the front of the room was draped with a white sheet, in case one of the girls with exceptionally good eyesight was able to read the European capitals and use this information on her exam.

Sitting at their desks with heads bowed in concentration, the girls looked relatively identical. All of the girls at Saint Regina's orphanage wore the same uniform: laced-up black boots, long navy skirt, white blouse with pressed round collar, and navy cardigan. Anna liked the predictability of the uniform.

With the beginning of another school year, she had been given a new set of clothes. Sitting at her school desk now, Anna slowly bent her ankles. She enjoyed the satisfying *squeak* of the leather of her new boots. This was her fifth new set of fall school clothes from the sisters. Her first set came when she was five, four months after her arrival at Saint Regina's. She was nine now, and life in the orphanage seemed like all she had ever known.

Looking down at her test, Anna spied Germany. She filled in the appropriate capital and then paused to listen to the music class next door. The teacher was simultaneously teaching and playing the piano, and Anna heard her say, "Girls, this is Chopin's Berceuse Opus number fifty-seven..." The high notes tinkled like bells down the octaves as the low notes kept a steady beat. Anna listened to the soothing lullaby until it ended. Then a vague but recurrent memory tried to surface; a beautiful face with brilliant golden hair came into her mind as she studied the map on her test. The vision was accompanied by the pulsing sound of a phonograph cylinder starting to spin and then a moment of thundering music. The face always sank back into a black fog before Anna could focus on it. When it disappeared, she reflexively glanced at the faded scar on her hand. These thoughts always confused and disturbed her.

Anna shifted her eyes to France, assuming this would conjure up more pleasant thoughts. Most of the sisters at Saint Regina's were from France, so the lessons concerning their homeland were delivered with great pride and passion. Sister Jeanne-Marie was from Verdun. She often described the picturesque beauty of the Meuse River that flows through the city under stone bridges and past turreted buildings. Then she shared in hushed tones about the battle against the German forces that killed most of her relatives. The war had ended less than five years ago and was still an ever-present part of most of the sisters' prayers. "Ah... *André*..." Sister Jeanne-Marie let slip once before snapping back to her more professional teaching demeanor. *"Et ils sauront que je suis l'Éternel, Quand j'exercerai sur eux ma vengeance,"* she quoted easily. "Irene, translate for me this passage from the book of Ezekiel."

Irene had shyly stood by her desk and said, "And they shall know that I am the Lord...when I exercise my vengeance upon them." She looked up for approval, then lowered her eyes and took her seat.

"*Bon*! That is correct," the sister had replied with relish as she wiped a stray tear from her cheek and re-assumed her full, towering height. Anna shivered slightly and wondered about this mighty Lord waiting with thunderbolts of vengeance to rain down on the Germans who had no doubt killed Sister Jeanne-Marie's *André*.

"*C'est fini,*" tweeted Sister Jeanne-Marie. Anna pulled her thoughts back from the events of the previous class and scanned her paper. All of the girls laid their pencils down and passed their tests to the front of each row. After collecting them, the Sister stacked the papers on her desk and stood by the long blackboard. There were three framed pictures hanging along the top. The first was a black-and-white headshot of President Harding. The second was a painting of Jesus, praying earnestly in the garden before his death. His hands were pressed together as he looked desperately into the heavens. The last portrait was of Saint Regina—the orphanage's namesake. She was a shepherdess from the third century who refused to denounce her celibate lifestyle and marry. She was eventually tortured and beheaded by her would-be betrothed. Anna always thought that the painting of the pretty saint—with the round cheeks and smiling eyes—looked like Sister Genevieve, one of the younger sisters at the orphanage. In the painting, Saint Regina wore a brown tunic and a hood that looked soft, like lamb's wool. She had her hands together in prayer, too, but without Jesus' look of despondency. Anna struggled to understand how Sister Jeanne-Marie's vengeful God, the suffering Savior in the painting, and the righteous virgin saint could all be working toward the same end. The Sisters' faith remained a mystery to Anna, but asking would admit doubt. It was easier to attend Mass, pray the right prayers, and memorize the scriptures the Sisters laid out for them.

"I have a new photograph to add to our wall today, girls," said the Sister as she removed the photograph of the president. "As you all know, President Harding died last month when he took ill on a cross-country trip." Sister Jeanne-Marie lifted a new, framed photo from her desk and hung it in President Harding's vacant spot. "And as with every tragedy, we face it and move on. So...this is President Calvin Coolidge."

Anna looked at the new black and white photograph of another balding man with lackluster eyes and joyless expression. She wondered if the three pictures represented adulthood: suffering and sacrifice or bland monotony. It didn't seem to Anna that being an adult held much happiness.

The end-of-class bell rang and the girls exited the room, single file. At the same time, Sister Genevieve was leaving the classroom across the hall where she taught French. She turned to Anna and smiled. She was the only one of the nuns from Saint Regina's who smiled easily and with regularity.

"*Bonjour, Anna, ça va?*" asked Sister Genevieve. Her brown eyes twinkled even in the dim stairwell.

"*Oui, ça va,*" answered Anna, softly. Several Sisters passed by them and glowered faintly. Most of the Sisters enforced a strict code of silence in the hallways. Sister Genevieve was more lax about this rule, as she was with many others.

"I am needing your help in zee sewing room. It would take but a few moments?" said Sister Genevieve in her lilting cadence. Whether she asked a question or not, at the end of every sentence, Sister Genevieve's voice swung up slightly, a chorus of tinkling bells to Anna's ears.

"Yes, Sister." Anna's heart fluttered. She was thrilled to be given a special responsibility by her favorite teacher.

Anna followed the Sister down a flight of stairs to a large

room with three long rows of sewing machines. Each sleek, black machine sat on a wooden table with a wooden chair scooted neatly beneath it. Though empty, the room still smelled of hot rubber from the bands that kept the wheels whirring on the sides of the machines. Stray threads wafted up in gusts and then settled on the wooden floor as Anna and Sister Genevieve passed each table.

"Did you remember all of your European capitals?" she said with an endearing imitation of seriousness.

"Yes, Sister. I hope so."

"As long as you remembered Belgium, you have no worries." Sister Genevieve winked and squeezed Anna's hand.

"Brussels?" asked Anna.

"*Bon!*" said Sister Genevieve.

The Sister picked up a box of rags and cast-off clothes and set it on one of the tables. "Mother Angelique asked me to examine zees box zee church collected and see what can be given away to zee poor," said Sister Genevieve. "Let us make *deux* piles. *Une* for zee poor families and *une*..." She picked up a dirty, threadbare shirt and tossed it on the floor. "*Une* pile for zee garbage."

Anna and Sister Genevieve worked together silently for a few minutes, adding to their piles.

"Sister, may I ask you a question?" Anna asked, timidly.

"Of course. What is on your mind, *ma petite princesse?*"

Anna asked, "How did you decide to become a nun?"

The sister smiled and stopped working for a moment. "My father was a very famous artist in Belgium. When fighting began with zee Germans, he sold all he could and bought us tickets to come to America. He took ill on zee ship and a few months later, he died."

"Oh, Sister, I'm sorry. I shouldn't have asked..."

"It is all in zee past, *princesse*," she said, soothingly. "Mama took in washing and did what she could to help us, but she too died, almost a year later. I had no one, so I came to Saint

Regina's looking for help. I was sixteen. I could only live in the orphanage for a few more years but Mother Angelique—*me Secourir*—taught me how to be a teacher and here I stay!" she said with triumph. "To teach sweet young ladies like you, Anna."

"I wonder...do you ever want to leave Saint Regina's?" Anna's real question was: *What is so frightening out there that we should want to stay forever inside these walls?* But she was too afraid to find out.

"Living in Belgium and when I first come to America, I am like most any girl. I like pretty clothes. I like to read books." Sister Genevieve whispered," I even have *un petit ami*."

Anna was shocked. "A boyfriend? Really, Sister?" Sister Genevieve giggled as if she was sixteen again.

"His name was Gil. I met him at zee Art Institute. We spent many afternoons together looking at paintings and sculptures. But when mama died, he could do nothing for me, so we say *au revoir*." A pained expression cut across the sister's face and Anna knew not to press the topic.

Anna returned to her task. After a moment, she lifted a small doll out of the box. It was entirely made of cloth, with yarn for hair and small black buttons for eyes. It looked very old, but it was in good condition—nothing was torn or mismatched. Anna stood holding the doll for several seconds, turning it slowly in her hands as if it were a rare and priceless relic from some ancient civilization, until Sister Genevieve said, "Would you like to keep it, Anna?"

"Sister?"

"The doll. She looks like she is needing a good home. Do you have any dolls?"

"No...but...may I?" Anna hugged the doll to her chest, feeling maternal devotion and responsibility—new emotions, but welcome.

"*Oui*. Zat will be your payment for helping me with zee box." The Sister placed all of the items that they had deemed worthy of distributing in the now-empty box. As she lifted it, the petite Sister stumbled slightly under the weight.

"Sister..." Anna leaned forward to help hold the box.

"I am fine, *princesse*. Zee dust is making my head spin." Sister Genevieve placed a hand on her forehead, a line of perspiration blossoming along her hairline. "Maybe I will lie down until my next class."

Anna carried the box to the door. "Thank you...for the doll," she said quietly after she placed the box outside of the sewing room. The Sister gave her a smile and walked unsteadily toward her cell.

Chapter 3

For years before Anna came along, Della was my only sister. Though I'm shamed to say that you wouldn't 'spect I liked her much on account of the way I treated her when we was young. There's only two years 'tween Della and me—twenty months to be exact—so you'd think I wouldn't have been able to get away with trickin' my little sister much. But she was 'bout the most gullible creature God ever made from dirt! Take the time our Aunt Hattie sent us gifts for Christmas. I was 'bout six so Della was four at the time. I'm pretty sure both the gifts was hand-me-downs from her grown children, but it was smack in the middle of the Depression, so gettin' any kind of present was somethin' special. I remember Della got the most beautiful doll—she called it Honey. Aunt Hattie's first husband worked in a doll factory in Louisville and that's where Honey was made. She had a hard, painted face with painted-on blue eyes and a little pink smilin' mouth. Her arms and legs was made of cloth and she had little stitched boots and brown hair painted to look like a Marcel wave. She was really somethin'. Me, on the other hand, I got a box half full of Tinker toys. I always thought Aunt Hattie confused me with the boys—bein' that my name

was Frankie—but then I knew for sure. I was so jealous of that doll, I couldn't hardly see straight. One day, Della was playin' with Honey out by the road and I decided to play a trick on her. I walked right up to where they was and I said, "Oh, Della, what happened to Honey?" She looked at me real odd and said nothin' was wrong. Then I commenced to talkin' 'bout Honey's bad colorin' and clammy forehead until I had Della believin' Honey really was sick. I worked all day on her like that and by afternoon I had Honey takin' her last breath. We gave her a real nice funeral and buried her right by the mailbox. When we come back in the house for supper, Momma asked why our fingernails was so dirty. Before I could stop her, Della told Momma we buried Honey. Momma knew in a wink I was to blame and she had me go and dig Honey up. We never did get her all the way clean, but that didn't stop Della from lovin' that old doll. She changed her name to Lazarus 'cause I told her it was a miracle and she was raised from the dead like Jesus' best friend. It's funny what we get attached to. Sometimes it don't make no sense. I reckon that doll made Della feel safe or somethin'. Maybe it was on account of the fact she never had another doll and she was tryin' to hold on to the only one she ever got.

SISTERS OF SAINT REGINA HOME FOR GIRLS, CHICAGO
SEPTEMBER 6, 1929

Her muslin dress was two inches too short and thinning at the elbows, but Anna stood tall and proud by her well-made bed. She cupped her right hand over her left and pulled in the fingers of her left hand—something she had done since she was a child—to conceal, as much as possible, the long, pink scar on her palm. She threw her shoulders back, like a cadet ready for inspection. She had learned early how to earn praise from the Sisters. "*C'est bon*," they would say with a nod and continue with their morning inspection in their sweeping black robes.

Then she would work hard at her chores to search out even more praise. Years of following rules had convinced Anna that her worth came from striving for perfection.

Anna was almost fifteen. Would anyone remember that tomorrow was her birthday? When Sister Genevieve was alive, she would look for any excuse to slip Anna a wrapped piece of candy or a small cookie to celebrate a special day. The thought of this sweet young woman quietly pressing a gift into her hand made Anna's back bow slightly. Sister Genevieve was the one who had held her as she cried for her mother on that first day. She had been the one to bathe Anna for the first time in months. Anna had been four and Sister Genevieve had been a teenager. Anna scolded herself for not learning more about her. She sighed as she imagined her birthday meal: stewed cabbage and watery gruel.

Sister Genevieve would have winked and told the girls in her most formal-sounding French that their meals were *la cuisine minceur*, food for staying thin. There was little joking in the orphanage now. The rooms were overcrowded with girls whose families could no longer afford to feed them. So many parents were unemployed and financially devastated in Chicago. It became a point of pride for some girls to claim that they weren't actually orphans; their mothers would soon return for them. Anna might have been able to make the same claim, but she was wary of questions. From the little she had heard from the Sisters—when they thought she wasn't listening—it didn't sound as if her mother would ever be back.

Along with the other older girls, one of Anna's responsibilities was to keep the younger ones in line. She silently walked down the stairs, head held high, always mindful that she was an example to them. A few of the new girls thought she was stuck-up, but she was just adamant about following the Sisters' rules. The muted gray and brown sea of girls' dresses made for jostling waves down the stairwell toward the dining hall. This was a change from the breakfast routine of the past. The new girls were unfamiliar with the idea of decorum and threw elbows whenever a girl merged in front of them. Anna knew this firsthand; she had the bruises to prove it. At the bottom of the stairs, she overheard Mother Angelique speaking in hushed French just inside her office.

"*Comme il faut,*" she said sadly. "What a shame."

Anna leaned in to hear more, just as Sister Bernice pushed her toward the door with the other girls. "*Allez, mes petit filles! Allez!*"

Anna wondered what the sadness in Mother Angelique's voice meant. She felt panic rising. What if some of the girls had to leave? What if *she* had to leave? The overcrowding of the dormitories was often suffocating, but she knew little else than what was inside these walls.

After one of the Sisters said grace, they all sat down on benches at the long tables. Bowls of boiled rye flour that the Sisters called *bouillie* were placed before them. Anna set the bowl to her lips and tilted it back. Swallowing it in one gulp was the only way to finish it. The Sisters imposed a strict policy about silence during meals. They wanted the time to be used for prayer and meditation, but Anna used this time to worry and chew the dry skin on the side of her lip as she looked around at her tablemates.

Across the table was Irene; she rubbed her red eyes incessantly, as if she hadn't slept well. She desperately needed glasses that the Sisters would never be able to give her, so Irene mostly kept to herself as she gradually became more invisible. To Irene's left was a set of twins about five or six years old. They were dully moving their spoons in the gruel with little intention of eating it. They were new to the orphanage. Anna silently scolded them for wasting their breakfast and smirked as she thought how soon enough they would be gulping down anything set before them. Dorothy was seated next to Anna. She had oily hair and a drawn face. Though at seventeen she was the oldest girl at the orphanage, she looked middle-aged. Dorothy absentmindedly picked at a sore on her arm.

The seat on the far end of the table was empty. This was normally reserved for Elise—the closest thing Anna had to a best friend. Elise was only a few months older than Anna, but she acted as if she was her senior by many years. She had come to the orphanage when she was ten, full of stories about the outside world. She and her mother had lived above a run-down furniture shop that was a front for an illegal bar. Elise claimed to have met Jake "Greasy Thumb" Guzik and other gangsters in the Chicago Outfit. She lived to shock Anna.

Two new girls whispered and giggled until Sister Bernice slapped the table with a yardstick. Anna jumped. Red-faced, the girls stopped talking and half-heartedly turned back to their breakfast. *Who are these new girls?* thought Anna. Looking around, she realized that many of the girls in the orphanage were thin, nameless figures to her. All of them had the sallow cheeks and cloudy eyes of undernourished children. Anna felt too numb to care about each one; she was overly occupied with her own concerns. How long could she hold off turning eighteen, the age when the girls had to move on? She simultaneously longed to leave the orphanage and to stay forever. Her instincts told her that the monotony and numbness of this place was not actually living, but she felt ill-equipped to face a world that seemed to hold only more worries and dangers.

Her mind leapt back to Mother Angelique's voice in the stairwell. Who had she been talking to? Why had she seemed so hesitant to heed whatever command or suggestion had been given to her?

As if she had read Anna's mind and her need for answers, Mother Angelique entered the dining hall and walked directly to Anna. "Anna, come with me, *s'il vous plaît*," she said with a warm whisper in Anna's ear.

Anna followed her to her office. Though she had been there

many times, she felt the weight of the heavy curtains and dark furniture pressing down on her this morning. Mother Angelique sat in her chair and shuffled through some papers on her desk. Then she began in a direct voice: "Anna, it is time for you to leave Saint Regina's. There is a movement to break up the larger orphanages and move some of the girls into cottages just outside of the city."

"Oh, Mother Angelique! I'm just fifteen. Don't you think some of the other girls..."

"I do not have confidence in many of these girls, but I know that you will do well. I am sending you to a home run by a good, Christian woman named Mrs. Sanders. She will teach you some skills and provide for you. I ask you to remember all that the Sisters have taught you, say your prayers, and mind your manners."

At this point, Mother Angelique finally looked up and met Anna's gaze. "Mrs. Sanders has asked that you be sent at once, and I see no reason to object. Go and pack your things." Anna fought back tears and her knees shook; she was afraid she might stop breathing at any moment.

"*Dieu vous bénisse, ma petit fille,*" Mother Angelique said this simple benediction softly, betraying an emotion that Anna had never seen in her. Mother Angelique had been given a directive—place the older girls or lose funding—so decisions had to be made quickly.

Dismissed to the hall, Anna took the long way back to the dorm rooms. As she walked past the silent row of classroom doors, she shivered. The silence felt ghostly—like an abandoned town. She imagined herself growing up in these rooms—sitting up straight, raising her hand to answer the Sisters' questions, passing in the countless tests that she didn't need to have checked because she knew all of the answers were correct. She felt betrayed by the realization that her blameless character had been her undoing after all. Perhaps if she had struggled with her chores more and fought with the other girls, Mother

Angelique would have kept her close at hand.

Anna climbed the stairs to gather her few belongings. In the dorm room, she spotted Elise, packing her things into an old carpetbag. "Are you leaving, too?" Elise asked.

Anna nodded and wiped a tear on her sleeve. She stacked her second dress, a nightgown, and a few undergarments on her cot. On top of these she laid an ancient-looking rag doll. She tied the entire bundle with a piece of twine, then stood looking at the doll through a blur of tears as she remembered the afternoon she had spent with Sister Genevieve. Anna sighed deeply as she pulled on her faded navy cardigan. Dejected, she dropped to her cot.

"I couldn't be leaving this place any sooner," Elise sneered. "No more porridge and praying for me. No sirree! I'm going to live with some lady named Mrs. Sanders."

Anna looked up, hopefully. At least she would be with someone familiar. "That's where they're sending me, too," Anna squeaked.

"It won't be so bad," Elise reassured her. "Mother Angelique said that Mrs. Sanders has a typewriter and will teach us how to be secretaries. Just you wait and see! Before you know it, we'll be able to get jobs and do whatever we want."

They carried their things downstairs to the foyer and waited for Mr. Johnson to take them to their new home. Elise chattered on without stopping, only waiting now and then for Anna to nod. She talked of grand times that she and Anna would have, but Anna's thoughts turned again to Sister Genevieve.

She had seen her both the first time and the last time in this exact same spot in the foyer. Her earliest memory of the sister was a secret from the others. No one knew that Anna had hidden away a few recollections of her first moments at Saint Regina. Actually, they were only pieces of memory: the sound of her crazed mother screaming, the feeling of a warm bath, and the taste of hot soup made of chicken and rice with chunks of carrots and celery. These memories were hers alone. She wasn't even sure if they were real, but she folded them neatly and stored them inside.

She never spoke of that night. Nor did she disclose to anyone how she felt the last time that she had seen Sister Genevieve—when her favorite teacher had been taken away. Of course, no one ever asked her how she felt anyway, so these feelings and facts were safe from discovery. Sister Genevieve had struggled with bouts of illness for years. The other Sisters told the girls that she had weak lungs, and asked for their prayers. Finally, after Sister Genevieve had labored with a high fever for several days, Mother Angelique had submitted to the Sisters and called a doctor, who recommended that she go to the hospital immediately. Anna had stood, rooted to the polished wooden floor and holding the doctor's hat for him in the foyer while he examined Sister Genevieve. Then Anna had returned the hat to the doctor as he left, leading the way for Mr. Johnson, who carried the Sister to a waiting car. Though Sister Genevieve had been terribly frail, she gripped Anna's hand with a surprising firmness as Mr. Johnson brushed past her. "Anna, à Dieu vat!" she said with a hoarse whisper.

It's in God's hands, thought Anna cynically, recalling the Sister's parting words. As she waited for her ride, Anna leaned against the long windowpane next to the heavy oak door of the orphanage, her cheek pressed against the cold glass. Contemplating her departure for the unknown wilds of the outskirts of Chicago, she wanted to ask Sister Genevieve: *If God's hands can hold us, why couldn't he hang on to you tighter?* With questions marks looming in her future, Anna didn't see Sister Genevieve or herself or anyone else in the hands of a caring, mindful God, but spinning without plan or purpose in a world where only the strong survive.

"Here's the car," Elise squealed, pulling Anna out of the doorway. Anna took a look back at the place she had called home for ten years—more than half her life. And now she was leaving without a hug or even a wave good-bye from the Sisters.

All her memories before age four being spotty, these serious and secretive women were the nearest she had to a family. Now she feared that she would be completely on her own.

Anna looked down at the cloth doll tied up along with the only things she owned. For the first time, she wondered why she had never given it a name. She slipped it out from the under the twine and dropped it on the ground before getting in the car. Anna felt a shifting in her life, an almost imperceptible tremor.

Oh to Grace

Most children today have plenty o' dolls and toys, I reckon. I know my grands have got heaps o' playthings—most they never get 'round to doin' much with. Extras weren't that easy to come by when I was growin' up. I got my first job when I was fourteen and I made twenty-two cents an hour. I was real good at arithmetic, so I kept the books for Mr. Padgett down at the grocery store. He used to tell me, "Frankie Jane, if Adell was as quick as you with numbers, I'd let her keep my cash drawer any day." Adell was his daughter and my best friend, but she couldn't add two plus two. Anyhow, I was still livin' with momma and daddy back then, so I could save up most of my wages. I'd buy fabric real cheap and I'd have a dress done up in one evenin'. I tried to help out my parents—you know, they had so many children—but by the time I was old enough to bring home anythin', most of the boys was moved out. It was just me and Della and George by then. I was the knee baby and that was a kind of puzzlin' place to be. I wasn't the baby—that was Della. But I wasn't a boy, so I couldn't tell nobody what to do. I always knew they loved me, but I also felt I had to get them to look on me as a real useful person.

Oh to Grace

That's all a person really wants, you know, to be loved and to have a job. FDR said, "Happiness lies not in the mere possession of money. It lies in the joy of achievement." I guess I was always lookin' for that kind of happiness. Heaven knows, I didn't find it by addin' up a column of dry goods for Mr. Padgett, but havin' a job was kinda like havin' direction.

CICERO, ILLINOIS
NOVEMBER 19, 1929

Anna soon learned that Mrs. Sanders wasn't above using her position as a "cottage mom" to her advantage. She was a resourceful widow with three daughters of her own, and when she heard that the city would pay her $16.50 every month for each orphan she took in, she saw a golden opportunity. She and her daughters had been paying their bills by distilling whiskey in their cellar at night. They mostly slept during the day, making deliveries difficult. With more helpers, they would be able to increase their output.

When Anna and Elise had been at their new home for less than a week, they began their shifts in the sweltering cellar. Mrs. Sanders led them down the rickety wooden stairs into a small room carved from chalky limestone. Anna's job was to keep the pot that held the milled grain and water boiling, while Elise frequently checked the copper coils and poured the condensed alcohol into barrels when the jars were full. The heat and late hours made Anna drowsy, but Mrs. Sanders forbade them to sleep. "You'll burn the whole house down if you don't pay attention to your duties, girls," she said. She allowed them to leave the small outside door open while they worked, so they wouldn't pass out from the fumes.

The girls never asked questions about the whiskey. With Elise's background, though, she could fill in any details about speakeasies and gangsters. "I'll bet Al Capone will be drinking this stuff some day with one of his lady friends. She'll be wearing a long silk dress, all curvy and low-cut. And she'll have a muskrat fur coat and buckets of diamonds—you know, like Norma Shearer in *The Divorcee*." Elise posed with one hand on her hip and the other hand thrust forward, ready to accept a gentleman's kiss. "What would Sister Bernice think if she knew we went to the picture show? She's probably never even seen a talkie!"

"Elise, the jar is full again, and I wish you'd stop talking about that movie," scolded Anna. "Gladys sneaking us out of the house is one thing, but if her mother finds out that we snuck into a picture show, she'll box our ears."

Mrs. Sanders was not unkind, but she was firm and single-minded in her task as a brew-master. She kept a tight schedule and a squeaky clean front for the neighborhood. It was unusual for a woman in the Chicago area to be a bootlegger, which was an advantage for Mrs. Sanders. As far as her neighbors knew, she was a benevolent widow who had opened her home to poor orphans. They would never guess that she kept a loaded pistol in her garter, under her calico housedress.

The very things that drew Elise to the life of bootlegging and rum-running—excitement, fast cash, shady men—were the things that pushed Anna toward the life of a secretary. Elise had been right about the typewriter. Mrs. Sanders had included the fact of its existence on her foster parenting forms, but she had no intention of showing them how to use it, and she always pushed Anna off when she asked where it was. It was an old Remington manual typewriter that her husband had won in a drawing at the 1926 World's Fair in Philadelphia. He thought the drawing was for a rifle, and he had been bitterly disappointed with the "newfangled gizmo."

During Elise's scene-by-scene retelling of the Norma Shearer movie, Anna made up her mind to look for the typewriter on her own. Anna had always followed every rule the sisters at St. Regina's laid out for them, but her time with Mrs. Sanders had convinced her that she would only be able to rely on herself.

Mrs. Sanders had probably been a happy housewife with a husband and a tab at the grocery store, but when her husband died, all of the principles of well-bred society flew out the window.

During her first few weeks at the widow's home, Anna had been in a state of shock, but the reality of the world was now seeping in. Real life was replacing the lessons of Saint Regina's—obedience and conformity to standards—drop by drop. Living in the Sanders' home taught her that breaking rules was acceptable, as long as no one found out.

After she finished her midnight shift in the cellar and took a quick nap, Anna was awake before anyone else in the house. She started in the neglected garden shed. After a series of sneezes and coughs, she found the typewriter under some dusty old boards. She cleaned it up and read the manual. Then she made a makeshift desk, constructed from fence pickets and upside-down buckets. She gingerly sat on an old three-legged stool and carefully balanced the typewriter in front of her across the pickets. At first, Anna lightly tapped her fingers on the glass keys, fearing they might crack if exposed to any kind of pressure. After she became more acquainted with the machine's sturdiness, she started by typing her alphabet on pages torn out of catalogs and any other scrap paper she could find. With mounting excitement, Anna decided to save up her allowance from Mrs. Sanders for ribbons and other replacement parts.

After she could type her alphabet quickly, she moved on to the Bible verses that the Sisters had made them memorize. Anna fed another sheet from last year's Sears catalog through the steel fingers of the machine. With her hands in ready position, she paused, then dropped them in her lap. She glanced around the shed, looking for words to type. Seeing uninteresting items like a cracked watering can, two spades, and several clay pots in varying sizes, she looked again at the catalog page. There she noticed a mesh bag purse for $1.45. This one was small and plain, a purse for a little girl. Then she saw one with butterflies for $4.75. It read: *For dress-up occasions.* She began to type:

I hope that some day I will go
To a dress-up occasion like a Broadway show
I will bring along my little girl
She'll mean more to me than the entire world
With our matching bags of powder blue
We'll smile and laugh the whole night through
Has silver chain and closes when it pinches
Measures 3 by 6 1/2 inches

Anna grinned and shook her head at the silly poem. She pulled out the page and flipped it over to see a picture of a woman and a young girl wearing helmet-like hats. Their cheeks were pressed together and they had the same smiling eyes. The heading read: *Grand style for every age.* The artist had captured a perfect mother-daughter moment. Anna sighed. She didn't miss her actual mother at that moment so much as she missed the possibility of having a mother with matching hat and eyes. She wanted a soft cheek to press against her own, but she wanted it to have always been so. The years of not having a mother could not be erased, so she didn't want Mrs. Sanders or anyone else to try to fill that position now. She wanted to pull the last fifteen years out of the typewriter with a loud *rip* and start with a fresh, blank page. Her one motivation for surviving was the hope that she could rise above her past—this new skill would be the answer.

Anna had a direction for her life and she was determined to find her own happiness.

Oh to Grace

Chapter 5

Morgan's Hat
1921 & 1926

As a boy, my brother George was always lackin' direction. The only thing that got him excited was his collections. He was what you might call a pack rat. He collected any number of things. There weren't a single thing in any of his collections worth a red penny. He had a shoebox full of dead moths, for one, and not even the pretty moths with the big yeller wings. Nah, just those ugly gray-white ones that do nothin' but fly around the porch light at night and make a powdery mark when you slap 'em against a wall. The worst one was his spit collection. Every time he ate somethin' he thought was real tasty or made his tongue turn a color, he would spit into a little glass jar, cap it, and put it in his shoebox. Momma finally threw it all out when he wasn't lookin' and it's a good thing she did. Gray stuff started a-growin' on them bottles and it gave off a terrible odor. It was my guess that the spit from the ice cream social was what done him in. Somebody had bought a couple o' Mr. Goodbars and crushed 'em up in their regular vanilla ice cream. That was George's first taste of that candy bar and I reckon he just wanted to remember it. It's funny how some people can see beauty in things the rest of us take for granted or are plum disgusted by. There's just no accountin' for taste, I reckon. Maybe George was some kind of an artist... or maybe it's on account o' the fact that Buddy rocked him clean out of his cradle when he was a baby and he hit his head on the floor. I reckon we'll never know. It's just nice to know that people can see past the ordinary and find somethin' special when the rest of us think we got it all figured out. It's like Pastor Cooley used to say, "Sometimes we feel 'bout as useful as a back pocket on a shirt, but one of these days we might get that shirt on backwards."

MORGAN'S HAT, TENNESSEE
APRIL 15, 1921

With the exception of Hobart Tipler, the last few stragglers had filed out of the classroom. Matt stood, stretching long legs that had outgrown the wooden school desk. He skirted around the large potbelly stove in the middle of the room and walked to Mr. Allen's desk, perfectly centered in front of the long blackboard. Matt cautiously glanced at Hobart, who was clapping erasers together near the chalkboard. This job was usually given to a younger student, but Mr. Allen had kept Hobart in after school today as a punishment. As clouds of chalk dust slowly settled on the plank floor, Matt read an exasperated expression on Mr. Allen's face, and he began to think that the only one being punished was the teacher.

"Hobart, take those erasers outside. Can't you see you're making a mess?" Mr. Allen snapped, brushing dust off his stack of McGuffey readers. Hobart grabbed up the erasers and leisurely walked out the side door.

Matt gently laid a book on Mr. Allen's desk, then silently turned to leave.

"Wait, Matt," said Mr. Allen. Reading the title of the book, he said, "*The Day Boy and the Night Girl.* What did you think about it?"

Matt swallowed hard. He had always been nervous to talk to his teacher. He was prone to silent adoration of anyone well-educated, and especially Mr. Allen. This young, lanky schoolteacher had spoken to Matt in a way that made him feel smart and special when he had been so easily overlooked by everyone else. "I think this might be my favorite one yet," Matt said softly.

"Your favorite book by Mr. MacDonald, or your favorite book ever?" questioned the teacher.

"Uh, my favorite one by Mr. MacDonald. I've read the one about the goblin, and *At the Back of the North Wind.* They was real good, but I reckon this one beat 'em all."

"Really? Why would you say that?"

"I like how the gal in the story thinks. She was never taught much by that witch that raised her but she used the little book-learnin' she had to figure out how to escape. On top o' that, she saved the fella with all the smarts and know-how and he shoulda been the one to save *her*. It's kinda a twist on what you 'spect, ain't it?"

"Isn't it," corrected Mr. Allen. He cocked his head to one side and looked intently at his burly scholar. "Matt, have you given any more thought about taking the entrance exams for high school? Your time here is about done and I believe you'd surprise yourself with what you've learned."

Matt had gone round and round with his parents over this topic since Mr. Allen had first proposed it several weeks ago. "My momma said I'm not the high school type. She said that God designed my body for hard labor on the farm, not porin' over books all day."

"Doesn't she want you to make something of yourself? I've been your teacher for the past four years and I've never seen a student progress as quickly as you have. Who knows what a few years of higher education could mean for you." Mr. Allen inhaled deeply through his nose and adjusted his wire-rimmed glasses. He spoke more softly now. "Do you *want* to go to high school?"

"Yessir, but Momma's got other plans for me...I reckon." Matt looked down at his feet. He couldn't bear the disappointed look on his teacher's face. He wasn't sure that he did want to go to high school but he *was* sure that he wanted to make Mr. Allen proud. Just the fact that Mr. Allen saw academic possibility in Matt bewildered him. In Morgan's Hat, people were put into categories practically at birth. No one but Mr. Allen had ever thought of Matt as a scholar. It was like the cucumber that Matt had coaxed into growing inside a glass Coke bottle. It grew until it fit perfectly into the bottle with no room left over. It never had a chance to be any longer than the length of the bottle.

Mr. Allen took Matt over to the rough, wooden shelf by the side door. Thirty-three metal cups or drinking glasses stood in a line, each bearing the name or initials of its owner.

"Matt, this is you," he said, picking up Matt's drinking glass. "When some people see you, they see just another empty glass. They see your life here in Morgan's Hat with all the limitations this town would bring. But when I look at you and all that you can do, I see an empty glass ready to be filled with great thoughts." Mr. Allen grasped a rough-hewn dipper in his other hand and plunged it into the wooden bucket that sat on the floor under the shelf. He poured the water into Matt's glass, letting it fill to the rim, with a few rivulets running over the side. "If you don't get filled with great things, you will dry up or get filled with trash. Don't waste this time and opportunity."

Just then, Hobart walked in, carrying the erasers. "I'll take some of that!" he said as he swept past them and grabbed the glass from Mr. Allen's hand. "I sure needed to wet my whistle!" Mr. Allen slumped his shoulders and cast his eyes up to the ceiling beams. He dismissed both of the boys and they walked out of the school together.

Matt had never enjoyed Hobart's company, but the Tipler farm was just to the left on the other side of the bridge. Matt decided he could endure this unwelcome companion by focusing on the knowledge that they wouldn't be together for long.

Just outside the door, they passed a gaggle of small girls having a tea party, with acorn caps for cups and slips of bark for saucers. They were using the shade from the white clapboard schoolhouse to protect their eyes from the afternoon sun. Matt noticed that the paint was peeling from the long horizontal boards. *Pa will have us out here scrapin' and paintin' this old building before too long*, he thought.

Two older girls sat nearby playing a slapping game. They clapped opposite hands together with the rhythm as they sang out:

Granny Silas built a school
She'd only a buckboard and a mule
Untied her bonnet; picked up her tools
Then she taught them the Golden Rules…

Matt had heard the rhyme so often he sometimes forgot that their schoolhouse was named after a real woman. He only knew about its recent history.

The Granny Silas Schoolhouse had been standing for more than fifty years, but not always in the same location. Originally, it had been built on acreage belonging to the Fuller family—a noisy brood with eleven children. Every last name on the roll of the school's inaugural class had been Fuller. When the Civil War broke out, school was cancelled and the schoolhouse was converted into an infirmary for soldiers. Fifteen years later, the building had been lifted and moved to the Wilton's farm when the Wilton family enrolled the largest number of students. Now it sat near Mosquito Spring, where it would stay. The county had purchased the land and hired the teacher, paying sixty dollars a month. The families in town still had to raise money to replace the red metal roof and buy more McGuffey readers, but the nearby spring was plentiful and the one-lane bridge leading up to the schoolhouse was in good condition.

"You gonna recite somethin' at the pie supper tonight?" asked Hobart in a lazy drawl as they strolled past a wild cluster of boys playing "Run, Sheep, Run." The boys were the foxes searching for the hiding herd of sheep.

"I reckon," said Matt. "Mr. Allen asked me to do *The Village Blacksmith*, but I told him I'd ruther do *The Wind*." Matt had claimed this preference because Robert Louis Stevenson was his favorite author, but it was really because *The Wind* was a short poem and *The Village Blacksmith* was much longer.

"My Pa said he ain't gonna let any of us boys recite. He said poems are for sissies and preachers and we ain't neither." As he spoke with great superiority, Hobart slid the strap of his overalls back in place on his bare shoulder. "Ma said what's the use of makin' up a basket of somethin' to sell for the school when your teacher'll probably be gone in a fortnight?"

"Be gone? What're you on about?" asked Matt.

"My ma's got a cousin in Nashville that heard he's up for a job there—some fancy post teachin' at a private school. He'd make nearly twice as much there," Hobart replied. "Why would he stay 'round here makin' next to nothin'?"

Just then, one of Matt's younger brothers ran over to Matt and Hobart. "Matt, I fin'lly got picked for the Fox King and now I cain't find them sheep," said Buddy, exasperated. Buddy was only five and the smallest boy in school. Matt knew the other, bigger boys would not have chosen him to be the lead searcher in the game unless they were playing a trick on him.

"Well, I reckon the other foxes are supposed to be helpin' you find them sheep," Matt said as he glared at the snickering boys behind Buddy. "Where all have you looked?"

Just then, Matt saw a group of boys moving in a tight fist across the field. Seth Morton, the Old Ram and thereby leader of the sheep, yelled out, "Run, sheep, run," and the whole group ran for the designated "sheep pen." The "foxes," led by Buddy, ran after them, but missed tagging any of the sneaky sheep.

Buddy returned to Matt's side, looking as if he might cry. "They's not helping me catch them sheep, Matt. They's just laughin' ever'time I go runnin' after 'em," Buddy whimpered, panting.

Among the "foxes," Matt spotted Arlen, Hobart's younger brother. He was bent at the waist, laughing, immensely proud of his joke. Every boy in the Tipler family went shirtless with worn overalls nearly every day of the year. This uniform, and their father's dominant gene structure, made it difficult to tell them apart. The sisters were unfortunate to look just like the brothers, apart from their longer yellow hair and calico dresses. Arlen was a chubby boy, just like his older brother. Wet from sweating, Arlen's pink, round face was plastered on the sides with stringy blond hair.

Matt walked over to Arlen and looked him straight in the eye. "You play fair or I'll give you a lesson on how it feels like to have a bigger boy whup up on you in front of all the fellas, you hear?" said Matt.

"Ah, lay off him," said Hobart, digging in the clay dirt with his fat big toe. Matt ignored Hobart and turned to Buddy.

"You ready to head home?" Matt asked. "Go grab your syrup bucket and let's get goin'."

After they crossed the bridge, Matt said, "See ya, Hobart," but Hobart continued on with them, turning right instead of left at the end of the bridge.

"I reckon I'll walk a while more with you boys. Ma's making cheese today and if I go home now she'll have me cartin' things all over for her. I reckon that's what my sisters are for," said Hobart with a grin.

They walked until they came to the place in the river called Fiddler's Bend. Matt stopped and stared off downstream for a moment. Then Buddy found a smooth stone by the bank and skipped it into the water, breaking Matt's concentration. It hopped twice before disappearing below.

"Well, that's no good," said Hobart. "Lemme show you

how's it done." Hobart threw a succession of stones into the river. The boys watched as each stone arced high and fell with a gulp into the still water. Each time Hobart would stick out his tongue and squint his eyes to aid in his concentration, but each time ended with the same outcome.

Finally, Hobart gave up on skipping stones and sat against the crooked tree next to Matt. "I reckon you'll be after Polly Clabo's supper basket tonight," Hobart said as he elbowed Matt's ribs.

"Where'd you get that idea?" said Matt, surprised.

"Ah, I seen how you look at her at school. And I seen you set your glass next to hers on purpose so you could fill hers up, you sly dog." Hobart lay back in the grass with his arms folded behind his head. The smell from his bare armpits made Matt dizzy.

"You're plumb crazy, Hobart," said Matt. He picked up Buddy's lunch bucket and herded him away from the bank. He hoped Hobart wouldn't see how hotly he was blushing. He never imagined that anyone had noticed the guarded attention he paid to his pretty classmate. He was fairly certain Polly Clabo had never noticed. *You can't pass gas in this town without somebody catchin' wind of it!* thought Matt.

The pie supper at the schoolhouse was to pay for a new hand pump for their drinking water. Having lugged buckets of water from the spring himself, Matt had originally thought this was a worthy cause. Little did he care how embarrassing it would be to stand in front of the whole town and recite some dead man's words, especially if doing it pleased Mr. Allen. Now he wasn't sure he could go through with it.

"Time to get home." With that, the brothers left Hobart resting against the tree. Before they had gone far, Matt and Buddy could hear him snoring.

That evening, Matt stood at the front of the schoolhouse, waiting for his turn to recite. The townspeople had moved back the front bench where the youngest students sat and brought in more benches for additional guests. Although it was cool outside, every seat was filled, so the room began to bake. Mothers fanned themselves with whatever they could find; fathers used their hats.

After Mr. Allen introduced Matt, he stumbled to the front. Staring out at all of the familiar faces, Matt felt sick. Like the melting icy tops of a mountain, sweat poured from the top of his head. It careened past his shortened sideburns, following his jaw line, until it dropped from the center of his chin and onto his dark gray shirt. He saw his mother and father sitting in the third row back. His mother repeatedly patted her chest as she rocked slightly in her chair and took long breaths, never looking his way. His father gave him a nod for encouragement. Matt hiccupped a breath and began his recitation. "The Wind. By Robert Louis Stevenson. I saw you toss the kites on high and blow the birds about the sky," he mumbled, barely audible to the large group.

Someone on the front row shouted, "Speak up! You got mashed taters in your mouth, boy?" Searching for the heckler, Matt locked eyes with Polly Clabo as she turned her head to giggle with the freckled girl next to her. Matt decided he would have to either finish or die on the spot, so he got louder and sped up. He ended his selection in thirty seconds flat. "O wind, a-blowin' all day long, O wind, that sings so loud a song." There was a smattering of applause and Matt found his seat.

Ernest, younger than Matt by just two years, was next. Ernest did not shy away from public speaking like his older brother. He had chosen Longfellow's *Hiawatha's Childhood* to recite. By the time he got to the section that begins: "By the shores of Gitche Gumee, By the shining Big-Sea-Water..." he had the audience eating out of his hand. At the close of the poem, the room erupted with whistles and applause, and the two boys who were to go on next shook their heads, indicating that they had changed their minds about volunteering.

The time had come for the auction of the pies and supper

baskets. The rule was that the man or boy who had the highest bid bought the item and was entitled to eat with the cook. The identities of the cooks were meant to remain anonymous, but the ladies usually found a way to reveal it to the fellow of their choice. Wives just glared at their husbands, who knew right away what to do next.

Zeal Cooley, the pastor from Berea Baptist, began the proceedings with a short prayer. "Lord, we thank Thee for this food and the hands that hath prepared it. We ask Thee for Thy blessings on our school. We ask Thee to keep us—Thy children—safe as we partake of these pies. Strike down any rotten eggs or curdled creams that may be a-hiding in these desserts, as Thou knowest your servant was a-stricken at the last pie supper, Lord. Protect us from the chess pies and lemon meringues just a-waiting to attack us, sweet Jesus. Guide, guard, and direct us. Amen."

Before the group could echo an "amen" back, Pastor Cooley began the bidding. They made their way through half of the pies and supper baskets, when a pretty straw basket with a light pink ribbon was brought to the teacher's desk. Polly Clabo began to giggle with her freckled friend again. Matt knew this must be her basket. He sat up straight, collecting his resolve. "Now this basket is a-hiding some good smelling stuff." Pastor Cooley lifted the dishtowel to see what was inside. "Looks like apple fritters and a pecan pie. What'll we start with, fellas?"

Polly's father raised a finger and said, "I'll give you five cents."

Matt pushed past the feeling that his heart would beat out of his chest and squeaked out, "Ten cents." Polly paused in wonder—her eyes round—then began giggling again.

"We have ten cents. Can I hear twenty?" asked Pastor Cooley.

A confident voice from the rear of the room called, "Two bits." Matt looked back and saw Ernest smiling his one-dimple smile. Polly giggled harder still.

"Twenty-five cents, can I hear thirty?"

"Thirty cents," said Matt, feeling his face grow hot as his heart beat faster.

"Forty," Ernest answered quickly, before Pastor Cooley could speak. Matt knew that Ernest didn't have that kind of money. He spent his meager earnings from working in their father's shop faster than he made it. Matt, on the other hand, had saved up everything he had from the last year.

"Sixty-three cents," said Matt with some certainty. He squeezed the two quarters, one dime, and three pennies in his pocket, letting their heft weigh in his palm one last time. The crowd made a little gasp and grew very still. All eyes turned to Ernest in the back.

"Sixty-three cents! Hallelujah! These are sure to be some mighty fine fritters," said Pastor Cooley. "Can anybody beat sixty-three?"

"Seventy-five cents," Ernest replied. At this, Polly succumbed to hysterics. Polly's mother pulled her out of her seat and marched her outside. After Pastor Cooley banged his hammer on Mr. Allen's desk, Ernest walked to the front to claim his prize. As he passed Matt, he gave him a wink as if they had been conspirators all along.

The auction continued, but Matt sneaked out the side door to find Ernest. He found him leaning against a gig parked under a flowery cherry tree. He had hung the basket on one of the oil lamps on the front of the carriage as he perused its contents. "Where'd you get that kind of money?" Matt asked before he even arrived by his brother's side.

"Well, I asked Momma if I could have a little of her rainy day money and she said it was alright. We put on quite a show, didn't we?"

Matt knew for a fact that their Momma wouldn't give seventy-five cents for one of Ernest's flights of fancy, but he decided to give him the benefit of the doubt. "You wanna piece of this pie? It ain't so very good," said Ernest in a whisper. "But I'm lookin' for that pretty cook to come over and eat some with me, anyhow."

"I never heard you talk 'bout Polly Clabo before. When'd you get sweet on her?" asked Matt, attempting to mask the raging jealousy that lurked just below the surface.

"Ah, she's been after *me* for months." Ernest looked around and whispered again. "Don't tell nobody but she give me fifty cents to bid on her basket. She was a-feared that only her pa would do any biddin'. Momma gave me another fifty cents to get a basket, so I ended up with a pie, a pretty girl, and a quarter to boot! Not bad!"

Now that she had gained control of herself, Polly found Ernest and came to stand next to him. She bobbed up and down, making her soft brown curls bounce like springs. "Come on, Ernie. Let's go find a quiet place to have a picnic," she said coyly. She grabbed his hand and started pulling him toward the woodshed. Ernest relented. As they passed Matt, Ernest shrugged his shoulders and smiled. Watching them walk away, Matt realized that he didn't envy his younger brother. Seeing the hungry look in Polly's eyes, Matt actually pitied him a little.

The auction was over now. Couples and families milled around the grounds, finding places to spread a blanket for their supper. Matt didn't care for any company just then, so he walked past everyone and crossed the old one-lane bridge. Just on the other side was a small grove of Osage orange trees. Many of the boys loved to spend their recess time here pelting each other with the bumpy yellow-green fruit. Matt heard the voice of his teacher, so he approached the trees.

"Wenonah, a tall and slender maiden, with the beauty of the moonlight, with the beauty of the starlight..."

"Oh, Napier..." said a female voice. Matt stood rooted to his spot, not wanting to be found out and accused of eavesdropping. There was quiet rustling, as if the branches were caressing one another as they shielded this couple of lovebirds.

"I'm just remembering what that Watson boy recited tonight—from Longfellow's *Hiawatha*," said Mr. Allen. "And Ruthie, *you* have the beauty of the moonlight and the starlight...and the sunlight...and candlelight..." Hearing his serious teacher talk this way to a woman made the tops of Matt's ears burn. He had never thought of Mr. Allen as anything but a teacher. He definitely hadn't considered the possibility of him as somebody's beau. "Ernest Watson surely overpaid for his basket, but I got mine at a bargain for a dollar. I would've paid all the money in the world to sit right here with you tonight."

"Hush, Napier. What if my daddy finds us here? He'll horsewhip you," said the voice that Matt now knew to be Ruth Evelyn Hoffman, the daughter of the Methodist minister.

"And what if he does? He knows what you mean to me. If he would only give you to me, I would make you so happy, Ruth."

"I've begged him and begged him, but he won't listen to me," Ruth said softly. "He says you've had the kind of book-learning that will drag you down to the devil. I wish you hadn't had that argument right off with him the first time you met him. You should've kept your opinions 'bout Shakespeare to yourself."

"I've regretted that every day of my life," he pleaded. "But what can I do about it now?"

"He's sending me to my aunt in Montgomery this summer. He says that since my momma died I need someone to teach me how to keep house and raise up children." Ruth started to cry a little. "How can I bear it, being away from you for so long?"

"I've been offered a job in Nashville, Ruthie," he said quickly. "What if I take it and save up my money? Will your father think I'm worthy?" She didn't answer. "Or maybe I can look for a job in Montgomery? Or some nearby place? Please don't cry, Ruth, I'll think of something."

They were both quiet now. Matt imagined that Ruth had her head on Mr. Allen's shoulder as he comforted her. Matt turned as quietly as he could manage on the bed of pine needles under his feet and started to tiptoe back toward the school. He saw Hobart Tipler walking in his direction, so he picked up his pace and cut him off before Hobart crossed the bridge.

"What's your gall-durn rush, Matt?" Hobart asked.

"Ah, I was lookin' for my kin. You seen any of 'em?"

"Nah, I jest got here."

Matt was grateful that Hobart had missed his recitation and his failed attempt at Polly's basket. "Let's go see what my momma brought for our supper," said Matt, slapping Hobart on the back.

"Don't mind if I do...'specially if there's biscuits with sorghum to be had." Hobart rubbed his pudgy hands together greedily as they walked back towards the schoolhouse.

Zeal Cooley was a real fine preacher—maybe the best in Davis County. He was at Berea Baptist nearly all my life. He even married me and Ronnie. Pastor Cooley grew up right here in Morgan's Hat. His mama named him Zeal after she found the word in the back of a Bible dictionary. "Come with me and see my zeal for the Lord." That's the second book of Kings, chapter ten and verse sixteen. Pastor Cooley made us all learn that verse in Sunday School. Yes, his mama had a bunch of kids, maybe eighteen or nineteen. I reckon she started having trouble thinkin' up names at the end. She always picked short Bible names—short enough so that they'd fit at the front of the family Bible. My daddy told me that she was forever tellin' the people in town that Zeal would be a preacher... well, either him or his older brother Toil. I wouldn't say that the people in Morgan's Hat were any better than the people anywhere else, but most of us did go to church on Sundays. And Pastor Cooley could make you feel awful sorry for what you'd done that week before. I still recall the time he preached out of Jeremiah, the 31st chapter. He said, "Brothers and sisters, the Good Book says: 'Everyone shall die for his own iniquity: every man that

eateth the sour grape, his teeth shall be set on edge.'" He went on and on about our iniquities and how our sins would ruin our teeth. I think about that now nearly every time I take out my dentures.

MORGAN'S HAT, TENNESSEE
MAY 10, 1924

Ernest and Matt reluctantly climbed the four short steps that led to the double doors of Berea Baptist church. "We done pretty good, Ernie," said Matt as he stroked the new coat of red stain on the doorframe.

"Don't remind me," said Ernest. "My back's still achin' from paintin' this whole durn buildin' last week. Now that we done painted the schoolhouse and the church, folks 'round here will be thinkin' that we're settin' up a paintin' business…and if our momma gets her way it'll all be done for free!"

Matt tried to peek into one of the long arched windows that flanked either side of the front doors. "I reckon we ought to get in there and see what Pastor Cooley's got us signed up for," he said.

"Yeah, we might as well get it over and done with."

The two boys—ages seventeen and fifteen—walked through the foyer and continued into the darkened sanctuary. It took a moment for their eyes to adjust from the bright sunshine. Hearing only the muffled sound of their footsteps, they strode past the rows of long wooden pews to the pastor's office situated just to the left of the pulpit.

After a quick knock on the door, Matt and Ernest entered into the cramped space.

"Come on in, boys," Pastor Cooley said in his booming bass as he rose to his full height of five and a half feet. He surveyed the boys with his brownish-gold eyes. These eyes had always baffled Matt. Pastor Cooley seemed to have the unique ability of controlling the color of his eyes during his sermons, darkening them when his sermons grew in intensity. Fires of hell? His eyes were like an old copper penny. Love thy brother? They softened to a dull amber. He had a few tufts of light brown hair over his ears and around the back of his head, but the top of his head was a shiny pink. "I can't tell you how blessed you're going to be today!"

Matt and Ernest looked at each other warily. That was what he had said just before he handed them metal scrapers and buckets of red stain last week. They both sighed.

"I know what you're thinking, boys, but hard work is a blessing. Proverbs six and verse six: 'Go to the ant, thou sluggard; consider her ways, and be wise.'"

"What you got in mind, pastor?" asked Matt.

Pastor Cooley snatched his hat from his cluttered desk. "Walk with me, boys." He set his hat on his balding head and walked out the door. Matt and Ernest followed him.

Though he was in the dead center of middle age, Zeal Cooley could run circles around most men with half the number of candles on their birthday cakes. Matt and Ernest had to jog at various times just to keep up with him. It was a wonder that Pastor Cooley could continue with this pace; his legs were quite a bit shorter than Matt's. The more remarkable part was how he could preach as he walked.

"'Whatsoever thy hand findeth to do, do it with thy might; for there is no work in the grave.' Ecclesiastes, chapter nine and verse ten. And that's just so, boys. Most people don't know this, but for a piece of time in my youth, I left Morgan's Hat— I must've been about your age, Matt—I went to Arkansas to help my uncle with his funeral parlor. Well, I can tell you for sure that none of those people lying in their wooden crates— God bless their souls—were doing much of anything but staying mighty still."

"What did you do in your uncle's funeral parlor?" Ernest asked, a little out of breath.

"A bit of everything. I laid the bodies out, arranged flowers,

I even did some hair and makeup work," said Pastor Cooley. "My mama, one of God's sweetest angels—God rest her soul—wanted me to be a pastor more than all the gold in California, but I had other plans for myself. My uncle had no children of his own and wanted to pass his funeral parlor business to someone in the family. I counted that as a real fine situation."

"Why didn't you stick with it? Did your folks make you come back and go to preachin' school?" asked Matt with some interest. He still hadn't forgotten his missed opportunity of higher education.

"I liked it fine. But I came to a realization that it wasn't for me."

"Was it them dead bodies?" asked Ernest.

"No, son, dead bodies don't bother me a bit, except...when I had to dress them and their arms and legs got stiff. That's a chore. No, I knew it wasn't for me because of the school children who had class upstairs."

"There was a school above the funeral parlor?" In spite of the heat, Ernest gave a shudder.

"Yes. There was a school just above us. Some of those boys would sneak down to where we had the bodies laid out and spoil our hard work. One rascal drew a moustache on an elderly lady we had just got in. Truth be known, she already had the beginnings of whiskers—but he made it entirely too prominent."

Matt and Ernest stifled a laugh, but Pastor Cooley continued with all seriousness.

"I saw that those boys needed some guidance, love, and understanding. And none of the corpses I dressed and made up really had any need of that kind of help. So, as I rubbed charcoal from the upper lip of the late Agnes Jebsen, I decided then and there that I was more suited to preaching to the living then tending to the dead. As it says in the Gospel of Luke, chapter twenty-four and verse five: 'Why seek ye the living among the dead?'"

A contemplative pause followed. Then Pastor Cooley said, "We're just a stone's throw away from where we're going, so I'd better let you in on our job today."

Up to then, Ernest had paid no attention to where they were walking, but he paused now and looked around. "Wait a minute, Pastor. This is Joe Davis' land, ain't it?"

"That's right, son."

Ernest stopped in his tracks. "The last fella I heard of who came in this neck 'o the woods was pickin' buckshot out of his behind for weeks. I ain't no fool. I'm leaving."

"Joe Davis wouldn't hurt a fly. Everyone in Morgan's Hat knows that," Pastor Cooley said.

"Joe Davis isn't the one we're worried about," said Matt. He wholeheartedly trusted Pastor Cooley with his salvation, but he wasn't so sure about his judgment this time.

"True 'nuff. It's his batty wife Versa who points the shot gun," said Ernest.

"I reckon Momma wants us helpin' out the poor and all, but she don't want two of her sons gettin' shot up," Matt reluctantly agreed.

"Now hold on, boys. Hear me out." Pastor Cooley put a hand on Ernest's arm. "I come by invitation. Versa has finally hit her limit and she's going to let some church-folk help her."

"Momma always said she don't accept nothin' from nobody," said Matt. "What's changed?"

"Versa's getting up there in years and she can't do all the planting and plowing and caring for the livestock and so forth by herself anymore. She's always been a powerful stubborn woman, but I believe she crawled inside that stubbornness when Joe came back from the war a cripple." As Pastor Cooley spoke, they began to walk the dirt road that led to the Davis farm. "They both married late. Of course this was Joe's second time round—his first wife died young. But Versa was accustomed to doing things for herself while she was single and living on her daddy's land. When they married, she was nigh forty and

Joe ten years her junior, but it seemed to work. They came to church and were real happy and then he went off to fight in the war. When they shipped him home from France with no legs to speak of, a weaker woman would've fainted dead away—not Versa. She lifted him up and carried him home. That was about seven years ago and she's been hauling him around ever since."

They arrived at the front porch of the Davis home. It was swept clean, but the graying bareness of the wood showed the need for a new coat of stain. Smoke rose from the crumbling chimney in a thin, wispy line. Pastor Cooley briskly mounted the porch steps and knocked on the screen door. A large woman came to the door, holding a dishtowel. She was taller than Matt and bigger around. Her hair was pulled tightly back into a small gray bun. Her pale blue calico dress hung on her like a tent. The only definition to her figure came from the short apron tied securely around her waist.

"Versa?" asked Pastor Cooley.

"Is that you, preacher? Speak up quick or I'll get my shotgun."

"It's me, sister. No need for the gun," answered Pastor Cooley without pause. "I brought you two strong boys to help with some work around the farm."

Versa opened the screen door with a loud creak, still standing inside. "You can start with this here creaky door," Versa snipped. "But don't think you can go openin' it and walk right in. Your shoes are filthy and I won't have you track Lord knows what into my clean parlor." She turned around, letting the door slam behind her. The three visitors stood silently on the front porch, awaiting orders. Ernest started to speak, but Pastor Cooley shook his head in warning. Versa returned in a moment, cradling something large against her ample breasts. As she approached, they recognized Joe in her arms. He looked like a toddler compared to his hefty wife.

"Howdy, boys!" Joe said with enthusiasm. "We don't get

near 'nuff company!" Versa set him down on one end of a metal glider bench. Joe smiled up at her and said, "I thank ya, honey." Versa feigned annoyance, huffed, and walked down the porch steps.

Joe Davis was dressed like a man of leisure. He wore a bright red, plaid shirt with the sleeves pushed up to his elbows. The legs of his dark denim overalls were rolled and pinned. Everything he wore looked perfectly cleaned and carefully pressed. He had a clean-shaven face and dark hair that Versa kept cut short. As Matt surveyed Joe, he thought the couple looked like an odd pair of opposites: big and little, sad and happy, strong and weak.

"What're you fellas doin' out here today?" Joe asked.

"These boys have been scraping and painting all over town, and they thought they might work on your front porch a while. How's that suit you?" asked Pastor Cooley.

"Well, Pastor, I believe that'd suit me fine." Joe looked past his visitors in the direction of his wife and whispered, "If'n the little lady don't mind, that is."

"Why, it was practically all her idea, Joe," he said.

Versa returned with buckets, scrapers, and brushes. "All right, boys. Here's your tools. Mind—if I don't like the job you do, you'll do it over. And if you break any of my scrapers or spoil my brushes, I'll have your hides. Get my meanin'?"

"Yes'm," both boys answered.

"Well, don't just stand there. Get goin'!" Versa re-entered the house with another creak, followed by a slam.

"Whoo-hoo. That woman's got more spit than a cobra!" said Joe with obvious pride. "They don't make 'em like that anymore!"

"Thank goodness," whispered Ernest. Matt elbowed him, hard.

The boys started scraping while the pastor visited with Joe. After twenty minutes, Pastor Cooley pulled his watch from his breast pocket and said, "I'd better get back. My sermon won't write itself! I hope to see you at services tomorrow, Joe."

"Well, pastor, when I was growin' up I would've caught a mess of trouble if I missed a Sunday. In fact, the Louisville Colonels wanted me to pitch for 'em when I was seventeen—I was all ready to sign the papers and everythin'—but my ma wouldn't allow it on account of they played some games on Sundays. That's how steadfast we was to services. Now...well, it all depends on Versa, you see," said Joe. "She ain't been too willin' to go since I come back from the war..."

"I understand, Joe." Pastor Cooley patted his hand. "Psalm thirty-seven and verse seven: 'Rest in the LORD, and wait patiently for him.'"

"I thank ya, pastor," Joe said as he shook Pastor Cooley's hand with tears in his eyes. "I thank all of ya."

The boys continued working throughout the day until Versa returned outside with lunch. "I got biscuits, cold ham, and applesauce. If that ain't good 'nuff for you, you should go on home."

"Ah, honey," said Joe, "that looks tasty 'nuff to feed President Coolidge himself." Versa rolled her eyes at her husband.

"Lands, Joe, your face is red. You're probably gettin' heat stroke, then what'll I do with you? You come on in the house for a piece." Before he could accept or decline, Versa had scooped him up in her arms to carry him inside. As she was leaving, she called over her shoulder, "There's a pump out by the barn and you each got a cup on that tray. I ain't pumpin' water for two full-grown boys."

As the boys ate their lunch in the yard, Ernest said, "I don't think I could abide havin' a woman haul me around like a baby. I would've ruther been killed in the war."

"I reckon." Matt looked up toward the house and thought about Joe and Versa. He tried to imagine having Polly Clabo or some other girl he knew from school carry him around town. It seemed ludicrous—but Joe surely never counted on it turning out this way, either. The humiliation of having to rely on someone else to provide for all your needs for most of your adult life was difficult enough, but for it to be a rough-edged, bitter woman like Versa Davis seemed like the greater insult.

After the boys had eaten and, with some difficulty, hoisted themselves off the dry grass in the front yard, they resumed their scraping.

Versa brought Joe back out to the front porch. "I thank ya, honey." Versa pulled the napkin out of Joe's front collar and performed her usual huff before turning around. Matt looked up just in time to see Joe swat Versa's sizable rump. Then *creak* and *slam* again.

Joe smoked his pipe as he watched Matt and Ernest shave off the gray, peeling layer of wood on the far end of the porch floor. Unexpectedly, Joe sneezed and dropped his pipe. Matt saw him struggle for a moment, trying to reach it where it lay on the floor. "I'll get that Mr. Davis," he said. Matt picked up the pipe and handed it to Joe.

"I thank ya, Matthew," said Joe. "Sit a spell, boys. Your ma and pa will be after me if you get overheated whilst a-workin' on my front porch."

Matt sat on the bench with Joe, and Ernest sat on the porch steps.

"Mr. Davis, can I ask you a question?" Ernest said.

"Sure 'nuff."

"What's it like…not havin' legs and all?"

"Ernie," growled Matt.

"It's all right, son. It's a fair 'nuff question." Joe puffed on his pipe for several seconds. "When I was a boy, there wasn't nothin' I'd rather do than play baseball. I played most every day—right out in them fields. I could throw a ball so fast it'd shave off your pappy's whiskers. I was right good with the bat, too. And runnin' them bases was like…well, I was as quick as a jackrabbit. So when I was called up to fight, I reckon I thought it was just gonna be like playin' ball—a game, you see—but it turned out to be hell itself. Boys dyin' all around me and me havin' to shoot men I couldn't even see—didn't even know them fellas from Adam. Then there was the battle in Belgium—when I lost my legs..." Joe puffed on his pipe again, choosing his words carefully. "After the explosion, they drug me down into one of them God-awful trenches and my legs stayed up on the battlefield. I thought my life was over. Even in the hospital when they was tellin' me I would make it, but they wouldn't let me look under the bed sheets, I was 'bout as low as a man can get. Then they sent me home and I saw Versa standin' there at the dock. She was a head taller 'n anybody, so she was easy to spot. She looked so strong and sure. She told me not to worry over nothin' and took me home. I been leanin' on her ever since."

"But don't it make you mad? You could've done so much, but now..." Ernest's voice trailed off.

"If I let it make me mad, then what good does it do me? I'm luckier than most. What if I'd been killed in Belgium or blinded by that German gas? Or what if I didn't have Versa to care for me? I've learned that we don't often get what we deserve—sometimes more and sometimes not all, but we get what we need. The Lord knew that I needed Versa." The screen door made a slight creak. All three of them turned to look, but no one was there. "Well, boys, it must be gettin' on near suppertime. Your ma will be wonderin' where you are. Why don't you get on home?" Joe pulled his wallet out of his back pocket.

"No, sir," said Ernest. "You don't owe us nothin'."

"We'll be back next Saturday to finish the job, if this nice weather holds out," Matt said.

"I'll be prayin' for sunshine, boys," said Joe. "That way I can set up a diamond in the cotton field and run the bases just like Babe Ruth." Joe winked at them mischievously. "So bring a bat 'n ball!"

Chapter 7

Pastor Cooley was just one of the colorful characters in Morgan's Hat. It stands to reason if you come from a town with an unusual name you may get unusual townsfolk. It's like namin' kinds of tomatoes. The stranger the names, the odder lookin' the tomato. You ever eat a Cherokee Purple or a Green Zebra? I never thought about it bein' a strange name when I was comin' up, but I reckon it is. I heard that before Mr. Lincoln's War, Morgan's Hat was called Skunk Pelt Cove. I don't know if that's true, though. All the children in Morgan's Hat had to learn their town history, so it was a natural thing to be named after John Hunt Morgan. He was a grand Southern general who led some successful battles in Tennessee, 'specially durin' "The Great Raid of '63," Eventually, he was captured by the Yankees. They sent him and a few of his men to a prison in Ohio. But no Yankee prison could hold General Morgan! He dug a tunnel, climbed down a wall usin' a rope made of his bed sheets, and boarded a train on its way out of town. He jumped off the train before it reached the depot and stole into Kentucky. He was quite the hero. Just like many men who gallivant all over and leave their wives home to do all of everythin'—at the

Oh to Grace

time he was escapin' from prison, his wife Rebecca was givin' birth to his daughter, with no help from him. The baby girl died soon after. Anyhow, one of his final battles in Tennessee was right 'round here. As the story goes, a young soldier was killed near the start of the fightin'. General Morgan rode up to him on his horse Black Bess, dismounted and kneeled by his side as he died. After the young soldier passed, Morgan took off his hat and held it to his chest in honor of the boy. The men were so taken by the act that they referred to the spot as "The Place Where Morgan Took Off His Hat" and later they just shortened it to Morgan's Hat. It may sound queer to some folks, but it's better than being from Skunk Pelt Cove, that's for sure.

MORGAN'S HAT, TENNESSEE
JULY 13, 1926

The vacant field next to J.T. Fuller's barn was never used for much. A few years back, he planted several rows of sweet corn, but after that, he decided to let it lie fallow and never got around to planting anything new. In the years since, it was taken over by blue dayflowers and tall white snakeroots. The latter spoiled his dairy cows' milk, so when some boys said they would pull them all out if he'd let them use it for the Anniversary Celebration, he quickly agreed. After being mowed down and the split rail fences all repaired at the beginning of summer, the field was now covered with white canvas tents and outdoor cooking fires.

Matt and Ernest woke up to the smell of their father cooking flapjacks on the spider skillet. Matt rubbed his eyes and stretched as he emerged into the bright July morning. He shook his head, trying to remember why they had spent the night in the middle of a dry and dusty field. Then it dawned on him: Old Cooter Brown.

Cooter did any manner of odd jobs in town and, about a

year before, had been hired to help a recently widowed mother unpack all her belongings in her grown son's parlor. While unwrapping an English vase with pictures of nearly-naked ladies holding great gray urns of purple grapes, Cooter had found an old clipping from a Pennsylvania paper describing "The Great Reunion of 1913." He was intrigued that more than 50,000 Northern and Southern soldiers would reunite to commemorate the battle of Gettysburg. He began talking about it all over town until the town fathers finally decided to give in and stage a mock battle. The Gettysburg reunion had fallen on the 50th anniversary of that famous battle, and they had missed an opportunity to use a solid round number like fifty for their event. They were downcast at the planning meeting until someone piped up that 1926 would be the 63rd anniversary of "The Great Raid of 1863"—the 63rd for '63. Seeing that their town's namesake, General Morgan, was the hero of that raid, they could use this formula to their advantage. After several hearty slaps on the back, plans were set in motion. Letters were written to elder Confederate veterans. Old uniforms were taken out of cedar chests. Banners and sashes were made. Battle scenes and speeches were scripted. Cannons were greased along with ancient muskets. Frank Watson and his boys were invited, along with every other able-bodied man.

When the time came for the event and the tents were constructed on the field, the organizers began to look around and see that there were only gray uniforms exiting and entering the flaps of the tents. Where were the Union veterans? Whose job had it been to invite them? Fingers were pointed in every direction. Then the mayor and his cronies fell back in their wooden folding chairs and fanned themselves with their straw boater hats. Fearing that all their plans for the event were in vain, the mayor sent men to search for those who would be willing to play the part of the Union troops.

After many rejections, including one man who threatened to sic his hound on them and another who poured his dishwater on their shoes, they passed J.T. Fuller's barn and heard a cacophony of snoring from within. In an empty but unswept stall, they spotted Cooter Brown. Here was their answer.

"Wake up, Cooter," said Carmine Baker, special assistant and brother-in-law to the mayor. He jostled Cooter and pulled him to his feet.

"What's happenin'? Why's I covered in straw?" Cooter jumped to his full height of just under five feet, dazed and disoriented.

"Why, Cooter, the mayor's been asking for you. He's got a real special job for you. He told us, he said, 'Go find me a good ole rebel who'll help us with this grand day.' So o' course, we first thought of you." Carmine flashed a toothy grin and let go of Cooter's arm. Cooter sunk down to his straw bed again.

"Ah, he's dog drunk!" said Harley Dickson, as he pulled out his old gold pocket watch to check the time. "Carmine, we got to go!"

But Carmine Baker was not one to give up easily. If he could get his sister's born-tired-and-lazy husband elected mayor, then he could do anything, in his estimation. They dragged Cooter out to the horse trough and dunked his head in it three times. Before the noon pistol was shot off to begin the battle, he had Cooter dressed in an old blue work shirt, overalls and a Union cap that Carmine's dad had taken off a Yankee soldier in the Battle at Chancellorsville. Cooter fluctuated in and out of consciousness during the preparations.

When the time came for the mock battle to begin, Cooter was positioned by an old cannon and a neat pyramid of cannonballs. After his arrangers had walked away and he was left alone, he groggily lifted himself up by placing his hands on the barrel and pushing, all the while fighting the pounding in his head. The visor of his woolen hat prevented him from seeing the "troops" facing him. Then suddenly, the starting pistol was fired. Still in a fog, Cooter feared he was under attack.

"It's them damyankees! My granddaddy wasn't foolin'!

They's back for the corn beer!" Cooter began haphazardly loading cannonballs into the cannon. He found a match in his pocket and lit the wick.

The committee for the mock battle had never intended to have the cannons actually fire the balls. Rather they had loaded them with gunpowder to make loud explosions, in order to recreate a battle-like atmosphere. Cooter was not on that committee.

When the spark had run the length of the wick, there was a split second, and then the barrel tilted down. With a sudden gift of common sense, Cooter threw himself behind a hay bale just before the explosion, his hands over his ears. The ground shook with the force of the blast. The end of the barrel was shredded, looking like a wilted flower pointing its drooping petals at a huge crater in the ground. The field was hushed. No rallying cries were heard, as everyone breathlessly awaited news about Cooter. Finally he rose up, covered in dirt. Everyone cheered. Many of the men ran across the field. Matt and Ernest hoisted Cooter on their shoulders.

"The South rides again!" they all shouted. Cooter could not hear their whoops for the ringing in his ears.

When the last speech was made at the end of that day, everyone agreed it had been a memorable event. Burnetta Watson brought a basket of fried chicken and corn fritters to her husband and two older sons. Running ahead of her were Buddy, Clarence, and Homer, who had been pestering her all day to go and join the men. She balanced Baby George on one hip with the basket on the other. After she passed out dinner to all her men, she brought a plate over to Cooter, who was sitting against a hay bale, poking and twisting his fingers in both his ears.

"I thank ya kindly, Miz Burnetta," Cooter shouted, too loudly. "Ooo! Fried chicken! I's happier than a dog wit two peters!"

Matt and Ernest ate their momma's dinner while they sat

on a log. As Frank Watson sliced open a watermelon and handed the juicy red triangles to his family, Pearl Montgomery and her cousin Eula Baker looked at the two oldest Watson boys—giggling and whispering all the while. Ernest gave them a wink and elbowed his brother in the ribs.

"Look at them sweet taters over yonder. They cain't get 'nuff of the Watson boys, I reckon," Ernest puckered his lips to imitate kisses, causing the girls to nearly tumble over in a fit of giggles.

"Who?" asked Matt, looking around, "Carmine Baker's girl has buck teeth big enough to eat corn through a picket fence and Pearl Montgomery has got to be a full head taller 'n you. Why, she could hunt geese with a rake!"

"Well, look at them lips that cover them big teeth—sweet as a suck o' sugar. Anyhow, I was thinkin' Pearl was for you."

"What you boys chinnin' 'bout? You stop that foolish talk, Ernest, ya hear me?" Burnetta gave Eula and Pearl a squinting, dirty look. The girls quieted down and turned around to face their circle of family and friends.

Harley Dickson was telling a hunting story to Eula's father when his wife Doris noticed the chain from his pocket watch was dangling from his belt loop.

Doris said, "Harley, where's your..."

"Doris, don't interrupt me!" Harley fussed. "Why do you always have to pipe in like that when I'm talking, woman? You know I'm just gettin' to the good part!" He had his hands up in the air, pretending to shoot an invisible duck.

"Well, I just know how much that old watch means to you on account of your daddy gave it to you on his deathbed..." Doris picked up their three-year old. "Come on, Bo-sugar," she said and walked away in a huff.

Harley pulled at the chain and saw an open chain link where the watch should have been attached. "Land-o-Goshen! I bet it got pulled loose when we drug that ole drunk out of J.T.'s barn!"

He took a posse over to the barn and started combing through the stalls. They worked for hours, but never came up with the family heirloom. Harley sat down and wept when they decided to give up the search. He loved his daddy—one of the most successful hunters in Davis County. He had once shot a 200-pound white tail deer with one bullet. Harley remembered this as he thought of the watch. It had an engraving on the back—a doe and a fawn standing in snow, looking off into the setting sun. A fellow soldier had given the pocket watch to his daddy during the Battle of Argonne in World War One. Harley would never forgive himself for losing it.

Oh to Grace

Chapter 8

Chicago
1932 & 1933

No matter where you lived, times was hard back then. At least in Morgan's Hat we didn't know any diff'rent so we could just go on workin' the land and makin' ends meet like our grandparents did before us and their grandparents did before them. But in big cities, people took advantage of the poor. I remember Ernest tellin' us about the mayor in Chicago and how he wanted to get rid of the bank robbers and moonshiners and all of them gangsters. He was Bohemian or Bavarian or Hungarian or one of them places in Europe where they eat a lot of beets. Anyhow, this Mayor, Anton Cermak was his name, he became friends with the black folks and the immigrants fresh off the boats. Loads of other politicians didn't care for them one whip. In '33, he went to Miami to meet with FDR. As he was shakin' hands with the president, somebody stepped in and shot him in the lung. They said the bullet was meant for FDR and as they carried him off, he told Roosevelt he was glad it was me and not you. Ernest said that was a bunch of goose grease. He said the I-talian who shot him was paid by the

Oh to Grace

gangster Al Capone. Capone wanted to get rid of Cermak. That I-talian fella was just an ignorant bricklayer who had a sick gall bladder. When they arrested him, he was spoutin' off about killin' the rich and passin' gas all the while. In the papers they said he went crazy due to his condition. After that, things kept getting worse and worse. The gangsters were killin' each other and anyone who got in their way, but even still, Ernest didn't come home to Morgan's Hat. He liked life in the Big City.

CHICAGO, ILLINOIS
APRIL 20, 1932

The *tap, tap* of her brown leather shoes was beginning to wear on Anna's nerves as much as the straps were wearing on the tops of her feet. The thought of buying her own new pair with the money she could earn from a respectable job was all that kept her moving down the black Chicago pavement. Thankfully, she had been able to borrow these shoes from Gladys. The daughter of her resourceful benefactress had heard about the job from a friend, and Gladys assured Anna that the typing job would still be available at Griffith & Sons Insurance Company if she could only make it there by eight o'clock. Anna wasn't sure what her cottage mom would think about the job or Gladys' help, but after her shift in the cellar was over, she dressed quickly and sneaked out of the house. She wasn't taking any chances; Mrs. Sanders might have forbid Anna from looking for work because it would take her away from the work in the cellar. Now that the government no longer paid her for her wards, Mrs. Sanders was tighter than ever with her money, and Elise was also planning to move out.

Anna wanted to stop and look at her reflection in one of the shop windows, but she didn't have time. She put a gloved hand to her simply-trimmed hat and the red curls that twisted around her ears. She was still adjusting to the short haircut Elise had given her. As she rounded the corner at Michigan Avenue, Anna was thinking about blotting off some of her red lipstick when her heel wobbled loose and she lunged to her right. She was caught in the arms of a man just leaving a grocery store.

"Whoa, ma'am. Can I help you?" said the stranger. He had dark eyes and a slow Southern drawl.

"I'm afraid it's my shoe." Anna said, panic rising inside her. She frantically thought, *It's broken and now I won't make it to the interview and I'll never get this job.* She tried to hold back her sobs. She was exhausted and nervous, and already felt defeated.

The man pulled a handkerchief from his back pocket and offered it to Anna. Holding up a *wait here* hand, he led her to an overturned produce crate and disappeared back into the store. In a moment, he was back with a small hammer and a handful of nails.

"Ma'am, my daddy can fix any shoe. It's God's truth. And though he's not here, I worked 'long side him for years, so if you'll let me, I'll get you right on your way."

As he unbuckled her right shoe and slowly slid it off of her foot, Anna chewed her lower lip and looked around to see who was witnessing this improper display. She allowed it, though, because she was short on choices. With a deft hand, the man had her heel back in place and her shoe put gently back on her foot.

"I can't possibly thank you enough," she said, her face warming. "Do you know what time it is?" Anna stood unsteadily, trying out the repaired shoe.

The man pulled out an ancient-looking gold pocket watch without a chain and said, "It's five minutes to eight, ma'am."

"Oh, I've got to hurry. Thank you, sir."

"My name is Ernest, ma'am, Ernest Watson, and it was my pleasure," he said with a tip of his hat.

As she walked away, Anna glanced back over her shoulder. She rewarded Ernest with a little smile and rushed off toward the tall building on her right.

With his hat back on and pushed up high on his forehead, Ernest stood watching the young woman go, all the while admiring the way her dark dress brushed against her legs.

Ernest had been in Chicago just over a year and had quickly learned to appreciate the tight cut of women's clothing in the big city. No flour sack dresses here—all the ladies he saw coursing up and down Michigan Avenue were dressed in professional-looking suits and wool dresses. They all had bright red lips and stylish hats. Of course, that's not counting the "Apple Annies" who sold their fruit on the streets and alleys until some tightfisted merchant shooed them away.

Ernest probably looked like an "Apple Annie" himself when he first came to Chicago. It had taken him several months before he could keep from just standing and staring up at the endlessly tall buildings. He had come up from Tennessee in Matt's old Dodge truck. His only possessions were a few dollars, a basket of food, and a desire to change the slow pace of his life. He had grown up seeing his father and other old men shrink into their later lives, sitting outside Mr. Padgett's General Store, whittling pieces of wood into nothing particular. He knew this was not for him. He wanted purpose beyond the daily necessities.

On his first day in Chicago, he drove out to the Central Depot and asked everyone in a uniform if he could make deliveries. Over and over, the railroad conductors said "no." After a week of sleeping in his truck in the rail yard, Ernest could divide the conductors into two groups: those who would kick dust and spit at him when he approached and those who began to admire his persistence. Ultimately, one of the men in the latter group gave Ernest a chance. With a tiny stub of a cigar between his brown teeth, the crusty old man pointed to a car at the back of the line. Soon, Ernest had a truck loaded with soybeans. After he dropped them off, he returned quickly and worked this way all day—seven days a week. He would transport everything from canned vegetables to animal feed, from small farm equipment to leather goods.

Today, his job was to deliver produce to the grocer on Michigan Avenue. Having done that and saved a lovely redhead in the bargain, Ernest walked around his truck to enter the cab.

"Hey, fella, what's your name?" came a gravelly voice from the alley next to the grocery store. Ernest walked back over to a man in suit pants and suspenders who was leaning against the wall.

"Ernest Watson." Ernest extended his hand. The man shook it vigorously.

"The name is Willy Conrad. Most around here call me 'Detroit Will,' though." Sticking his thumbs in his suspenders and gesturing his head in Anna's vacant direction, he said, "She's a real twist, ain't she? I've seen her beating up and down these streets—another dame looking for a job."

"I reckon," said Ernest, anxious to get back to the depot.

"You got a job, boy?"

"Yessir, I deliver goods for the Burlington Q rail," replied Ernest with pride.

"Boy, that ain't no job! What do you make? A dollar a day? Dollar and a half?"

"What's it to you?" Ernest's pride was now melting into aggravation. He turned to go, but Willy grabbed his arm.

"Come on, boy, don't get sore. I wanna help you. I was once a young fella like you, just looking to make a buck. Listen here. I know a delivery job that'll keep you rolling in the dough and I ain't talking about bread. Alls you gotta do is make some deliveries for some friends of mine. They'll pay five dollars a day at first. If you're good at it, it'll be more."

"What kind of job is it?" asked Ernest, suspicious but hopeful.

Willy pulled him closer and looked around. "You're from the south, yeah? What do you like down there? White corn whiskey? Tennessee bourbon? We make all kinds of whiskey. The boss just needs the stuff delivered to some snazzy clip joints and speak-o's right under the schnozzle of the fuzz, see? I figure you been all over town in that jalopy and they won't know what's what."

Ernest didn't want to break any laws, but he did want to improve his lifestyle. He took a deep breath, leaned back against the wall next to Willy and flashed his one-dimple smile. "You know, back home, we got a preacher who drinks sour mash whiskey every winter for head colds. I reckon if Pastor Cooley does it…"

"Hey, Jesus Christ hisself preferred it over water, so no biggie, yeah?" Willy recognized the hungry look in Ernest's eyes and knew the country lad was ready to sell his soul.

"O' course, I saw Pastor Cooley one Christmas higher than a Georgia pine trying to hang stockings on the toes of the Crucified Savior statue at the back of the sanctuary…"

"Well, we all gotta have our fun, even holy men, yeah? So what do you say? Are you in?" Willy was ready to close the deal. Ernest was not aware that Willy's regular delivery boy had just been pulled over and his truck confiscated.

"I'll do it, Mr. Conrad. When do I start?"

Willy put his chubby hand on Ernest's back and directed him toward the alley. "First, you come back here with me to my office and we'll get set up. Did you ever carry a gun before, Ernest?"

Ernest stopped walking. "Now what would I need a gun for?"

"Hey, you never know what might happen out there on the road. There's a lot of not-so-friendly competition in the whiskey business, you might say. You could meet up with some dumb cluck late at night and whammo! It's all over." Willy finished his remarks with his hand shaped like a gun, then he grinned.

He enjoyed introducing young men to their first taste of the criminal underworld. "And I'm thinking it would help your cover if you keep on at the Central Depot every day or so. That way nobody will be the wiser, yeah?"

    They walked in through a door off the alley. Willy's office consisted mainly of a table and a chair. It looked as if he had kept it simple in case he needed to be relocated in a hurry. Willy hopped his plump rear onto the desk and began writing down addresses for pick-up. He reached for a smoking cigarette sitting on a heap of ashes and took a drag. "Here's where you need to go today. Most of our distilleries are just outside the city. You do just what I tell you and you'll be fine, got it?"

Oh to Grace

Chapter 9

We never went to visit Ernest when he was in Chicago. Travelin' was a lot harder to do years ago than it is now. Momma and Daddy didn't even get a car 'til after I was born. It was a dark red Buick and Daddy loved it like it was his baby. He washed it every Saturday—the same time we was all gettin' our go-to-Sunday-church baths. Travelin' makes me think of the "Gypsy Queen." You ever hear of a man by the name of Frank Heath? Well, on the day I was born—November the 4th, nineteen and twenty-seven—he finished up his trip across all of the forty-eight states. It took him two years and more than 2,000 miles to do it. Imagine that—just Heath and his horse Gypsy Queen. She walked all that way—'cept for when they rode the ferries and a couple hundred miles in Texas that was quarantined due to tick fever. Matt told me that story a million times with all kinds of adventures thrown into every state. He kept clippings from newspapers that described all about their trip. He even made a book of 'em. When I got older, I remember thinkin' Gypsy Queen must have been the most wonderful horse ever. O' course, Heath got most of the credit on account of he had the idea to do it, but any way you look at it, it was a miraculous thing. You know, it's like FDR said, "There are many ways of goin' forward but only one way of standin' still." Some people feel they gotta keep moving, keep moving and that's okay, but oft-times, after awhile, they see they been goin' in the wrong direction. If only everybody was ridin' Gypsy Queen, then we'd get where we need to be! It puts me in mind of my old next-door neighbor, Miz Golden Walker. Miz Golden was as blind as a bat and got confused pretty easy. Back when I was still drivin', I carried her to her doctor's appointments and the drugstore and such places. Every time she got in my Oldsmobile, she said, "I don't know where we're goin' but we're on our way!" She just enjoyed the ride even without gettin' any of the scenery!

CHICAGO
OCTOBER 20, 1932

Despite her shaky self-confidence after breaking a heel on the way to her interview, Anna was able to type fifty-seven words per minute on the Underwood Portable Typewriter in the back office of Griffith & Sons Insurance Company. Mr. Griffith's aloof personal secretary gave her the dictation test. Her name was Gertrude Blum and she had been with Griffith & Sons for twenty-five years. She possessed no other aspirations in life than to please the elder Mr. Griffith, crack down on the young secretaries in the typing pool, and obtain more cats for her apartment. Over the years, she had evolved into a human version of her favorite pet. She had soft, pale hair growing all along the edge of her cheeks, across her lip, and around her chin, framing it with smooth fur. She had the cool demeanor of a cat, too, but none of the playfulness.

Anna only hoped that Miss Blum never found out that the typing school on her application was fictional and she had actually honed her skills in the garden shed of a bootlegger. Her main source of confidence was that she could type well and fast—she could knock out the Lord's Prayer in less than two minutes with only two fingers.

On the morning of the six-month anniversary of the start of her job, Anna was called in to the office of James Joseph Griffith, Jr., also known as J.J. Unlike his father in almost every way, J.J. was tall and lean where James, Sr. was short and plump. He perched his athletic physique on the edge of his mahogany desk in a meditative imitation of *The Thinker*, while his father always sat in his leather chair, never standing unless absolutely necessary. James, Sr. had only one son, but when J.J. joined the company, he had preferred "Sons" for the company name. He felt it gave it a more stable sound in a financially uncertain time.

"Close the door behind you, Anna," said J.J.

Anna walked briskly into the room, pad and pencil in hand. She held a single-minded devotion to her job. She refused to take any shortcuts in her work and was always the next-to-last person to leave the office; Miss Blum would sooner spend the night under her desk than leave before one of her subordinates.

J.J. twirled his wedding band on his ring finger while he was thinking—an involuntary habit he had developed over the eight years of his marriage. "Take a letter…" He paused here and looked at Anna's crossed legs hanging over the edge of her seat. Suddenly distracted, he said, "Anna, I hope you don't mind me asking, but do you have a special fellow?"

Anna blushed, unsure of what to say.

"I mean, a pretty girl like you should have a string of men in line. I know it's none of my business, but I just want you to be happy. I want that for all of the employees of Griffith and Sons Insurance Company." Here, J.J. slid over to the seat next to Anna. "Are you happy, Anna?"

Anna realized that no one had ever asked her that question before. In fact, she had never placed much of a value on happiness. Who had time to be concerned about being happy when there are so many more immediate worries?

"Yes, sir. I'm very grateful for this job." Anna placed a hand on her chest to show the extent of her feelings.

"But are you *happy?*" he pressed. She struggled with another answer, and before she knew what had happened, J.J. was telling her of his *un*happiness: he was a frustrated actor and a frustrated husband. He never wanted to enter the insurance business, but it had been a foregone conclusion by his father. He revealed things to Anna the likes of which she had never expected even her closest friends to divulge.

Suddenly, there was a sharp knock at the door and Miss Blum entered. J.J. sprang up before she could see anything unprofessional, but Miss Blum could sniff out scandal and she was on the trail of something socially unacceptable. She furrowed her brow and placed a stack of letters on his desk. Exiting, she left the door wide open.

"Thank you, Anna. That will be all for today. Uh, please get that out in triplicate form," said J.J. as he rounded his desk and sat in the chair. Anna looked down at her empty notebook and swiftly glided out the door, nearly running to her seat. Her heart was pounding, but why? She was unfamiliar with this type of attention from a man of his importance. She moved on through her day, completing all of her tasks adequately, but eager for a word or look from her boss.

THE SAME DAY
CICERO, ILLINOIS

Ernest had been on the job for Willy Conrad for six months. Work was slow at first, but he kept busy with his deliveries for the railroad. He liked the money he was making with Willy. It was no more work than his other job, but now he could more than triple his earnings. He had heard rumors that President Roosevelt might lift the ban on liquor sales as soon as next year. Unhappily, he wondered if his services would become obsolete.

At the rail yard this morning, he had seen the two men who

worked for Willy. Their presence was the signal for him to look under the foot pedals of his truck for the details of his next job. After they drove away, he nonchalantly strolled to his truck and opened the envelope. The paper had a home address just outside of Chicago and the name *Sanders*. He patted his right leg to check that he had his small pocket pistol with him this morning. There hadn't been any reason to need it so far and he hoped that wouldn't change today. He loaded his truck bed with pumpkins to deliver on the round trip back into the city.

As soon as he had saved enough money, Ernest installed a Roger's Majestic Batteryless Radio in his truck. As he crossed wires and re-read the instructions, he wished that Matt was there to help him, but he eventually got it humming. As he made his way down Michigan Avenue, then headed west toward Cicero, he turned the dial, searching for a strong signal.

"*It is our honor to present for your entertainment, Cecilia Chambers and her associates as they bring you the Powder Room Review. An announcement of unusual importance for every woman in the audience will be made later in the broadcast...*"

"Nope," Ernest muttered as turned the dial again.

"*Campbell Soup brings you Amos 'n' Andy...*"

"Now we're talkin'," he said. Pleased, he put both hands back on the wheel.

"*How-de-do, everyone. This is Bill Hayes...*"

"How-de-do to you, Bill Hayes." Ernest waved to the invisible broadcaster.

"*For many years, Campbell Soups have been a staple ingredient for any discerning housewife. How would she cook without them? We are now pleased to introduce Campbell's Cream of Mushroom Soup—a soup for every member of the family. People who love mushrooms have taken to Cream of Mushroom. Those who have never tasted mushrooms in any form are just as enthralled by the unique taste...*"

"Ya lost me, Campbell Soup," he said, disgusted by the long advertisement. He turned the dial again, wishing he could hear Uncle Dave Macon or Fiddlin' John Carson—the music from his youth in Morgan's Hat. Today, he would be happy just to whistle to a familiar tune. Finally he found Duke Ellington and his band.

It don't mean a thing if it ain't got that swing…

Suddenly, Ernest heard something *whiz* past the window. Then, *whoosh*, a rear tire burst and deflated. The truck swerved to the side. He looked out the back and saw someone pointing a gun at him. He ducked down and drove his truck into a bumpy ditch. The car behind him followed, but veered wildly to avoid the pumpkins that came flying out of the truck bed. The largest pumpkin eventually became dislodged and rolled toward the tailgate. Ernest hit a sharp bump and the mammoth gourd was airborne, crashing into the windshield of the car behind him. As the glass spread everywhere, the driver lost control and drove up out of the ditch into a field. The car burst through a fence and ran into a tree at full speed. The man inside the car maintained the momentum as he flew out the window.

Ernest stopped his truck. He sat, trying to catch his breath and regain his wits. He looked behind him and saw the crumpled body of his assailant. Shaking violently, he opened the door and walked over to the man. Ernest booted him gently with the toe of his shoe and saw no movement. At that moment, a police car pulled up on the highway next to the ditch where Ernest was standing.

"Stay right there, son," said the officer. He slid down into the ditch and stood by Ernest. He gestured toward the dead man. "Now what happened to him?" Ernest attempted to explain while the officer looked at him suspiciously. "Son, do you know who that fella is?"

"No," Ernest said honestly.

"That's Dan Fitzgerald. He's one of Bugs Moran's men…or

at least he was."

Ernest looked blankly at the officer.

"He was a mean one. They called him 'Slappy Dan' cause he liked to rough up anybody that crossed old Bugs. We've been looking for him for weeks. A witness saw him running away from the pier the night Leo Giovanni was shot," he explained. "Now why do you think he would be chasing you?"

"I can't rightly tell you, officer. I reckon he must've mistaken me for somebody else," Ernest said, looking as innocent as he could.

"Well, I'll have to take a look in your truck, son," said the officer. He looked it over carefully. Ernest was relieved that he hadn't gone to pick up the liquor from the bootlegger yet.

The officer squinted at Ernest. "I'll tell you what, son. You get that tire fixed and get on your way and I won't write you up for anything. But you better keep your nose clean, you hear me?"

Ernest declared his innocence again, said good-bye to the police officer, and walked back over to his truck. His hands still shook as he looked for something to patch his tire before pumping it back up. The officer stood by his squad car as he filled out the necessary forms, while Ernest nervously glanced in his direction. More than once, he fumbled the wheel nuts, forcing him to crawl under his truck to retrieve them before reattaching the rim.

Ernest finally got back on the road, hours later than he had intended. When he reached the address on the paper, he was surprised to see an older woman answer the door and direct him to the back of the house. There was a shelter built over the outside entrance to the cellar. He backed the truck right up to the door. She had her tall, beefy daughter help to load the barrels in the back of the truck. Then she gave him an old mattress and other household items to camouflage the liquor. "Now you bring these back, understand?" said the older woman, wagging her finger at him. "Gladys, you ninny! That's my best coverlet!" She fussed at her daughter and grabbed the quilt from the arms of the chagrinned girl. "You know that was the wedding ring quilt I was saving for your hope chest, stupid girl! Not that you really need it—the way things've been going! I had four young girls living here less than a year ago and she's the only one left. What about you? You gotta girl?"

"I'd b-b-better be going, ma'am." Ernest stuttered as he turned to leave. She jogged up to him and put a hand on his shoulder, roughly spinning him around.

"Well, you tell Willy that if I don't get my money in full, I'll be back with the others before you can say 'narker,'" she said in an effective whisper. "And tell him I don't need a boy to pick up my stuff. I've been making my own deliveries for years." She looked around and saw a neighbor walking out to his garbage can. She closed the opening of her housecoat more securely and called, "Oh, hello, Mr. Jefferies! How are you? This nice young man is taking some things to the poor for me. 'Share with those less fortunate'—that's what I always say!" Mr. Jefferies waved and walked back into his house. "Nosy old crackpot..." she grumbled.

Ernest forced himself not to speed as he left the house, hoping he never had to return to the Sanders' home again. *Good luck to Gladys*, he thought. He couldn't imagine how the towering daughter would ever find a man who could stand her mother.

That evening, Willy stopped by Ernest's tiny apartment. Ernest told him all about the pumpkins and the accident. "Everybody's talking about Slappy Dan," Willy said with obvious pride in his voice, "but they're saying that Officer Kensey did the job. Looking for a reward, I figure. Won't the honorable Mr. Kensey be surprised to know that Bugs has a contract out on him?" He chuckled at the irony.

"Willy, what if they find out I did it?" Ernest had three smoldering cigarettes all going at the same time, and he picked them up alternately with a trembling hand.

"Ah, don't worry, kid! You got good luck. Has Willy gotten you into trouble so far...I mean anything really bad?"

"I was nearly shot today, Willy. That sounds like trouble to me!"

"Calm down, kid. I been telling the big guys all about you and they wanna give you a raise." Willy looked around the bare apartment. "It looks like you could use some more money. Here, take this." Willy handed him a rolled wad of bills and slapped him on the back. "Just have fun, kid. You're doin' great!"

Oh to Grace

Chapter 10

I didn't mind drivin' when I still had my license. My husband taught me how to do it. That was one of the few skills I learned that weren't taught by my brother Matt. I loved riding in Matt's truck—'specially when it was just the two of us. When I was eight, Matt took me to Gallatin to the Palace Theater to see my first picture show. It was Modern Times *with Charlie Chaplin. I screamed to high heaven when the little tramp— that was Chaplin's famous character—put on that blindfold and skated 'round the toy store. I really thought he was gonna fall past the railing down to the bottom floor. I still remember hee-hawin' in Matt's truck on the way home while we was talkin' 'bout the tramp gettin' caught up in the cogs of the machine and slidin' through like a snake. Boy-howdy, that was funny. I asked Matt when we could go again and he said we should save up our pocket money for a while and see another show after we had the two bits we needed for both tickets. That made me a mite mad on account o' I knew Matt had a heap more 'n two bits, and I told him so. I think I even stomped my foot and huffed a little with my arms across my chest, as eight-year old girls are prone to do. He pulled his truck over*

off the road just then and said, "Frankie Jane, when you gonna learn? I just took you to see a picture show and here you are a-fussin'. Why, you'd gripe with a ham under each arm! Is that all I am to you? Just somebody to carry you to the picture show and buy you a ticket? You say 'thank you' to me right now, ya hear?" O' course I thanked him right then and I felt truly sorry for actin' so ungrateful. Matt was the best big brother I coulda asked for and I didn't want him thinkin' that he had to do anything but be hisself to get my love. It's like FDR said, "Self-interest's the enemy of all true affection." When all you do is think of yourself, it'll eventually catch up to you—one way or another.

CHICAGO
SEPTEMBER 5, 1933

Anna looked around her apartment in wonder. Her own place! If it hadn't been for J.J., she would never have been able to afford it. She laid her magazine down on the tiny wooden table. In the quiet of her room, Anna indulged in her favorite pastime—a mental recounting of the circumstances that led to this moment. Maybe it was J.J.'s influence on her, or maybe it was because she had just seen Greta Garbo, glamorous and regal in *Queen Christina*, but she began to think of their romance as acts in a film.

Act one: After that first tender encounter with J.J., the days and weeks had continued for Anna with subtle flirting and heart-racing clandestine conversations in his private office. During one such meeting, Anna had accidentally dropped a pencil. When they both reached down to pick it up, J.J. had grasped her hand and brought it to his lips. He closed his eyes as he held it there. Slowly, reluctantly Anna had pulled it away.

Act two: Her mind tripped to the first time he kissed her. She was sitting on the windowsill, bouncing her foot up and down. They were talking about Chicago weather or some other benign topic, when J.J. crossed the room, pulled her up abruptly, and crushed her in his embrace. She looked up at him, a willing recipient of his kiss. They held this pose as long as they dared until Anna reminded him that she was supposed to be taking a letter to be sent to the First Chicago Bank and Miss Blum would surely want to see it.

Anna felt a wonderful stirring in her stomach as she remembered that kiss. These were the dramatic gestures this handsome man in his mid-thirties showed Anna. She was overcome by his admiration of her. The delight she experienced was almost strong enough to remove any thoughts about the similarities she might have noticed between their encounters and certain scenes she saw at the movie theater. On one occasion she did find it strange when J.J. attempted to feed her lines straight from the film *Grand Hotel*.

"Do you play anything?" J.J. had asked.

"The typewriter," she had said, shrugging.

"Ooh. You're a little stenographer. Fascinating. I don't suppose you'd take some dictation from me, would you? No? Well, how about some tea then?"

"I suppose so..." Anna said, slowly. "But I've just finished my lunch break and I don't think Miss Blum would approve..."

"No, no. You're supposed to say, 'Tea would spoil my dinner.'"

"What do you mean?" Anna asked.

"Oh...well, nothing, dear. I was just...hmm...thinking of something else."

"Do you still need me to take dictation?" Anna began to retrieve her pad and pencil from his desk.

"No. I've got several letters to read over." He sat in his chair, dismissing her with a wave back to the typing pool.

As she left, Anna remembered the scene from *Grand Hotel* when John Barrymore meets Joan Crawford: A baron meeting a secretary. She dismissed the thought with a shake of her head.

Act three: After a few months, their intimacy accelerated.

Soon, J.J. rented an apartment for Anna so she wouldn't have a roommate and they could spend more time alone.

"So you're really moving out?" asked Elise, Anna's long-time friend and roommate, on the last night Anna stayed in their shared one-room apartment.

"Yes," Anna answered. "But I'm sure you'll be able to find a new roommate—one of those girls you work with." At times, Anna had felt envious of her friend when Elise laughed about the stories she brought home from Marshall Field's department store. At first, it sounded like a much happier place to work than the insurance office. Now that Anna had J.J. in her life, she knew this was the place she was meant to be.

"Is it a man?" Elise was filing her nails, wearing her winter coat over her slip, with her hair set in waving combs.

"Elise, I told you. I got a raise and I want to live closer to my office," Anna lied.

"Whatever you say, honey," said Elise, unconvinced.

Anna knew Elise would never stop her, let alone judge her, if she knew her real reason for moving out, but she was afraid of her mouth. Elise had never been able to keep a secret. What if she waited on J.J.'s wife at the perfume counter? Anna didn't want anything to spoil this. She was afraid she would never find love like this again.

Now that she had settled in her new place, she realized her apartment was exactly what she had always wanted—complete privacy. It was the first time in her life that she was able to be alone. She arranged and then re-arranged her meager furnishings frequently, just because she could. It was a one-room apartment, with a bed serving double duty as a sofa—though Anna called it her divan. She had a hot plate to prepare all her cooked meals, but mostly she ate the bread, fruit, and cheese that she bought nearly every day. She had a little table and a chair she used for meals and one lamp that she moved to different parts of the room in the evening—on the table at dinner, by the bed at night.

Her understanding with J.J. was flexible. He would come over at least one night a week, usually Wednesdays. Since he would eventually be missed at home, he never spent the night, so Anna was guaranteed her solitude once again. She didn't press for a definition of her role in his life—girlfriend? Pal? Mistress? To her way of thinking, the latter could not be true, because he had never spent the night, whatever that would involve.

She was just settling down to read her September McCall's magazine—she frugally paced her reading in the magazine to last the whole month—when she heard a click in the keyhole. As it was Tuesday, she was not expecting J.J. To her surprise, he opened the door holding a bunch of pink roses.

"J.J.! Roses? For me?"

"It's your birthday, doll. You didn't think I would forget, did you?"

Her birthday wasn't actually until Thursday and she almost said this, but quickly decided against it. The fact that he even came close was an earth-shattering realization for Anna. For a handsome, sophisticated man to remember an exact day on the calendar some nineteen years ago was asking too much. Anna tossed her magazine on the floor and ran to him. Without thinking, she threw her arms around his neck and gave him a forceful kiss. J.J. was always the instigator in intimate moments, so this was an unexpected pleasure. He dropped the roses, lost his balance, and almost fell on top of her. They both fell to the bed, laughing.

Up to this point, their "dates" consisted of his reading poetry to her, followed by intense necking. He often brought her a small gift—candy, perfume, and once, a little French figurine of a shepherd girl. He knew she spoke French, so the little girl seemed like a perfect gift. He told her the girl's name was Fifi. This had made Anna smile and kiss his cheek.

Tonight was different, though. As their laughter trailed off, she looked down at her arms and saw goose bumps covering them. There was an odd kind of tension in the room. She wanted to ask him how he was able to get out of the house on a Tuesday, the night he usually joined his wife and another couple to play bridge, but Anna didn't feel as if she had a right to ask anything at that moment. He had remembered her birthday!

She stood to pick up the scattered flowers, then filled a pitcher with water and methodically placed the roses in it. J.J. watched her with great interest as she walked to the table and set the pitcher down.

"She's at her sister's," he said quietly.

"What?" Anna was surprised by the comment. Could he read her thoughts?

"Belinda. She went to her sister's house in Indiana. Her sister just had another baby and she went on the afternoon train to see it." J.J. patted the bed next to where he was sitting and Anna obediently joined him. It was only a moment before they had renewed their passionate embrace. J.J.'s hands moved with confidence as he unbuttoned the back of her dress. His movements were tender but without any of the hesitancy that Anna felt. At times during the rest of the evening, Anna considered asking J.J. to stop, but she was caught up in the moment and the ease of their physical chemistry. Her mind was able to shut down and let her instincts completely take over. On the rare occasions when her conscious thoughts did swim to the surface, Anna reminded herself that J.J. loved her and this was his way of showing his love.

The next morning, J.J. was up early, dressing to leave. He kissed her forehead and tiptoed out the door. Anna had only pretended to be sleeping. She didn't know what to think of their relationship or J.J. or herself, so she didn't want to have an awkward conversation with him this morning. She rolled over on her side and wrapped her arms around herself, staring at the door that had just closed.

Chapter 11

Morgan's Hat
1918 & 1931

Are you hungry, honey? If you'll wheel me down to the cafeteria we can get us some dinner. I believe they've got chicken-fried chicken today. So if you like meat that's flat and mushy, it'll be right up your alley. Go on and keep that recordin' machine runnin' while we're in the elevator and I'll tell you more about the picture shows we saw when we was kids. (sound of elevator door opening) *Push number 1, honey. We're headin' to the first floor.* (sound of elevator door closing) *Well, we finally got a movie theater of our own in Morgan's Hat when I was about fifteen. It was really nothin' more 'n a big hot room with a white sheet, a reel-to-reel projector, and a bunch a foldin' chairs, but it was better 'n drivin' all the way to Gallatin every Saturday night. When I was seventeen, my friend Adell and me went to see the movie* Bathing Beauty *with Esther Williams. There's one part when she's got a lot of swimmin' gals around her then she raises up above 'em all, lookin' like a queen. Yep, I reckon she was the most talented movie star in the world. Besides swimmin,' she could sing and dance and act. I saw a program on her the other night. They said she broke her neck when she* was makin' Million Dollar Mermaid *and it's no wonder with some of the stunts she did. Adell and me saw that one, too. We just sat there and imagined that we was her, swimmin' the English Channel and gettin' famous. Growin' up near a river, Momma and Daddy made sure we all knew how to swim. Daddy took all the boys out to Fiddler's Bend and showed 'em what to do, but Matt taught me and Della. Matt usually cut up with us girls, but he was serious as a pallbearer when he was teachin' me how to swim. I was a real good swimmer ever after that. You know in that television program, they said Esther Williams was married four times—that's one more 'n Della!*

Morgan's Hat, Tennessee
January 28, 1918

"Momma, I wanna go out!" Clara wailed for the fifteenth time that morning.

"I told you to stop that catterwallin', missy, and I meant it! You gonna wake your brother."

Clara defiantly put her hands on her hips. "I wanna go out!"

"You're fixin' to get a Momma-whoopin' to beat the band!" Burnetta menacingly waved a wooden spoon at Clara with one hand, while using the other to hold up her considerable belly. Burnetta was almost nine months pregnant and her impish three-year old was stretching her patience to the limit. "It's too cold for you, girlie."

"It not waining no mo, Momma. I wanna go out!" Clara was unfazed by her mother's threats. Her parents had not been able to find an effective form of punishment for this strong-willed sprite. Clara was an intensely burning flame of personality that could charm any friend or stranger, but she wore her mother to a frazzle. Burnetta had stayed up all night with her teething toddler son, and this pregnancy was taking its toll on her lower back. She sent Ernest to the shop with his father, Buddy was napping, and Matt was old enough to amuse himself. Now Clara had to be dealt with.

Burnetta exhaled loudly. "I think Matt's out in the barn. I reckon you can go and see him, but that's it!" She bundled Clara up and watched her walk ten of the twenty yards to the barn. Clara loved to be outside—no matter what kind of weather. They were experiencing an unusually warm afternoon and the above-freezing temperature was melting the few remaining patches of snow. Clara stopped to investigate a frozen puddle created by the last night's sleet, intrigued by the twigs and leaves suspended in ice. Burnetta stuck her head out the door and shouted, "Go on, girl! You're as slow as Christmas!" She realized Clara would never make it to the barn without a minor bottom-swatting, so she threw a shawl over her shoulders and got her the last few feet to her destination.

"Matt, watch your sister for me," she said. Without waiting for a reply, she turned and walked back to the house.

Upon entering the barn, Clara began looking for her brother. "Ma-att! Where is you?" she called.

"I'm up here, Clara-Bell," Matt said from up in the hayloft. The nearly ten-year old Matt was intently reading *Treasure Island*, a book borrowed from his teacher, Mr. Allen. He had made himself a nest out of potato sacks and hay and anything else he thought would keep him warm while he read.

Clara put her hands on her hips, looking just like her mother. "Come on down here, Matt." She also sounded like her mother.

"You ain't my boss," he said, without even looking up from his book.

"I gots to ask you somethin'." She pleaded with her dark eyes.

"Ask me now."

"No, you come down 'cause I cain't come up!"

"That's 'xactly why I's up here! So you'd best go ahead and ask me now."

Clara stuck out her lower lip, but knew she was beaten. "Is we gonna get any mo snow?"

Oh to Grace

"What?" Matt was barely even listening to his baby sister.

"Is we gonna get any mo snow?" she said louder. "That's what I's askin' you!"

"Why?"

"You said you'd hep me make a man and I wanna do it now, but we ain't got much snow."

Matt sighed and looked at his sister for the first time since she came in the barn. "Yep, we'll get lots more snow. It's still winter."

"Oh. Now I gots to ask you somethin' else."

"What?" he said in exasperation.

"When's Sassy gonna get a baby?" she asked, pointing to the horse in the nearby stall. "You said she and Mr. Fuller's horsey done got married this summer so's them can have a baby."

"I reckon it'll come 'round springtime."

"Now, I gots to ask you somethin' else. Who did Mr. Fuller bwing for momma so's she can have a baby?"

"Clara! That ain't how it works with people!"

"Well, then how's come Momma's got a baby under her apron?"

Matt tried to think how to answer her question and then looked back down at his book. He had read the same sentence five times in a row since she came in. He was halfway through the book, in the middle of the attack at the stockade. If Clara continued to interrupt his reading, he would never find out if Jim finally digs up the treasure. He would have to return the book the next day to Mr. Allen without finishing it. He studied the drawing of Jim Hawkins in a sword fight with two cutthroat pirates and grew more disgusted by the second.

"Well..." she tapped her toe on the barn floor.

"Clara, get outta here! I'm tryin' to read!" he fumed.

Her lower lip began to tremble. "But, I wanna go down and toss wocks in the wiver with you!"

"Go on by yourself and leave me be!" he shouted.

Clara ran out, crying. Matt furrowed his brow in righteous indignation and snuggled down deeper into his little nest. He read a few more pages and then sighed heavily. He shook his head, grumbling about the trials of being the oldest brother of so many young nuisances.

Suddenly his breath caught in his chest. He remembered what his father had told him that morning about the late January thaw and the rising levels of the Tennessee River. A shiver ran through Matt's entire body. He threw the book aside and quickly slid down the ladder. Bursting out the barn door, he ran toward the river. The water was higher than he'd seen it all winter. It overflowed the bank and reached the lower part of the tree trunks. Frantically, he called out to Clara, but all he heard in reply was the rushing voice of the water.

He stood on the bank at the U-shaped Fiddler's Bend. In the summer, this was his favorite fishing spot and the place he always brought Clara. They would dangle their legs in the water here and lean against the smooth bark of the crooked tree. Now he stood, calling for her, with soaking shoes and socks, the water lapping at his ankles. He slipped in the thick mud and then turned to run back to the house.

"Momma, Momma!" Matt yelled as he reached the back porch.

"What're you hollerin' 'bout, son?" Burnetta asked. "And why're your britches muddy?"

"I cain't find Clara!" he panted. Burnetta saw the worry on his face. "I think she mightta gone down to the river."

"My baby!" Burnetta screamed. She gave Matt a wild, angry look and said, "Go and git your daddy!" Matt ran outside and vomited in the grass. He stood bent over with his hands on his knees, trying to still his spinning thoughts and catch his breath. As soon as he had finished retching, Matt started off for the town square.

It wasn't until two days later that they found Clara's body. She was tangled in some branches far downriver by Greer

Sidebottom's place, just outside of Morgan's Hat. His dogs found her body that morning and howled until Greer came out. It had snowed the night before, and her dark hair was barely visible under the white frosty blanket.

When Greer brought the news to Frank and Burnetta, Burnetta's contractions started and Baby Clarence was born that night. Matt stayed in bed for the next several days. Doctor Jameson said he had pneumonia brought on during the long, feverish search for Clara, but his guilt was what nearly killed him. His Grandma Dingus, Burnetta's mother, came to stay with them. She split her time between caring for Burnetta and the new baby, keeping an eye on Ernest and Buddy, and nursing Matt back to health.

Granny Dingus was a legend in the ridges of the Pine Mountains—in the center of Appalachia country. She had doctored many newborn babies, elderly rheumatics, and everything in between. Momma Orpha—as she was known by the Appalachian locals—could find the necessary ingredients within a half mile of her home to make a remedy for just about anything. Now she would heal her own grandson. She made a paste of black mustard powder, flour, and water. With a skillful hand, she applied it to his chest and covered it with pieces of muslin soaked in hot water. When his suffering didn't subside, she placed hot, steamed onions in a cheesecloth pouch and pressed them on his chest. Then she mixed up her special remedy of lemon juice, honey, and homemade brandy and poured it down his throat daily, with no change.

"Son, I reckon, Momma Orpha knows what's the matter," she said as she sat on the edge of his bed. "The problem ain't your lungs, but it *is* in your chest...right *here*." She thumped him on the chest with a calloused thumb and middle finger. "You gotta forgive yourself. Clara's an angel now and she loves you. She ain't mad." Granny kissed his forehead and left the room.

In the darkness of his room, Matt closed his eyes and

whispered a prayer. "Jesus, I'm awful sorry that I wadn't nicer to Clara. Please don't send me to hell with the devil. And please let Momma love me again." He wiped his face on his pillow and fell into a deep sleep.

That night, Matt dreamed that he and Clara were rowing in a boat. They made it to a tiny island and pulled the boat ashore. Matt stood in the sand and looked around. Everything shone with a blurry brightness. Then Matt started checking his pockets for a treasure map. Clara smiled and shook her head. She pointed in one direction and ran off. Matt followed without question. At one point, he looked around and couldn't find her. "Clara!" he called. The same sick feeling he'd had in the barn began to spread inside him until he saw her again, standing next to a huge wooden chest near a hole in the sand. Clara opened the chest. It was overflowing with pearl necklaces, dark red jewels, and golden coins. She threw a handful into the air and squealed with laughter. She reached out to grab Matt's hand, squeezing his fingers and smiling at him with her dark, piercing eyes. At that moment, Dream Matt felt bathed in forgiveness. He knew that Clara loved him and always would.

Suddenly, Matt's newborn brother wailed loudly in the room next door and Matt awoke from his dream. The warm wash of forgiveness fled away, like stepping out of a hot bath onto the cold kitchen floor. Matt closed his eyes again, but the accusing face of his mother pressed into his mind. He tried to retrieve the dream, but this time Clara stayed lost and the chest was full of ghostly figures. He attempted to clamp shut the guilt, like closing a chest and locking it, but it just wasn't that simple.

Oh to Grace

Chapter 12

That chicken-fried chicken weren't too bad after all. They have to cook everythin' around here 'til it's nearly pass eatin' on account of so many of us don't have the teeth nor the stomach to get real food down no more. That's the reason why Della won't move in here with me. She said she'd ruther die at home after eatin' a good roast than live to be a hundred and eat food that she can't make out what it is. My sister Della Mae is somethin' else—I tell you. She married young—too young if you ask me. She was barely sixteen. Her and Blakely had hardly 'nuff sense to come in outta the rain, so when they had Dillon, Della's oldest, Blakely was gone faster than a knife fight in a phone booth. He cut out to North Carolina when Dillon was a week old and Della got the divorce papers before Dillon was walkin'. A couple of years later, Della married an older carpenter named Lynnwood. They was married for 'bout four years. Della had Annie and Ginger with him. He was a good sort of fella—always covered in sawdust with bruises and scrapes all over his knuckles. But he died of a heart attack when he weren't yet forty. After that, Della swore she'd never marry again. She got a job at a bakery and lived in Momma and Daddy's old house. When she was more 'n fifty years old she carried Dillon's boys

to Silver Dollar City—that's an amusement park in Branson, Missouri. That's when she met a good-lookin' Yankee fella named Vic. Her grandsons was watchin' one of them Hatfield vs. McCoy shootin' shows and Della started gettin' upset. Vic came over and pulled her out a chair. He helped her calm down on account of Della didn't see they was all actors pretendin' to shoot each other out in the street. He explained the blood and bullets was all fake. Della said Vic patted her hand real gently and he had the softest hands and prettiest nails of any man she'd ever knowed. They kept up callin' and visitin' each other—mainly meetin' up in Branson. They was real good friends. They had heaps in common. They both loved Marvel Cave and singin' shows and Andy Williams. Vic kept a-beggin' Della to marry him but she said she wouldn't. She figured she'd made it that far without a husband, so why get one now? He asked her, "If I get Andy Williams to ask you for me, will you do it?" She said sure, knowin' that the chance of him ever gettin' to meet Andy Williams was pretty slim. But, sure 'nuff, after Andy opened his theater there in Branson, he got Vic and Della up on stage and proposed for him. She couldn't say no in front of all those people. Della was sixty-two years old when she got hitched that third time. You know that sayin' 'Third times the charm?' Well, it sure was true for Della. They had a real nice ceremony at the house and they played "Moon River" when they was walkin' out. They even found somebody who made a cake that looked like Andy Williams' face for the reception. I never saw Della so happy.

MORGAN'S HAT, TENNESSEE
MAY 20, 1922

There was an unusual commotion at 508 Jefferson Street. The home of the redoubtable Methodist minister was normally a peaceful, if not fiercely silent place, but today was the wedding day of Reverend Hoffman's daughter, Ruth Evelyn. He had fought the chaos at first, but eventually succumbed to his domineering sister and retreated to his study.

"What does an old widower like you know about a wedding, Danford?" Rev. Hoffman's sister had asked. "Go stick your nose in a commentary and leave me to Ruth's trousseau. I've married off four daughters of my own. I believe I know what I'm doing!" There was nothing left to say. Rev. Hoffman was to stay downstairs until he was called to put on his suit and take them to the church. He used this time in his study to polish the sermon he had written for the ceremony. Ruth had only wanted her father to walk her down the aisle, but her father insisted that he would perform the ceremony, too.

Ruth stood in front of a long, oval mirror, wearing a plain white chemise over her corset, and her new navy crepe housecoat over both. Her coal black hair was fastidiously swept up and fluffed in the front, but her tiny bun was desperate for additional hair. Ruth stood holding a lock of false black curls with a hairpin at one end, screwing up her pretty mouth into a frown.

"Aunt Beth, I need you!" Ruth called down the stairs.

"Ladies don't holler, Ruth Evelyn!" her aunt yelled back. "I'll be there as soon as these buttermilk pies come out of the oven."

Feet pounded down the stairs. "Auntie Beth, what am I gonna do with this piece?" Ruth moaned in frustration.

"Ruth Evelyn Hoffman, you get back up to your room! There's all manner of men in and around this house that have no business seeing you dressed like that!" Aunt Beth pulled a straw out of a nearby broom and pierced one of the pies in the center. "That'll have to do," she said to herself as she pulled the golden pies out of the oven. "March upstairs, young lady."

Before they could leave the kitchen, there was a loud clattering in the yard. "What in heaven's name?" said Aunt Beth. She looked out the window and saw one of the hired workmen attempting to right a birdbath he had knocked over. "If that's cracked, you'll be seeing the cost of it come out of your wages!" she yelled out the open window. Then she herded Ruth up the stairs.

"Your guests will be arriving in two hours. We'd best get your dress on." She slid the simple, ecru satin under-dress over Ruth's head and buttoned the back. Then Ruth stuck both arms out as Aunt Beth carefully slid the airy, white overdress of tambour net lace on top and fastened the back. Seven ecru satin flowers with seed pearl centers formed an upside-down U-shape across her chest and created a flattering balance for Ruth's slim waistline. Aunt Beth tugged the net material to eliminate the wrinkles as it spread two feet behind Ruth on the floor. Ruth fluffed the puff sleeves at her shoulders and pulled the cuffs just below her elbows.

"Now...let's take a look at your hair," said Aunt Beth, calmly. She had regained control of the chaos and her renewed poise gave Ruth some needed self-confidence. Aunt Beth tucked the false hairpiece in the bun and pulled down several small curls along Ruth's forehead. "Where's your hair wreath, sugar?" Aunt Beth asked. Ruth pointed to the circle of velvet ribbon sitting on her bureau. It was decorated with the same seed pearl flowers as the dress, with velvet and gilded leaves sewn to the ribbon headband. Aunt Beth deftly set it on top of the black cloud that was Ruth's hair, then stepped back to survey her work. "Lovely," she said at last.

She turned Ruth to face the mirror so that she could see her own reflection again. Ruth smiled, then her lip quivered. "Oh, Aunt Beth...do you think I'm making a mistake?"

"Whatever do you mean, child?"

"How do I know he's the one?" Ruth looked frantic.

"You know because you know," Aunt Beth said matter-of-factly, as she adjusted one of the tiny forehead curls. She was not one to put up with any kind of wedding day jitters. When her daughter Tilly had threatened to walk out on her groom, Aunt Beth had stripped Tilly naked and poured creek water over her head. Aunt Beth didn't take weddings lightly. "You're gonna walk down the aisle at your daddy's church, smile and say 'I do,' then come back here for a very genteel, refined reception. Then you're gonna live a truly happy life, sugar."

Ruth smiled at her wise aunt. Ruth had lived with her in Montgomery for the past year and Aunt Beth had yet to steer her in the wrong direction. But there was a thought that nagged at the back of Ruth's mind: *Napier*. No. She just couldn't think of him now. As Ruth pulled on her white canvas pumps with the glass buckles, her aunt went to the spare room to get dressed. Ruth stood up and looked in the mirror again. "I will marry Verlon McKendree and I will live a truly happy life," Ruth said with determination. She pinched the apples of her cheeks and went downstairs to find her father.

As she descended the stairs, Ruth heard a faint knock at the back door. She paused to see if her aunt or her father would see to the visitor. After a moment she went herself. She opened the door, and standing before her was Napier Allen.

"Oh, Ruth...you look b-b-beautiful..." he stuttered, pulling his cap off and twisting it in his hands. "You look exactly as I dreamed you would."

"Napier. What are you doing here?" Ruth was horrified and yet somehow relieved by his presence. "I'm on my way to the church this very minute!"

"Ruth, you can't! You are my Wenonah...my Juliet...my Penelope..."

"Hush, Napier..."

"Robert Burns said what's in my heart: *Till all the seas run dry, my Dear, and the rocks melt with the sun: I will love thee still, my Dear...*"

"That's enough, Napier. You've gotta get. I don't know what my daddy'll do if he finds you here!" Ruth pushed Napier out the door so she could close it.

"I'll go, Ruth, but tell me one thing. Tell me why you're marrying him when you know you still love me."

Ruth was speechless. With every second she didn't answer,

Oh to Grace

Napier's hopes grew. He reached for her hand.

"Ruth Evelyn," called her father. "Where are you? It's time to head over to the church."

"I've gotta go, Napier." Ruth pulled her hand away from Napier's grasp. "I'm sorry." Then she shut the door.

Following the afternoon ceremony, family and friends found the happy couple at 508 Jefferson Street. There was a large canvas tent set up in the minister's backyard. Under the tent were long tables covered with platters of food and glass dessert plates. A variety of milk glass vases sat on every available flat surface both inside and out, filled with bright yellow and white daisies to match Ruth's bouquet. In the back yard, there was a modicum of laughter and tempered revelry. No one in the party would raise his or her voice or spirit too high—such was the commanding aura of Reverend Danford Hoffman. He didn't knowingly impose this regulation on his guests, but since most were of his flock, they were all too familiar with his superior standards.

There was one in attendance who shouldn't fear that his happiness would become overly raucous—Napier Allen. He wasn't counted among Rev. Hoffman's church parishioners, but Ruth Evelyn had asked he be invited. Her father had been unsure of the reason for the invitation, but he had agreed if for no other reason than to prove to this heretic that his romantic chances with Ruth Evelyn were finally lost forever.

As the party moved around him, Napier Allen—local schoolteacher and Ruth Evelyn's most ardent admirer—sat on a cold stone bench in Rev. Hoffman's small vegetable garden and contemplated his misfortune. Such was his evident misery that no one dared approach him.

A clutch of young ladies stood nearby. Among them was Vera Baker, Ruth's closest friend and maid of honor. "Look at Napier Allen. He's the most pitiful thing I ever seen!" she whispered to her two companions. "Imagine Ruth having two fellas mad for her at the same time. Who would've thought it possible? You know I'm her best friend so I can say this with charity in my heart—she's not what you'd call a classic beauty. Her eyes are terrible far apart and her hair was about as frizzy as I've yet to see it. But watching Verlon during the ceremony and seeing Napier now, it makes you wonder what men are looking for in a wife, don't it?" The unmarried girls nodded as they listened to Vera's comments with great satisfaction, glad to re-package their jealousy into a shared bewilderment at the turn of events. "Oh, excuse me, girls. I gotta get my picture taken with the wedding party. Comin', Ruthie!"

Vera left to join Ruth and Verlon and the rest of the group; Napier's eyes followed her as she walked. Vera was directed to sit next to the already seated Ruth. Other friends and family crowded around and Aunt Beth directed them where to sit or stand. "Ya'll smile!" she said and the photographer snapped the picture.

After the first flash, the photographer drew out from behind the short curtain and frowned. "Let's do another one, folks," he said. "This time, how 'bout a smile from the bride?"

Ruth hadn't noticed the photographer's actions or much of anything that had happened after her father said, "We are gathered here today..." And the reception was a dizzying series of handshakes, hugs, and kisses on the cheek from nearly everyone she had ever known. Since the moment she'd been instructed to sit in the wooden folding chair next to Verlon, she'd been watching Napier in the vegetable garden. As soon as she caught his eye, Napier clambered over the picket fence, into the back alley, and past the row of trashcans. Then he disappeared into the growing dusk.

After Aunt Beth was satisfied with the photo session, Pastor Cooley approached his fellow minister at the reception to congratulate him on his daughter's wedding.

"Reverend," he said to Rev. Hoffman as he pumped his hand in an energetic handshake, "Praise the Lord for this blessed event."

"Thank you, Pastor. It's good of you to come out." Rev. Hoffman braced himself. He knew Zeal Cooley well and anticipated a theological battle.

"I admit to being a trifle puzzled over your selection from Deuteronomy for your homily."

"'All scripture is given by inspiration of God, and is profitable for doctrine, for reproof, for correction, for instruction in righteousness.'" Rev. Hoffman pressed his small leather Bible to his chest. "Which part of God's Word are you opposed to, pastor?"

"You read nearly all of chapter twenty-five, even the verse about what to do when two men are fighting and let's see... 'the wife of the one draweth near for to deliver her husband, and putteth forth her hand, and taketh him by the secrets'... Is this a major point of consideration for your flock, reverend?"

"I'm of a belief that Deuteronomy is filled with instruction that can be helpful to Ruth Evelyn and Verlon. What would have been your passage of choice, pastor?"

"Well, Reverend, I'm mighty partial to Nehemiah ten. After I've read some ninety names of the Levites, they're ready to hear: 'And that we would not give our daughters unto the people of the land, not take their daughters for our sons...'" The color of Pastor Cooley's eyes deepened as his pulpit voice surfaced. "The Lord had sanctified his people..."

"At my niece's wedding," Rev. Hoffman interrupted, "I borrowed from the twenty-ninth chapter of Jeremiah: 'Build ye houses, and dwell in them; and plant gardens, and eat the fruit of them; Take ye wives, and beget sons and daughters; and take wives for your sons, and give your daughters to husbands, that they may bear sons and daughters; that ye may be increased there, and not diminished.'" Rev. Hoffman's voice was quieter but with a much deeper growl. The battle was on.

"Danford..." Aunt Beth approached the men who were encircled by a group of guests, like school children watching a playground fistfight. "Ruth is fixing to leave. You and Pastor

Cooley can do this another time." The men knew better than to argue with her. They slumped their shoulders in defeat and smiled at each other.

"You coming Monday for chess, Dan?"

"I believe so, Zeal." Rev. Hoffman pulled out a small pocket notebook where he recorded his weekly schedule and thumbed through it. "I've got an appointment to do some counseling at nine, how's ten o'clock sound?"

"Sounds all right to me, brother." Pastor Cooley slapped the reverend on the back as they watched the new couple being showered by handfuls of rice. "You'll be in my prayers this week. I know it'll be hard to lose her."

"I appreciate that, Zeal. I really do." Rev. Hoffman gave his friend a two-handed handshake and Pastor Cooley left the yard by a side gate.

While he was in the neighborhood, Pastor Cooley decided to walk the extra couple of miles down the county road and call on the Watson family. It had been more than four years since the death of Frank and Burnetta's young daughter Clara, but the pain was still evident in all of their faces every Sunday morning. Pastor Cooley had no wife or children of his own—he took very literally Paul's advice to the Corinthians to remain unmarried—so all of the members of Berea Baptist were his kith and kin.

As he approached their gravel driveway, he met Matt digging a hole in the corner of the front yard where the drive met the road. Matt was working with such concentration that he didn't notice the minister's arrival.

"You'll be halfway to China 'fore too long, Matt," said Pastor Cooley. "What's the hole for?"

"Evenin', pastor. Daddy says we can get the mail in a box by the road now. So I'm diggin' a hole deep 'nough for the post to go in."

"It's getting dark now. Why don't you walk me up to the house so we can visit for a spell?"

Matt was glad to stop working, but he wasn't sure how a job half done would be greeted by his mother. "I don't know, pastor…"

"I believe I can square it with your ma and pa, son."

Matt picked up his shovel and leaned it over his shoulder. "Yessir," he said, and they began to walk in the direction of the house.

"How's your ma doing?" Pastor Cooley asked. "I know it's been mighty hard on the family since Clara passed."

Matt winced slightly. "I reckon she's all right."

Pastor Cooley let a cool silence settle before pressing on. "And how're you doing, Matt?"

"We all miss her a terrible lot, pastor." Matt said, somberly.

"Matt, do you recall the story about the sinful woman who bathed Jesus' feet with her tears and wiped them with her hair?"

"Yessir," Matt replied.

"When the people rebuked her and scolded Jesus for allowing it, Christ said: 'Wherefore I say unto thee, Her sins, which are many, are forgiven; for she loved much: but to whom little is forgiven, the same loveth little.'" Pastor Cooley paused to let his words sink in. "Matt, I know you feel it's due to you that little Clara drowned that day…"

"Oh, pastor, I…" Matt tried to stop him from speaking any more about Clara. He wasn't aware that others knew his role in the events of that day.

"Now, listen, son. It's time to forgive yourself. Whether your folks believe it or not, it's time for you to believe it. Your ma may seem mad at you, but you can bet your horse and the wagon too that she's madder at her own self." They were almost at the front porch. Pastor Cooley put a hand on Matt's shoulder to stop him from walking any nearer to the house. "Just think of the blessing you'll get, Matt. It's like Christ told that sinful woman: the more love you get that you don't deserve the more you can give it out without wanting anything back. That's grace, son."

Matt lowered his head to hide the tears. Pastor Cooley said, "Now you run in and put up that shovel. I'll go and see your folks."

"Yessir," Matt managed to squeak out. As he rounded the back of the house to enter the barn, he heard Pastor Cooley's loud greeting: "Evening, ya'll. What a fine night for visiting with such a handsome family!"

Oh to Grace

Chapter 13

I really thought Della would never get over Blakely leavin' her and Lynnwood dyin'—but the heart can be a mighty queer thing. And hers bounced back like a rubber band! Della and Vic stayed in a real nice hotel in Branson for their honeymoon. Della's kids wanted 'em to stay somewhere fancier, but they was just glad to be together. I reckon places like Silver Dollar City and Dollywood are pretty common nowadays, but it wasn't always that way. Sometimes it was powerful hard to find somethin' to do, 'specially somethin' that wouldn't get you into trouble. People will crowd up to see some of the strangest things! Did you ever hear of an elephant hangin'? Well, before I was born, there was this circus that come to a city in Tennessee called Kingsport. They had a big ole elephant there named Mary. Accordin' to the stories I heard growin' up, that elephant killed one of her handlers—stepped on his head and squashed it flat. They never did find one of that man's ears. Anyhow, the people in town were so hot over it they wanted to kill that poor ole thing. So they took her to a little town called Erwin because they had a big rail yard and cranes and such. They hoisted her up and the first chain broke, then they did it again. She hung there for half an hour before they decided she was

dead enough. Thousands of people showed up to see the hangin', which is a poor picture of human nature, if you ask me. Why would anyone want to see a dead animal hangin' like that? I reckon circuses have changed a lot. You never knew what you was gonna see back then, 'specially in them sideshow tents. Momma never would let us go in those.

MORGAN'S HAT, TENNESSEE
AUGUST 26, 1922

"Come on, Matt. This is an opportunity of a lifetime!" Ernest spread his arms apart with a flourish, pleading.

"You heard what Momma said. She's gonna raise sand if we go to that freak show," replied Matt, lazily. Matt held his fishing pole as he sat leaning against a crooked tree. He had come to the river looking for a cool place to sit and read *The Red Badge of Courage*, a novel he had borrowed from his former teacher. He didn't really care if he caught any fish. The fishing pole was just a prop to avoid being labeled "bookish" by others.

"Now, Matt, don't call it that. We're just gonna go to the circus, is all. We ain't gonna do nothin' wrong, unless you count takin' our two little brothers out for a day of fun *wrong!*" Ernest's excitement was evident.

"Ah, Ernie, you know as well as me the only reason you're bringin' Buddy and Clarence is 'cause Buddy can flip his shoulders back and wrap his arms all around himself and Clarence has that extra pinkie finger on his hand. You're plannin' to use their peculiar ways to make some money."

Conceding a partial defeat, Ernest gave a lopsided grin and slid his back down the tree to sit by Matt. In all his thirteen years, Ernest's motives had become fairly transparent to his older brother. There wasn't much Ernest could sneak past Matt. "It woulda been fun, though," Ernest continued. "I heard Jackson Fuller sayin' he saw a lady that weighed more'n five hundred pounds. She had a moustache and a full beard, too.

They also saw a pig with three tails and a sheep with two heads. Ah, well, maybe next year…"

"Alright," Matt said in exasperation. "I'll go with you to look it over, but you have to promise me if'n it seems shady, we'll skee-daddle."

Ernest agreed with the conditions and ran back to the house to fetch the boys. He told his littlest brothers they were taking them frog gigging. Burnetta overheard him and asked, "Why're you takin' 'em giggin' in the middle of the day?"

"Momma, I just figured they was gettin' in your hair with all you gotta get done and we'd just take 'em out for awhile," Ernest coaxed. "You just work so hard feedin' and carin' for all us boys."

"Well, I do have a heap of beans to can today. …You just keep an eye on 'em, ya hear?"

"Yes, ma'am." Ernest flashed his one-dimple smile and pushed the boys out the door. Matt remained outside the entire time. He knew the truth almost always found Burnetta, and he didn't want a lie on his conscience. He didn't have the same kind of relationship with his mother that Ernest did. Matt was much more like his father, both in temperament and character.

They started off toward the clearing past the square. They didn't want to run into their father, who was working in his shoe repair shop, so they took the long way to get to the other side. Matt and Ernest took turns carrying Clarence piggy-back. As they wound up and down the residential streets, they talked about the exciting sights they would see once they got to the circus.

Upon arriving at the clearing, the two older brothers' expectations deflated. There were a few large, high-quality circuses touring the country at the time, but no Ringling Bros. or Barnum and Bailey operations were going to make their way to a city without a major train depot. Instead, they were treated with a second-rate imitation. There was one large dilapidated tent in the center with several pioneer-era wagons

Oh to Grace

circled around it like the spokes of a wheel. A couple of men hawked chameleons and bugs in handmade cages and exotic-looking fish in bowls. To the side of the wagons, a woman sold popcorn she had made in a dingy copper kettle over an open fire. Long logs created a sidewalk to queue up customers to the opening of the tent, but this crowd-control device was unnecessary. Attendance was low. It consisted mostly of curious boys in their teens who were keenly interested in the unusual and the grotesque.

Outside the tent, the owner, Clyde Hagenbeck—who was also the barker and the ringmaster—called out to the few patrons standing just out of his reach. Ernest approached him to begin his sell. "Excuse me, sir. I'd like you to take a gander at my younger brothers. For the right price, I think they'd be a real plus for your show here."

The owner ignored Ernest as he took money from a gaggle of boys passing by.

"Aw, come on, Ernie. Let's just pay and go in," Matt whispered.

"Buddy, come here," Ernest said. "Show 'im your trick."

Buddy pulled off his shirt and threw his skinny arms back. His shoulder blades jutted forward, then he wrapped his arms around his back with his hands grabbing each opposite shoulder.

"Alright, kid. Are you gonna pay or what?" snarled Mr. Hagenbeck.

"Wait! We got more. Clarence, show 'im your hand!" said Ernest, pulling his youngest brother forward. Clarence wiggled all six of the fingers on his right hand. The owner snorted.

"Kid, that's nothin'!" he said to Ernest and his brothers. Then turning to those milling around the grounds, he yelled, "If you wanna see something to shock the senses and astound the mind, pay two bits extra and visit the creatures in our wagons."

"I wanna see the horsies," said Buddy, pointing to the tent.

"Just a minute, Buddy," Matt said. "Let's go in the tent,

Ernie."

"Alright..." Ernest relented. As Matt paid for their tickets, Ernest gave a backward glance at one of the wagons. It shook, and a girl and her boyfriend ran out, screaming and laughing. Buddy grabbed Ernest's hand and pulled him into the tent.

The ground was covered with sawdust and horse droppings. Kerosene lamps burned at every corner of the tent, giving off an acrid odor. They easily found seats on the front row and waited for the show to start. When the horses came trotting out, Buddy and Clarence cheered. A man wearing a cowboy hat and chaps jumped on the back of one horse and stood as it continued to jog around the ring. He jumped off and continued with the next horse. Ernest leaned near Matt and whispered, "I'm goin' out to see what's in them wagons."

"We used up all the money just gettin' in here. You heard what that fella said. It's extra to see the freaks," Matt whispered back.

"Well I gotta get in there." Ernest ducked down and exited through one of the side flaps. The owner was arguing with a lady who held a tiny poodle shaved to look like a lion. She was an act in the show, and while she complained about her missing equipment, Ernest used the diversion to run into one of the wagons.

It was dark and musty inside. Once his eyes adjusted to the interior, Ernest saw that it was a crude wooden wagon with a canvas roof. On the bottom, he saw piles of blankets and pillows. He scratched his head, wondering what sights he would witness. Would it be a tiny person with superhuman strength, or identical brothers attached at the backside? Would they be covered in tattoos, with pins in their ears? Finally, he spotted a little girl in the corner. She wore a pretty pink taffeta dress, and her hair was neatly pulled back with a large black bow. She was quietly playing with two dolls, making them talk to each other in high-pitched voices. It was as common a scene as if she were sitting in her mother's parlor, waiting to be called for dinner. Assuming this couldn't be the act, Ernest said, "Hey, little girl. Where's your momma?" At that moment, she shifted to reveal that she had two extra legs. The two outside ones were longer than the two on the inside, but no two legs seemed to be exactly alike. All four were covered in knee-high stockings, and she wore black patent leather shoes of varying sizes. Ernest hopped back for a second, then he slumped his shoulders in disappointment. This was it? She looked up and smiled at him. He gave her a wave, which she returned.

Just then, Mr. Hagenbeck snatched the back of Ernest's shirt and yanked him out of the wagon. "Trying to get past me without paying, huh?" Ernest was so surprised he could only stammer incoherently. "Well, I don't have much patience for thieves, boy, and that's just what you are. I'll be getting the sheriff down here directly!"

"Nah, sir! I wasn't hurtin' nothin'!" Ernest shouted.

At that moment, Matt ran up with the little boys. "What's goin' on here?" he asked.

"Well, it looks like your friend here is gonna spend a night in jail for stealin'. He didn't pay to see the Amazing Four-Legged Girl and I can't abide thieves!"

"The Amazing Four-Legged Girl? Uh, well…our daddy is Frank Watson—he repairs shoes. He's got a shop right across from the courthouse. And he, um…asked us to check on your four-legged girl to see if she needs anythin' fixed b-b-by way of shoes," Matt sputtered out.

Ernest caught on to Matt's strategy and continued. "Yeah, I was just makin' sure her soles were alright and everythin'. You gotta keep celebrities like her happy, I reckon." Ernest couldn't stop now. "Our daddy will fix anythin' you got—on the house—all free."

"Ernie…" Matt punched his arm. Their father would kill them if every strange and misshapen member of this traveling band walked into their father's shop demanding free repairs.

"Daddy," came a small voice from inside the wagon. "This

shoe does pinch a little and the strap is nearly broken. Do you think that boy with the black hair could get it fixed for me and bring it back tomorrow?"

"Okay," answered Mr. Hagenbeck reluctantly. He climbed in the wagon and came out with one of the black shoes. "I'd better see this looking as good as new tomorrow." He slapped the shoe hard into Ernest's hand.

The boys backed out of the clearing with "yessirs" and "see-you-in-the-mornings" at every step as Mr. Hagenbeck watched them leave.

"Phew! That was a close one!" said Ernest with relief when the circus tent was out of sight.

"Ernie, when are you ever gonna learn? I s'pose I'll be gettin' you out of scrapes the rest of your life!" Matt was mad at both his brother and himself. "We should've never gone to that show in the first place." Matt looked down at his two little brothers and saw their tired faces. "Well, let's get on home, boys."

"I'll run past daddy's shop and fix this shoe," Ernest said. "It's just a little job. I'll be done in time for supper." The boys parted ways at the square and Matt took Buddy and Clarence home.

Matt dropped them off on the back porch and gave them each half an apple he cut with his pocketknife. He decided it would be better if he had a mile or two between him and his mother when she noticed they were back from their afternoon adventure. Buddy and Clarence were guaranteed to confess about the circus.

He walked past Fiddler's Bend again, pausing for a moment by the bank. This had been a secret ritual for him for the past five years. He would stand with his back upstream, watching the sharp curve in the line of water as it flowed downstream. The spot where he and his little sister Clara had spent so much time seemed like a fitting place to think about her, but it was also the first place he had searched for her that cold January day. As a part of the ritual, Matt always used this time to talk to Clara. He'd try to calculate how old she would be and imagine how she would look. After several minutes, he continued his walk until he came to the narrow bridge leading to his old schoolhouse.

Matt had graduated more than a year ago, but he still valued any time he spent with his former teacher, Mr. Allen. He could see from the bridge that the door was open, so he walked down the path to the front steps of the schoolhouse. Inside, he saw Mr. Allen opening the large wooden drawers of his long desk, pulling the contents out in armfuls and dumping them into a wooden crate.

Matt cleared his throat to alert Mr. Allen of his presence. "Oh, hello, Matt," said Mr. Allen in a weary voice. "Come to see me off?" Matt noticed for the first time that the hair of Mr. Allen's sideburns was beginning to gray and there were lines around his eyes.

"If I'd-a known you was leavin' today, I'd have brought you back your books I borrowed."

"You can keep whatever you have, Matt. Nashville has a public library where I can get all the books I can carry for free...as long as I bring them back."

"Well, can I at least help you pack up?" asked Matt.

"I'm nearly done," he said." Not much to pack, really. Most of the things will stay here for the next teacher...Miss Bennie Lee Waddle is her name, I believe—all the way from Alabama."

"I reckon your new school in Nashville will have all sorts of fine maps and books," offered Matt, looking for a ray of sunshine in the suddenly darkened room. Was a storm cloud passing by or was it the sad look on Mr. Allen's face that was pulling all of the joy from the room?

"I suppose..." Mr. Allen said in a far-off voice. Matt grabbed a broom and started to sweep bits of dried leaves and chalk dust into a pile. He always preferred to stay busy when a situation grew socially awkward. As he swept, it was hard not to think about why his schoolteacher looked so forlorn and heartbroken. In a town as small as Morgan's Hat, it was impossible for people to keep their business private. That was true for Mr. Allen, too. Matt had hated hearing the hushed whispers about Mr. Allen's misfortune. His sweetheart—Ruth Evelyn Hoffman—had been dispatched to Montgomery the summer before last. Everyone knew it was because her father, the local Methodist minister, thought the match unwise. While she was there, staying with her aunt, Ruth met Verlon McKendree, a recent graduate of Howard University in Birmingham who was on track to be a Methodist minister. Just three months ago, they were married in her father's church. Napier Allen's Ruth was now Ruth Evelyn McKendree and living in Montgomery. Some of the wedding couple's guests claimed to have seen Mr. Allen lurking in the vegetable garden during the reception at the minister's home. They said he was sitting on the stone bench with his head in his hands, crying and yanking up carrots and string bean plants. Matt had doubted this at the time, but the sorrow in his teacher's eyes made him believe it might have happened after all.

As he swept his collection of dust out the door, he noticed a thunderstorm boiling above them and decided he should rush home ahead of it. "I reckon I'll be gettin' home, Mr. Allen."

Mr. Allen looked up from some old letters scattered across his desk. He had forgotten Matt was even there. He pulled a small book from one of the drawers and walked over to where Matt was standing. "I'm so glad you came by. I was wanting to give this to you." He handed Matt the book.

"Thank you." Matt was moved that his teacher would think of him—a former student who hadn't come near to realizing his teacher's hopes and expectations for him. They both looked out at the darkening sky.

"Do you know why they call this Granny Silas Schoolhouse, Matt?" It had held that name for all of Matt's life. He had never bothered to wonder much about its origins.

"No, sir."

"Granny Silas—Adelaide Silas was her given name—was a pioneer woman. Both her parents were dead by the time she was ten, but their deaths didn't stop her from moving on through the unclaimed countryside. She made her way by helping other families with their children. Before he died, her father had taught her how to read and she sat in covered wagon after covered wagon teaching other children the same thing. When she finally settled here, she helped start a school. She taught here for forty-five years. Can you imagine that? She did exactly what she was made to do for nearly her entire life. She was never married or had any children but the people called her 'granny' anyway."

"Down in Cannersville they named their school after a fella who rescued a drownin' baby," said Matt. "I reckon that's different but only a little."

Napier Allen turned to Matt and smiled, looking more like his old self. "How do you figure that?"

"I reckon I might as well be drowned if I couldn't read books—life wouldn't be worth much," Matt said with conviction. "And Granny Silas made it possible for heaps of young 'uns to learn to read and do figurin' and writin'."

Mr. Allen patted him on the back. "I suppose you're right, Matt." He wrote down the address for the boarding house where he would be living and gave it to his former student. They shook hands on the front porch and Matt darted out from under the awning. The rain had begun to fall in heavy drops and he had a soggy jog home.

That evening, by the time they sat down for supper, Matt had completely forgiven Ernest for the events at the circus. Even Burnetta seemed reconciled with the false circumstances of their outing. Ernest told his mother that Buddy and Clarence had heard the whinnying of the horses and so wanted to see them that he and Matt couldn't deny them a trip to the circus. After supper, Ernest had Clarence riding on his back, pretending to do the equestrian tricks they had seen in the tent, and

Burnetta clapped and cheered with the rest of the family.

That night as they lay in bed, Matt asked Ernest to describe the girl in the wagon. By the end of the story, Ernest had convinced himself that the Amazing Four-legged Girl actually needed his help.

"That strap was 'bout to fall off, Matt. I reckon travelin' people like them just don't have time to take care of their shoes." Ernest sighed a weary, self-important sigh, bemoaning some people's lack of responsibility. "I'll carry it over to her tomorrow and see what else needs mendin'." Matt looked up at the ceiling and smiled. He was never able to stay mad at Ernest for very long.

Oh to Grace

Chapter 14

Momma had heaps of rules for us kids growin' up. I reckon most mommas do. Our momma was funny, though, 'cause her rules were mighty specific—like she was just sittin' 'round studyin' on scrapes we might get into and comin' up with a rule for 'em before we got there. Take the one she once told me and Della 'bout climbin' trees. She said, "If'n somebody dares you to climb a pine tree, don't do it 'cause you'll be covered in sap for weeks, but if they say to climb an oak or maple, it's alright. Just don't climb too far out on them branches." Or there was the one 'bout us cuttin' our hair. She said, "Don't go a-cuttin' your own hair or your sister's or your cousin's or anybody else you got a mind to. But if you do, be sure that you bury all that hair 'cause if a bird makes a nest of it you'll have a headache for a month." Ooo-wee! I could go on all day like that! Momma was just so scared of what was happenin' outside of Morgan's Hat, and some scared of what was goin' on right in our own town! She was just born a worrier. Momma's momma—our Granny Dingus—most likely filled her head with all kinds of omens and superstitions when she was growin' up in Appalachia. That would account for her tellin' us to never look in the mirror with two older people

'cause the youngest one will die soon. Or the time when George dropped an umbrella at Aunt Cecilia's and Momma said, "I didn't know'd there been a murder here!" Aunt Cecilia didn't think that one was too nice. She was Daddy's sister and didn't know 'bout some of her queer ways. Queer or not, that was just Momma's way of lookin' after us kids, and, of course, we all need some lookin' after from time to time.

Morgan's Hat, Tennessee
February 15, 1928

The view from the window of Frank Watson's shoe repair shop was monotonous. No one had passed by in nearly an hour. Ernest stood—back bent in a long curve—with his elbows on the counter. His father frowned on the practice of sitting in front of customers during work hours, so Ernest rested his chin on his hands and let his eyelids slowly drift closed.

"Ernest," Frank called from the back room, abruptly startling and awakening his son. "Have you shelved all them tins of Bixby's?"

Ernest stretched before answering. "Yessir." Given the choice between building vegetable beds in the barn to sow starter seedlings for radishes and onions or going in to town to work in the shoe repair shop, Ernest had chosen the shop. Now he wished for the companionship of his brothers on this dreary winter day.

Despite its unexciting appearance, Frank Watson's shop had changed over the years. It seemed the longer he was in business, the less the customers wanted to see what went into fixing their shoes. Three years ago, he built a wall that cut the shop in two. In the "customer" half there was the front door, a window, and a counter. Behind the counter, against the dividing wall, Frank had installed shelves to hold the tins of oil polish and shoe wax, various sized shoehorns, and a new display of socks from the True Shape Hosiery Company. The back half of the shop housed an old potbelly stove and a wooden folding chair with a small footstool between them. There was a low, long bench along one wall with a parade of finished and unfinished shoes in a line. The room was sooty and dark, but the wall of cobbling tools was neatly arranged.

"I'm headin' over to Padgett's," Frank said as he grabbed his hat and coat. "Mind the store for me, son." Frank opened the door, letting in a chilly blast of air before closing it again and leaving.

Ernest tipped his head back and stared at the ceiling. He envisioned his father and the other elder statesmen of Morgan's Hat huddled around a checkerboard or the grocer's lead stove, talking about their bean crops or the outgoing President Coolidge or their mares' new foals. Or worse yet, not talking at all, with only the sound of whittling and an occasional phlegmy spit to fill the void. At a restless nineteen years old, Ernest couldn't imagine a less worthwhile way to spend an afternoon.

He glanced back out the window, mercifully rewarded with a welcome sight. Dorcas Hogg—alone today, though usually on the arm of her brawny but dense boyfriend, Charlie Duncan—checked her reflection in the glass of the shop door. She pulled both of her long brown braids over her shoulders and adjusted her woolen tam o'shanter. She pinched the apples of her cheeks and opened the door. Ernest was thankful for such a lovely distraction on this gray winter afternoon. He stood tall, with an engaging customer service stance.

"Well, if it ain't Miss Dorcas Hogg!" Ernest showed off his winning smile. "Have you come out in this cold weather just to see me?"

"Ernest Watson, you are a fool." Dorcas blushed and giggled. "My Ma sent me to fetch my daddy's rubber boots. Are they mended yet?"

"Well, he only brung 'em in yesterday, but it's been mighty slow so we mightta got 'em done. Don't go nowhere. I'll be back in a jiff." Ernest ducked back to the workroom and found the boots quickly. Not wanting to send Dorcas away and return to his shift of lonely boredom, he set them back under the low bench and returned to his customer.

"Well, Miss Hogg, I cain't find them boots just yet. I 'spect my daddy will be back in shortly. If you can stand my company for a few minutes, you and me can visit for a spell while we wait." Ernest winked at Dorcas with confidence and authority. "We'll get your daddy in his boots 'fore you can say 'bob's-your-uncle.'"

Dorcas smiled coyly. "It's mighty warm in here," she said.

"I reckon it's the stove in the back room. We gotta keep it burnin' real regular."

Dorcas pulled off her thick wool sweater and laid it across the counter. She smoothed the front of her gray chambray apron dress. It was a plain dress, but neat, with darker gray trim around the curved collar and along the top of two square pockets. Her hemline hit just above her knees and she wore dark socks pulled just below them. "I was hopin' you'd be workin' in here today, Ernest. I just passed your daddy as I was leavin' Padgett's." Dorcas slid her hand in her pocket and pulled out an envelope. "I got you a valentine card over yonder and I was wantin' to deliver it to you personally…and alone."

Ernest opened the envelope and pulled out a card with a picture of a puppy wearing a bright blue ribbon around its neck. Threaded through the ribbon was a heart-shaped tag that read: "I have a little secret. Can I be so bold? This is not just puppy love. My heart is yours to hold. Be My Valentine!"

"Why, Dorcas Hogg! I do believe you're sweet on me!" Ernest said in mock surprise. "What'll Charlie think 'bout you givin' me a card like this?"

"Charlie Duncan is the most tiresome boy in all of Morgan's Hat!" Dorcas fumed. "I had my birthday last month—I turned seventeen, you know—and Charlie didn't so much as kiss my hand. Then yesterday was Valentine's and do you think Charlie remembered me? I declare he did not. He had nary a thought for the gal he's been goin' with for almost a year!"

"If Charlie Duncan ever had a thought it would die of loneliness," Ernest said, attempting to pour gasoline on her flaming fury. "Only a full-out moron would take no notice of a girl as pretty as you…or maybe he's just too sure that he's got you hook, line, and sinker."

"He's got no such thing," she answered quickly. "I'm as free as a bird."

Dorcas propped her elbows on the counter, rested her chin on her hands, and leaned forward. She stared at Ernest in a way that made him feel like a hunted animal—and oddly enough, Ernest realized he liked the feeling.

"Polly Clabo told me last week that you was the best kisser she ever had," said Dorcas.

"Polly Clabo? I ain't kissed her in years. She was the first girl I ever kissed, though. I must've been 'bout twelve." Ernest assumed a similar position, inching closer to Dorcas' button nose. "I've had heaps more practice since then, so I reckon I'm an even better kisser now."

"I only ever kissed ole Charlie, so maybe you could give me a lesson…"

Just as their lips were about to touch, the door was thrown open. "Get away from my gal, you egg-suckin' dawg!" Charlie Duncan bellowed from the doorway.

"Charlie!" Dorcas cried. Her face was lit up with pure delight. "What are you doin' followin' me all over town? Get on out and leave me to tend to my own business."

"But Dorcas," Charlie whimpered. "You told me to meet you here at four o'clock and that's just what I did." His voice grew louder as he looked in Ernest's direction. "But what do I find but this fella tryin' to love you up right in front of all of Morgan's Hat!" Charlie looked confused and hurt. He also looked as if he could lift a tractor with one hand, so Ernest was beginning to feel nervous. "Ernest Watson, you come out from behind that counter and fight me like a man."

Dorcas' eyes grew wide with anticipation. Ernest added together the talk of Polly Clabo and Dorcas' feelings of underappreciation and came up with her manipulative plan to make Charlie jealous. He had been a pawn in her scheme and now it looked as though he would be a beaten and bruised one.

"I said come out, Watson! I'm gonna give you such a lickin' that you'll never look at my gal again." Charlie roared louder. Just at that moment, Matt passed by the door.

"What's goin' on here?" Matt asked, closing the door behind him.

"Charlie thinks me and Dorcas have been up to somethin', but Charlie—of all people—should know Dorcas is just as pure as the driven snow," Ernest said anxiously.

"Ah, Ernie, you don't have to stick up for me," said Dorcas, a little annoyed. She obviously wanted to see them fight.

Matt drew up to his full height and squared his shoulders as he approached Charlie. He wasn't quite his equal in size, but it was close. Charlie advanced on Ernest and Matt stepped between them. He put a firm hand on Charlie's shoulder, keeping him from coming any nearer to his brother.

"All right, Charlie. Slow down a minute," said Matt, "What 'xactly did you see?"

"I come in here at four o'clock—just like Dorcas said—and I catch this hound dog 'bout to smooch my gal…"

"Now, Charlie," Matt interrupted. "How do you know they was 'bout to smooch? Why, there's a whole counter between 'em. Not much neckin' can be done from that kinda distance."

Charlie thought a second, rubbing his forehead with a fat finger. "I reckon so," he said, finally. "But it did look awful friendly for a shoe repair shop." He shook a mammoth fist at Ernest.

"I hear what you're sayin', but you better have more to back up them falsehoods 'bout my brother," said Matt in a fatherly tone.

Ernest watched on with appreciation for his older brother. He had known Charlie for years and knew him to be a follower more than an instigator of any kind of trouble. If Matt could talk him down from his initial flare of temper, he hoped Charlie would forget why he was even mad. If his plan didn't work, Ernest knew at least one of them would have to fight this giant plowboy.

"Well, when you put it that way..." Charlie trailed off as he thought about his case against Ernest. Silence sat heavy in the room for a few seconds as Ernest felt the adrenaline leak out of the argument.

"Ugh!" Dorcas cried, staring at Charlie. "Is that all you got? Ernest Watson was tryin' to court me! He was wantin' to steal me right out from under your nose! How was I gonna 'scape his manly advances—just an innocent girl of seventeen?"

"When'd you turn seventeen?" Charlie asked. Dorcas screamed an incoherent reply.

Matt spied the valentine card on the counter. "Innocent, huh? I reckon that card there is for Charlie, right?" asked Matt. "Why don't you give it to him so we can all see his face when he reads it?"

"You can just hush up, Matthew Watson!" she said as she snatched her sweater and the valentine card off the counter. "Polly Clabo was right 'bout both of you Watson boys—one's dull and the other one's dashin' but in the end neither's worth a girl's time!"

Dorcas stormed out, leaving Charlie standing in the middle of the shop. He stuck his hands in his pockets and rocked back and forth on his heels. "Charlie!" Dorcas screamed from the sidewalk a few seconds later.

"Comin'!" Charlie called back. "See ya, fellas," he said with no obvious or lingering ill will for Ernest.

Oh to Grace

After they had left, Matt turned around to face his brother. "Ernie, one of these days, you're gonna get whupped and I won't be 'round to stop it from happenin'."

"Ah, Matt. You worry too much!"

"Were you really fixin' to kiss Dorcas Hogg?"

"Why not? I'm sick and tired of sittin' in this store waitin' for somebody to hand over their stinkin' shoes so Daddy can sweat over 'em and fix 'em for a couple of bits. It's a wearisome way to live and I ain't gonna keep on doin' it."

"What's that got to do with kissin' another fella's girl?"

Ernest smiled as he considered his answer. "It just seemed like a pleasant way to pass the time, I reckon."

"Well, didn't you figure that bein' knocked out cold by the likes of Charlie Duncan would be a mighty *un*pleasant way to pass the time?"

"Like I said, you worry too much."

"Well, if this gets 'round to Momma, you'll be in a heap of trouble. You know how she feels 'bout them girls who get fresh with boys."

"Yeah, she says they're loose women who eat their supper 'fore sayin' grace.' I reckon she means that in the way Danny Haslem and Vera Baker were in the family way 'fore their weddin' day, but that ain't gonna happen to me."

"Don't be too sure. Them girls have got a powerful pull on you. It's clear to see."

"Kissin' a girl don't make her a momma."

"Don't you wanna settle down and marry a nice girl and have a family?"

"O' course I do. I just wanna have a little fun first."

Matt saw that reasoning with Ernest was pointless. No matter what he said to him, Ernest would counter with a stream of plausible yet ethically hazy logic.

"Just you wait," said Ernest. "Some day I'll leave this town and when I come back to see the folks, I'll be such a big shot that people won't know me. They'll think I'm a city boy just lowerin' myself to visit my poorer relations."

"So that's all we'll be to you? Your poor relations?" Matt said, a little hurt. "Well, then you can stay in the big city and leave us country folk alone!"

"Ah, Matt. I didn't mean you!" Ernest tried to undo his tactless boasting. "Anyhow, you'll be with me."

"No sir, the big city's not for me. You can have it."

"Well, I reckon you'll be singin' a different tune one of these days!"

Matt glanced out the window at the dark sky. "It must be quittin' time now. Let's run over to Padgett's and get daddy. I brought the Gypsy Queen. I'll give you a ride home."

"You got that ole truck runnin'?" Ernest was easily impressed when it came to Matt's natural ability to fix things.

"Sure 'nuff," Matt said as Ernest slipped on his coat and hat and they walked toward the door together.

"Well, what are we waitin' for?" Ernest turned the sign on the door to read CLOSED and they shut it behind them. "I'm hungry, and momma made gingerbread today."

They jumped in the truck and drove to the grocery store to get their father. Frank was sitting in a circle of men, listening to one of Silas Padgett's war stories.

"There was enemy fire comin' in all over," Silas said. "It seemed like it was on every side of us…like it was rainin' artillery shells from the sky…"

"Daddy," Ernest whispered as Silas continued his story, "you ready to head home?"

"Just a minute, son." Frank had heard the story many times, but he didn't think it would be polite to leave in the middle of it.

Matt and Ernest went to stand near the door to wait for their father. Harley Dickson was already there, waiting for Joyce Padgett, Silas' wife, to bring out the new suitcase he had ordered through the store.

"Evenin' boys," said Harley.

"Mr. Dickson," they answered back.

"Yup, I'm 'bout to get the finest piece of travel luggage money can buy," Harley said with his chest puffed up high. "Made of pure walrus hide, hunted in the Alaskan territory."

"Is that so?" asked Matt with no real interest.

"We're leaving for Memphis next week—me and the wife and our boy—and we don't want to look like we come from nothing."

"Memphis?" Ernest perked up. "You're leavin' town for good?"

"Sure 'nuff. I'm gonna work for my uncle—he's in cotton, you know." Harley picked at an invisible piece of lint on his sleeve. "Don't reckon I'll be back to this one-horse town any time soon."

Matt caught the look on Ernest's face and knew this was just the beginning of a long conversation with him.

"Let's go wait for Daddy in the truck," said Matt. He hustled Ernest out the door so Harley couldn't fill his head with any more thoughts of leaving. The only problem was when Ernest had an idea, there wasn't much anyone could do to dissuade him. The seed had been planted.

Chapter 15

People would come and go over the years, but I always knew I'd live out my whole life in Morgan's Hat. I reckon some people want to leave their hometown folks and search out somethin' new. My momma knew a girl like that from the town where she grew up. Her name was Grace Moore and she lived in a little town called Jellico—it's up in the Appalachian mountains of northern Tennessee. She was a wonderful singer. Grace went off to New York City and Hollywood and made a big name for herself until she was killed in a plane crash in Denmark in '47. They called her the Tennessee Nightingale. Even Elvis liked her so much he named Graceland after her—so you know she had to be special. Now, Elvis—he was another story entirely. Elvis always remembered where he came from. He still ate his favorite foods that his momma made him. He kept on livin' in Memphis even after he made all them movies and sang all over the world in concerts. Della and me went to see his house a couple of years back. Oooh, it was fancy! I oughta show you that picture of Della and me in front of his Cadillac. I wonder what I done with it...I reckon it's in that shoebox over yonder on my bureau. Yes, that's it...the one that says Easy Spirit on the side. Bring it here and let's see if I can find it. Anyhow, Ernest was just like Grace Moore. He had to stretch his legs a bit in Chicago. Morgan's Hat just wasn't fast enough for him, I reckon.

MORGAN'S HAT, TENNESSEE
MARCH 30, 1931

Burnetta Watson had been in a perpetual state of tears all morning. Monday was normally washday, but today she was also doing some extra baking for Ernest's trip. She made his favorite gingerbread, cut it into thick slices, and wrapped it in an old dishcloth. Now she was up to her elbows in sticky popcorn. Ever since Ernest was a little boy, Burnetta had always made molasses popcorn balls for him at Christmas, and even though that was months ago, she was making a batch for him to eat in the truck. She had both of his shirts pressed and folded along with his winter underwear and every other article of clothing that would fit him, including some of Matt's.

Frank was at work. Ernest had promised to stop by the shop on his way out of town. Matt was helping Ernest change up a few things on his old truck parked behind the barn. George and Homer had already left for school and Clarence and Buddy were looking for jobs in the barn. No one wanted to be around Momma when she was this upset. She was a short, round woman with plump, red cheeks. Someone outside of the family might assume only maternal affection could be communicated from her big, friendly eyes, but her sons all knew when to avoid crossing her path. Frankie Jane and Della Mae were playing on the floor near the warm oven with a set of smooth, wooden blocks that Matt had whittled for them during the slow winter months. As she worked, Burnetta mostly talked to herself, but occasionally she looked at the girls to find something to fuss about.

"Law, Frankie Jane, pull your dress down, I can see clear to the Promised Land! Oh, I nearly burnt the poppin' corn! Gad night a livin'! A rat's been in my sugar again! You give that back to sister now, or I'll jerk a knot in your tail! Where's them boys? I need them to git me some more eggs. Maybe if'n I had somebody to help me I could get these forty 'leven things done before...before..." Here, she stopped talking and wiped her moist eyes on her flour-covered apron.

Matt was under the truck, shouting directions to Ernest as he ran back and forth from the driver's seat to under the hood. Occasionally Matt handed him a wrench. Finally satisfied with their work, they stopped and sat on the cold ground, leaning against the truck door.

"I'm sure grateful to you for lettin' me take the Gypsy Queen," said Ernest, pointing to the old truck.

"So you're really gonna leave, huh?" Matt rubbed his greasy hands on his red handkerchief.

"Matt, whyn't you come with me? I reckon there's gotta be jobs for the both of us in a big city like Chicago."

"Momma needs me here to work the fields."

"What about Clarence and Buddy? They's old 'nuff to do the heavy stuff now. It's time to get outta this one-horse town. 'Ventually you gotta chew your own tobacco, Matt!" Ernest could have been a preacher or a salesman with his talents for persuasion, but he and Matt had been through this all winter and Matt's mind was made up.

"What if you cain't find a job once you get up there?"

"Well, I just will is all. I ain't gonna come crawlin' back here with my tail tucked between my legs so daddy can tell me he was right, that's for sure."

"I just hope you don't get in with some rough fellas. They say Chicago is full of criminals, and I hate to think of you bein' as helpless as a turtle on his back..."

"You sound just like him," Ernest interrupted.

Oh to Grace

While they were talking, Frankie Jane sneaked up to where Ernest and Matt were sitting and listened to their conversation. "Ah, Matt, you know what I'm most wanting to see?" Ernest put his hands behind his head and stretched out his legs. "Them city girls! I'm terrible tired of the same ole Pearl Montgomery and Dorcas Hogg and Eula Baker! I want to have me a city girl, all curves and long legs..."

Frankie popped out from her hiding place. "Is you gonna see her wuv bubbles?"

"Consarn it, Frankie Jane! What're you doin' sneakin' 'round like that?" Ernest said, teasingly wagging a finger at her. "And who's been tellin' you 'bout 'love bubbles?'"

"You know what we do with peepin' Frankies, don't ya? Come on, Ernest, let's git her!" said Matt.

Matt and Ernest grabbed her and tickled her furiously until something shiny fell out of her pocket.

"Look what you done now, Uh-nest! Me and the boys got this for your leavin'-home pwesent!" Frankie Jane gave them her best three-year-old frown.

"Frankie Jane, where'd you get that watch?" asked Matt.

"The boys tol' me to say they saved up their coke monies, but I knows they just found it and cleaned it up with a wag," she said conspiratorially.

"They don't get no coke money! What a couple of liars!" said Ernest, shaking his head.

"Uh-nest, don't you like the watch?"

"'Course I do, Frankie-Puddin'! It's the best watch I ever did see! It'll be awful useful to me in Chicago, too." Ernest pulled her into his lap and flipped the watch over to see the back. "And look at them pretty deer—a momma and a baby, I reckon."

"That watch looks awful similar to the one Harley Dickson lost a few years back at Cooter's Great Raid," said Matt.

"Ah, he musta found his ages ago. Anyhow, he moved to Memphis to sell cotton for his rich uncle, so he ain't needin' it now!" Ernest could always talk himself into believing whatever was the most convenient reality at that moment.

Ernest put the watch in his pocket and stood up. "I better get movin' if I want to make it to Chicago before I'm too old to have any fun!" He drove Matt and Frankie Jane over to the house in the truck and honked the horn at the back porch. Burnetta came out with her arms full of supplies.

They packed up the truck and Ernest passed out hugs and handshakes just as George and Homer walked up. "Wait, Ernest, we got a present for you!"

"Frankie Jane gave it to me. Thanks a-plenty boys! Sorry you had to spend all your coke money on me!" Ernest said with a wink.

"What did them boys git you?" asked Burnetta. Ernest pulled out the watch to show her. She narrowed her eyes at her mischievous boys. "That best not be stole! Where'd you git that?"

"At the gittin' place," sassed George. Matt slapped him on the back of his head.

"Ow!" said George, rubbing his head. "Homer found it out in J.T. Fuller's field!"

"Why, you liar...*you* found it! I's gonna hit you in the Adam's apple so hard you'll be spittin' cider for weeks!" yelled Homer.

"Well, I'll knock you in the head and tell God you died..." countered George. They fought to get to each other as Matt held them apart.

"Hesh up, both of you! Here we is sayin' bye to your big brother and all you can do is fight." Burnetta began to cry again.

"Oh, Momma, I ain't dyin'. I'll be back with pockets full of money before you know it!" Ernest grabbed her around her sizable waist and picked her up. He spun her around until she was laughing and smacking his hands to put her down. Soon the watch was forgotten.

Oh to Grace

Ernest jumped in the truck and started it up. He slapped the door where Matt had carefully stenciled the name "Gypsy Queen" and shouted, "Giddy-up!" Then he saluted all of his waving family. A strong early spring wind blew dust up behind him as he drove toward town. Everyone watched until he turned a corner and the truck was out of view. A feeling of melancholy that always lingers with those left behind hovered over them like a rain cloud. Slowly, the well-wishers dispersed, but Matt stood watching a little longer. He knew he didn't want to leave Morgan's Hat, so he didn't feel left out of the adventure, but he would miss Ernest. For the past twenty-two years, it had been his job to keep his clever but overly trusting brother out of trouble—trouble with brazen girls and trouble with their burly boyfriends. Now he would be on his own. Matt wondered what compromises of conscience Ernest would make in order to live the life he wanted and felt he deserved.

As he was about to leave the driveway, Buddy ran to the spot where Matt was standing.

"Did I miss him? Did Ernest leave already?" Buddy panted. His pants were torn at one knee and he had a cut on his forehead.

"What happened to you?" Matt asked.

"Ah, nothin'," Buddy said, embarrassed. "So, did I get here in time?"

"Nope, and it's no wonder, from the looks of you. Did them Tipler brothers rough you up again?"

"I don't wanna talk about it, Matt."

"Ah, come on now. You know I won't say nothin' to Clarence or Homer or George."

"I know but I still don't wanna talk about it."

"If it was that no-count Hobart Tipler then I need to know, that's all."

"It wasn't Hobart, Matt."

"Then who did this to you? Was it Arlen or Milton?"

"No."

"Then who?"

Buddy looked around to make sure they were alone. "It was Ida Mae."

"Ida Mae Tipler?" Matt yelled.

"Hush, Matt," Buddy scolded. He pulled Matt away from the house. "She followed me out to the woods where I been diggin' up chicory root for Daddy's coffee."

"Then what? Did she knock you out and rob you?"

"She snuck up behind me and asked me for…well for something, and when I said no she started hittin' me with a stick. I couldn't hit her back—her being a girl and all—so I just run off." Buddy sat down in a crop of tall weeds, pulling them out one by one.

"What did she ask for?"

"She asked me for…a kiss. She's awful sweet on me and it's the most terrible thing that's ever happened!"

Matt tried to keep his face from contorting into a smile. His fifteen-year-old brother was by far the meekest of their family and he had exceptionally sensitive feelings. "Well, what're you gonna do 'bout her?" Matt asked.

"What can I do? I'll just try and stay out o' her way, I reckon." Buddy brushed the weeds from his lap and stood up. "I'm powerful hungry but I got no chicory to give to Momma. Reckon she'll still give me some o' dat gingerbread she made for Ernest?"

"You can try and see," Matt said, dubiously.

Buddy went in the house and Matt stood contemplating what job to tackle next. There was always something to mend or build or sow or reap on a farm. In addition to his regular chores, for the past year Matt had been working on a project all his own—a modest house situated on a corner acre lot his father had given him. It was small, but Matt knew he didn't need much. He was ready to shingle the sloped porch roof, but there wasn't much daylight left for that kind of a job.

Instead, Matt walked into the woods behind the barn and

sat on his favorite log. He pulled a small book out of his back pocket and smoothed the bent cover: *The Complete Poetical Works of William Wordsworth*. He turned to the title page and read the inscription: *To Matt.* "*Thanks to the human heart by which we live. Thanks to its tenderness, its joys, and fears. To the meanest flower that blows can give thoughts that do often lie too deep for tears.*"—*W.W. Warm regards, Napier Allen*. His teacher had pressed this book into his hands on the porch of the Granny Silas schoolhouse nearly nine years ago.

He turned to the first poem in the book. This one always reminded him of Clara. At first, he had read it as a part of his self-imposed penance. Now he had read it so often, it felt like being reminded of a fading dream. *A simple child, that lightly draws its breath, and feels its life in every limb, what should it know of death?* The young girl in the poem refused to subtract her dead brother and sister from the total sum of her family, insisting that there were still seven children.

Matt understood the feeling. No matter that Clara had been dead for thirteen years, he still thought about her every day. Only now, he was learning to move past the guilt and be blessed by the memories. He remembered what Pastor Cooley had told him so many years ago: "The more love you get that you don't deserve, the more you can give it out without wanting anything back." Matt still felt responsible for not keeping Clara away from the river that day, but it wasn't the gnawing, sickening kind of grief anymore. His awareness of being forgiven took the edge off of the regret. Now Matt understood how grace operated. It wasn't logical or quantifiable. It flew in the face of reason, but it was real and Matt was learning to love the equally flawed around him the better for it.

Chapter 16

Chicago
1913 & 1919

Ah, here's that picture of us at Graceland. Look at that God-awful shirt Della's got on. She never could wear that shade of orange, you know. Don't you wonder what Elvis Presley's kin thought about him after he got famous? Folks like his Sunday school teacher and their milkman—folks that knowed him before he was a big star. I reckon it's kinda amazin' when somebody from a tiny town like Jellico or Morgan's Hat can do somethin' to get famous. I didn't get much of a chance to do any performin' or play-actin', growin' up. They put on a nativity pageant every Christmas down at the Methodist church, but I never was in it. Now, my girls was real good at actin'. They was identical twins so they spent a lot of their time tryin' to act like the other one to fool everybody, so I reckon that was good practice for them to be on the stage. I recall one year…I think they was six or maybe seven…they was in a play about Johnny Appleseed. Dinah was playin' the part of a townswoman who Johnny gives some seeds to start some apple trees. It was a real small part and she didn't have

Oh to Grace

any lines to say. Lou-Ella loved to rub it in that she got to be the first one to talk in the whole play. Lou-Ella was supposed to walk up the side steps onto the stage wearin' a white nightgown. Then she was supposed to say, "Grandpa, Grandpa, read me a story." Grandpa was actually Timothy Chandler wearin' a furry beard and sittin' in an ole rocker. Anyhow, I made her gown, and thinkin' it would wear longer, I gave it a real long hem. When Lou-Ella climbed them stairs, she stepped on the front of her gown and tripped right on the stage. She busted her chin on the floor. Everybody gasped. I could hear her teacher sayin', "Psst. Psst," tryin' to get her to come off stage so they could patch her up, but Lou-Ella was a real professional. She stood there with tears a-flowin' down her cheeks and blood all over the pretty white collar of her gown and said her lines anyway. I was real proud of her. Even Dinah— as jealous as she was—loved on her all the way home that night. I guess bein' a star's all in how you look at it. It's like FDR said: "You're just an extra in everyone else's play."

CHICAGO
NOVEMBER 6, 1913

An usher walked over to the redheaded man seated in the uppermost row of the balcony. The opera had ended fifteen minutes ago, but the young man still sat, leaning forward with his elbows on his knees and his chin resting in his hands. He was staring at the crest on the closed curtain with a wistful look in his eyes.

"Show's over, son," barked the usher.

Embarrassed, the man stood quickly and made his way down the row of seats, hitting his knees on every other one. He hurtled down the steps of the ornate staircase, then paused in the foyer. This was the third time he had seen the German opera *Tristan und Isolde* at the Auditorium Building. He had taken his students from Holy Trinity Boys School to a matinee the week before, then he had come again, alone. He read in the morning paper that the touring company was leaving on Friday to take the production to Toronto. He knew he had to see *her* again.

He had been instantly struck by one of the actresses—not the long-suffering and long-winded Isolde, but her maid Brangäne. He scanned the program to find the actress' name: Emma Bäcker. He could tell she was younger than the gray powder in her hair and charcoal lines drawn on her face were meant to portray. She played her part with such sincerity that the grief spilt by Isolde at the death of her lover Tristan seemed overplayed, compared to the love and compassion showed by Brangäne, her maid and close friend. He was anxious to meet this woman; unable lately to think of little else. He chewed on the inside of his lower lip as he contemplated what to do.

Resolutely, he squared his shoulders and took a deep breath. With firm determination, he walked out the door and onto Congress Parkway. It was drizzling and windy. For a moment, he tried to talk himself out of doing anything foolish. Then he flipped up the collar of his overcoat, pulled down the brim of his bowler, and propelled himself forward. He walked around the building, looking for a back door that might lead to the dressing rooms. The Auditorium Building housed a hotel and many offices. It was the largest building on the block and seemed endless in this weather. After tramping around the entire exterior of the massive building, he devised a plan. He ran over to a nearby florist and bought a bouquet of flowers. He wrote "Emma Bäcker" on the card and went into the hotel, guessing that she was staying there with the opera troupe.

"I have a delivery for Miss Bäcker," he told the concierge.

"Leave it here and I'll see that she gets it," said the man behind the desk. A name plaque at his right read "Mr. Hendler."

"I was given specific instructions to deliver it to her myself," he lied badly. "The Duke of…Württemberg telegraphed the order to our shop with the stipulation that someone from the shop place it in Miss Bäcker's hands and hers alone. The Duke wants to congratulate her on her performance, and not with an arrangement that has wilted in a lobby for lack of a timely response." He tried to sound official and persuasive, but the soggy bunch of pink carnations and purple sweet peas interspersed with stalks of bear grass weren't convincing.

A wealthy-looking couple walked up to the desk at that moment and the concierge turned to help them. He called for a bellboy to carry their bags.

"Room 219," Mr. Hendler said as he marked the couple's name from his registry.

The bellboy took the couple's bags, while the young man continued to drip on the mauve carpet. More guests stood, waiting to be attended by Mr. Hendler. The concierge screwed up his nose as if he caught a suspicious scent, then reluctantly allowed the wet delivery boy to deliver the flowers. "It's Room 307," he said between closed teeth, trying to maintain his best customer service smile.

The man took the elevator up to the third floor and found the room quickly. He swallowed hard, then knocked on the door. Emma Bäcker answered, wearing a faded floral kimono, golden hair hovering at her shoulders.

"Yes?" she said quietly.

The young man was overpowered by her presence. He had been so preoccupied in the last hour, formulating and then carrying out his plan, that he had forgotten he would have to talk to her eventually.

"Uh, hello. My name is Thomas Simmons. I'm a language teacher at Holy Trinity School. I've seen your performance three times and may I say that you were...are... um...enchanting. I mean your performance was enchanting—perfect, really."

Emma cocked her head to one side and looked at him with a confused expression.

"Well, these are for you, of course." He handed her the soggy flowers. "I just wanted to tell you how much I enjoyed the opera..." He began to feel the burning heat of his cheeks spread to his neck—a redhead's curse. Emma continued to look at him without speaking.

"Sorry to interrupt your evening, Miss Bäcker," Thomas turned to go.

"*Ich spreche leider kein englisch,*" she said.

Thomas spun around quickly. "You don't speak English?" he said to her, beaming. "Of course you don't." He smacked his forehead. "Idiot!" he said to himself. "Not you, me! Uh, *Ich spreche nur ein bisschen Deutsch,*" he fumbled.

"*Sie nass sind!*" she said as she pointed to his dripping overcoat and hat.

"Wet? Yes...I mean *Ja.*"

"*Hereinkommen.*" She fussed at Thomas as she ushered him into her room.

"*Danke,*" he replied.

She bade him take off his drenched coat and hat. Then she asked him to sit in an armchair as she threw a coverlet over him. Thomas was made slightly uncomfortable by her forceful consideration of him, but he was under her spell.

Throughout the following hours, Thomas learned that Emma was from Munich. She told him about growing up in the culturally progressive Bavarian region under the leadership of their beloved Prince Luitpold. Emma had loved her homeland, but she had sensed a restless aggression in other parts of the German empire and feared what it might mean for her fighting-age brothers. Seeing that the topic caused her pain, but relishing that a variety of facial expressions only heightened her beauty, Thomas tried to change the subject.

He pressed her to tell him about being in the show. Emma explained that she was actually the understudy for the role of Brangäne, but the actress who was supposed to play the part had become ill and lost her voice. Thomas expressed regret over her departure in the morning for Canada, but she corrected him. Her manager had told them that he was closely watching a storm over the Great Lakes that could prevent them from traveling by boat for a few days. Thomas' heart lightened. He told her that he would show her around Chicago all weekend. First, he would take her to the Palace of Fine Arts that was built for the Chicago World's Fair. And if it wasn't raining, he wanted to take her for a walk through Jackson Park. He wanted to show her the Tiffany glass dome at the Chicago Cultural Center, and the now-empty Comiskey Park. She told him that she would spend as much of the weekend with him as she could.

Noticing the late time, they made plans for the next day. Thomas picked up his coat and hat and headed for the door. "*Auf Wiedersehen*," he said, standing in the hotel hallway.

"*Bis morgen, meine leibe*," Emma said as she slowly shut the door.

Thomas walked out of the hotel and back into the rain, though he didn't feel a single drop. His mind was busy remembering how she looked when she called him "my dear."

Chapter 17

Rememberin' ole times like this sure can be taxin' on the mind. I could use some help tellin' these stories and gettin' the facts all straight. That's the shame of out-livin' a lot of your kin. 'Course on the other hand, then there's no one to dispute the details. I'm seein' the more memories I got, the less I got time to make more of 'em and that'll cause anyone to get sentimental. It 'specially makes me miss Ronnie-Boy. He was my late husband, God rest him. His daddy was also named Ronnie, so when he was born, they all took to callin' him Ronnie-Boy. That name stuck to him like a tick on a hound dog. When I met him, his folks had just moved to Morgan's Hat and he was sellin' popcorn and cokes at the new movie theater. He said his name was Ronald, but he had so much kin that moved to town with him and kept up callin' him Ronnie-Boy... well he just didn't have a chance to change it. We were sweethearts all through the rest of school. After we got married, Ronnie-Boy got a job at the Baby Kakes factory. They made all sorts of cakes and cookies—each one wrapped up separately so you could put 'em in a lunch pail. For the first couple of years we was married, he ran the machine that shot the icing into the sponge cakes that was shaped like baby rattles. Most of their cakes was shaped like somethin' for a baby. Ronnie-Boy worked there 'til it closed ten years later. I reckon the white cupcake in the shape of a diaper was what did 'em in. They called 'em "Dandy Doodles" and they had chocolate fillin'. I cain't imagine many truck drivers or construction workers wantin' to open up their lunch pails and eat a baby diaper for lunch, can you? Every night when Ronnie-Boy'd come home I'd smell all that butterfat and sugar on his clothes and it'd just make me wanna eat him up! I still get a little stirred up every time I open a Twinkie. Them first years was awful hard, but they was awful sweet too!

CHICAGO
DECEMBER 18, 1916

Emma slid the yellow wax cylinder onto the mandrel of the phonograph and turned the crank on the side of the wooden box. She carefully placed the gear in the appropriate spot on the far left of the cylinder, and the stylus began tracing out the grooves in the hard wax. The tinny sound of an orchestra began playing, then a woman's voice sang *"L'amour est un oiseau rebelle"* from the opera *Carmen*. Emma hummed along as she buffed the already glowing bell-shaped horn with a rag. Music filled the tiny apartment like smoke from a stovetop griddle. Two-year-old Anna looked up and smiled at her mother. Emma had played the two cylinders they owned almost constantly over the last week.

"Sweet Papa," purred Emma as she inhaled the music tumbling out of the bell. Thomas had given the phonograph to Emma as an early Christmas gift. He knew she tremendously missed singing onstage, but she had put aside her dreams for Thomas and Anna. He had saved all he could to buy it for her. Now Emma was bound to find an equally ideal gift for him.

She struggled to think of something to give him and agonized over how to pay for it. This morning, though, she had an epiphany. She had spied Thomas' book *The Four Million*, a compilation of New York short stories by O. Henry. Thomas had been using the book to teach Emma her English lessons in the evenings. His favorite was *The Gift of the Magi*. The couple in the story, Jim and Della, relinquished their most prized possessions to give each other gifts that became obsolete due to their sacrifice. Emma's practical nature made her scoff at the notion, but she was inspired by the pocket watch. Yes, she would give Thomas a pocket watch, and to pay for it she would sell her hair combs. Her combs were tortoise shell with a bird design made of tiny jewels—a description similar to Della's in the story. They had little sentimental value other than to remind her of her days of traveling with the opera troupe. She had bought them in Paris, and she knew they were worth a great deal.

"*L'amour...l'amour...*" she sang with the phonograph. She lifted Anna in her arms and spun her around. Anna shut her eyes and let her head fall back with glee.

"*Mutti!*" Anna squealed her German name for Emma and grabbed her mother tighter as the dizziness overcame her.

"*Ja, doch, meine liebe!*" said Emma, "We go." Emma tucked her combs into her purse. Then she bundled Anna against the brisk Chicago wind and they left their apartment. In the hallway, they spotted Mrs. Lancaster, their portly, middle-aged neighbor.

"Good morning, Mrs. Simmons. Anna, dear," Mrs. Lancaster said. "It's a cold day to be heading out-of-doors. Where are you ladies off to?"

"Uh..." Emma hesitated, looking for the right words. "Present for Thomas."

"Aha. A Christmas present for Mr. Simmons. Well, don't let any of them rascals try to pull the wool over your eyes, dearie, and keep your pocketbook right under your arm. Anna, you mind your mother and stay clear of them carriages. All right, off with you then."

Emma only understood a small fraction of Mrs. Lancaster's words, but she knew the spirit in which they were said. Their nosy neighbor's intentions were as well-meant as her advice was unsolicited.

Emma followed Madison Street until she found Schmidt's Pawn Shop on the corner. She knew the owner was German, so she was sure she could haggle with him in her mother tongue.

They entered the shop, glad to be out of the cold. An elderly woman stood by the counter, with her back to Emma. The owner, a dwarfish, balding man, sat on a tall stool, examining a brooch of black stones through the magnification of his jeweler's loupe. He looked up at Emma and Anna upon their entry and turned his eyepiece up to his forehead. At once, he appeared to Emma as a Cyclops—a creature straight out of one of the stories Thomas read to Anna every night. Emma wondered if Anna thought the same thing, as the little girl hid behind her mother's long woolen skirt.

"Good morning," he called out.

"*Guten Morgen!*" answered Emma, letting the owner know that she would prefer to speak in German.

The man turned back to his customer and said, "I can give you fifteen for this." He set the brooch down on the counter and removed his loupe.

"Only fifteen?" the woman said. "Mr. Schmidt, you must be mistaken. I know what it cost my father some fifty years ago, and that is highway robbery."

"Frau Tilden, this style is not popular today. Victorian pieces are not selling. No one wears mourning jewelry anymore."

The woman sighed and pulled something wrapped in a handkerchief out of her small brocade handbag. She set it on the counter and unwrapped it slowly, as if a live animal might burst out and scurry away.

"How much can you give me for this watch?" she asked in a reverent tone.

Emma, who had been pointing out objects to Anna to keep the toddler occupied, looked up at the mention of the watch, and she took a step nearer. Mr. Schmidt methodically examined the gold pocket watch and chain. He opened it, listened to its ticking, and checked its reading against his own watch. "I can offer twenty-five dollars for both."

"Truly, you are a hard man, Mr. Schmidt. That will barely pay my notes for a month." She began to put the watch back in her purse.

"Thirty," he said.

The woman paused. "Done."

After he placed the bills in her hand, the woman hesitated again, delaying her departure as she chose her next words. "Mr. Schmidt, I must confess...I feel so odd giving up that watch."

"Frau?"

"I bought it for my brother many years ago—during the War Between the States—but he never received it. A man—a close acquaintance of mine—was to deliver it to him. It was a foolish request, a truly selfish dare from a spoiled girl." The lines in the woman's face deepened with the memory. "At the end of the war, it was found and sent to me with a scrap of paper that had my name and address and that was all. I never heard from my brother...or my friend...again. That watch," she said, gesturing to the object as if it held powers of voodoo, "was meant to be a gift but instead it has been a reminder of such loss..." Her words floated, suspended in the air. "I have held on to it, somehow hoping it would be given to someone...perhaps passed down as a family heirloom, but I am an old woman now. Too old for impractical dreams." She used the handkerchief to dab the fan-shaped wrinkles that extended from each eye. "Good day, Mr. Schmidt." She nodded to him and left.

When Emma approached the counter, she knew in her heart that the watch would be hers. Mr. Schmidt tried to wrangle more from her than the equal exchange of the combs, but in the end, she won him over with her beauty and cleverness. Herr Schmidt never had a chance.

On their walk home, Emma carried Anna against her chest, wrapped inside her unbuttoned coat. As they walked, Emma thought about Christmas morning and Thomas' face. She knew it would be a glorious holiday.

Chapter 18

Me and Ronnie-Boy had some good Christmases over the years, 'specially the ones with the kids. Openin' presents and family traditions take on a whole new meanin' when you're doin' 'em with your own little family. I had some good Christmas memories growin' up too. One of the hardest Christmases was when I was fourteen. That December was when the Japs bombed Pearl Harbor. We spent the next day listenin' to President Roosevelt's speech on the radio, and that Christmas was mighty somber 'cause we was all wonderin' what was gonna happen next. Most of my brothers and their friends ended up fightin' in that war. It was a terrible time for us back home. Every mother, sister, sweetheart, and wife was just a-feared they'd get a telegram from the war department. Thank heavens most of the boys from Morgan's Hat came back home. Some even had medals. Momma cried and cried the day Homer and Clarence came home. O' course, they started fightin' just like they used to... they was always in a competition. It didn't help none that Homer got a silver star and Clarence got nothin' but a constant ringin' in his ears. That's when Clarence would tell the story of the pigeon who got a medal. The bird's name was Cher Ami. He was a homing pigeon that saved the Lost

Battalion in W-W-one. You see, the men were surrounded by Germans in the Argonne Forest and on top of that, they started takin' on friendly fire. They wrote out a note and tied it on a pigeon's leg. They sent that bird up, then another—both were shot down. Their last hope was Cher Ami. He got the message to the others to "for heaven's sake—stop your shootin'" and that saved 'bout two hundred soldiers. The poor bird was all shot up but the medics worked on him and they ended up makin' him a little peg leg and he come home a real hero. After he'd finished tellin' the story, Clarence would pull down the poem Ernest wrote 'bout the bird that his teacher had sent in to the newspaper. (Momma had framed it and it was hangin' in the kitchen.) I don't recall most of it but it ended somethin' like: "A bird like you could stand up to the Huns/ Though when it comes to legs, you've just got one." Clarence said that if'n a bird could get a medal it must not be so much of a thing so Homer should stop flashin' it around like that! It weren't his fault, not really. Folks all over town wanted to see it, so what else could he do? So many of the older folks in Morgan's Hat still remembered the first Great War. It musta felt like a nightmare to have to relive all that worryin' and frettin' all over again.

CHICAGO
MAY 27, 1919

Four year-old Anna never knew what her mother would be like from day to day. Emma mostly sat in the same chair, wearing the same dress, and holding the same folded and re-folded piece of paper. There were some days when she never moved from that spot at all. Her hair, once soft and golden, was now falling to her shoulders in oily gray-yellow strands. Her face was sunken, and there was a remote look in her eyes. She stared at the unlit stove. Ashes were scattered on the floor.

On those days, Anna crept around her, afraid of rousing her

from her catatonic state. Other days, Anna would awaken to see Emma manically pacing the floor, muttering to herself. Anna wasn't sure which version of her mother was more frightening.

Once, Emma had picked up the framed photo of a happy couple with their little daughter, standing at the Navy Pier. After staring at the picture—concentrating on the image as if seeing it for the first time—Emma impulsively hurled it on the floor and the glass shattered. Stricken by her *hasty* action, she knelt on the floor, cutting her fingers on the shards of glass. Emma picked up the photo and stared at it through glassy eyes. The black and white picture didn't capture the brilliant red hair of the man or the jewel-like green eyes of the woman—or the bliss of the carefree moment.

Some of the times that she had stirred in the past months, Emma had let loose a barrage of German phrases that frightened Anna. The little girl didn't know that Emma was reciting verses from the book of Job. "*Aber der Mensch stirbt und ist dahin; er verscheidet, und wo ist er,*" she would cry out. Then Emma would wildly open and shut drawers until she found the English translation and read it aloud with her heavy accent: "But man dieth, and wasteth away: yea, man giveth up the ghost, and where is he?"

With her melodious and lilting mezzo-soprano voice, the words sounded like a plaintive arioso in a tragic opera. "*Ach daß du mich in der Hölle verdecktest und verbärgest, bis dein Zorn sich lege, und setztest mir ein Ziel, daß du an mich dächtest!*" she would implore. Then she would stumble over to Thomas' worn King James Version and read: "O that thou wouldst hide me in the grave, that thou wouldst keep my secret, until thy wrath be past, that thou wouldst appoint me a set time, and remember me!"

In better times, Emma had sung songs in other languages to her little Anna. She would move around their tiny apartment with the grace of a dancer as she sang about love's triumph over all. Now Emma's strong voice sang out about death and loss. Her most frequent tunes were dissonant Wagner pieces that poured out of her like melting wax.

Most days, Anna could be found sitting as still as possible in a dark corner of their living room, watching her mother. She hoped that if she stayed completely motionless, she could freeze time for everyone. Then her mother's agony would stop. If they stayed still long enough, maybe her father would return and make everything right. It was like the story her father had told her about Sleeping Beauty. The kingdom slept, carefree, while they waited for their prince. Once, Anna thought she had achieved this perfect state of statue-like immobility. Emma sat in her rocker, staring blankly at the wall. It wasn't clear if she was even breathing. Anna concentrated. Her ears started to buzz and her eyes burned but she wouldn't blink. *It's working*, she thought. Then a rat ran across her still legs. Anna felt the tiny claws and shrieked. She looked at her mother, but Emma didn't even twitch.

Anna also spent her time staring at the letter her mother held, in turns loosely and unyieldingly, with thin, bony fingers. Though only four and unable to read, Anna remembered the look of her father's neat schoolteacher script and the sound of the words as when they had first been read aloud. She longed to hold the precious letter herself, and worried that it would be fed to the fire, if her mother chose to light it again. It read:

My dearest Emma and darling Anna,

I have safely arrived in France. I am enjoying the changing of the seasons in this part of the world, though I wish with all my heart that I could spend the holidays with my two best girls. I am meeting fellows from all over here. Most in my division are from the Illinois Guard like me, but I have met so many men from other states as well. The 82nd came in to relieve some of us who have been here since September. Those boys are from Georgia, Alabama, and Tennessee. I got to know an older man named Bo, with a farm in Tennessee. He told me about his son who wanted to join up with him even though he was only fourteen. His son reminded me of some of my students at Holy Trinity. We talked a lot about hunting and fishing. Emma, I hope you won't be angry with me, but I gave him my pocket watch. A lot of the soldiers trade trinkets when making a new pal and he gave me a real nice lock back knife with deer antler grips. It's hard to explain, but trading up gave me a good feeling. It keeps me from getting homesick when I find fellow soldiers with stories of their own homes. I also didn't need the watch to remind me of the minutes that pass by without you near me. My heart ticks those away by the second. Well, I had better go now. If you get a chance, send me some more socks. They say the winter here will be a hard one.

I love you both with all my heart and I long for the day when I can hold you again.

With deepest devotion,
Thomas

When Thomas' letter first arrived, Emma had excitedly knocked on the door of their neighbor, Mrs. Lancaster, who gladly read it for Emma and Anna. Emma pursed her lips when she heard the part about the pocket watch. Mrs. Lancaster just laughed her deep, throaty laugh and said, "Men!"

Another letter came the very next day, but no one had been called to read it. The War Department letterhead and the briefness of its content had made it unnecessary to bother their neighbor again. That letter sat on the table for a few days, until Emma burned it in the stove. Mrs. Lancaster and the other ladies from their hall brought food and sympathy for more than three months, but eventually Emma's paranoia prevented her from accepting any more of their charity. She slowly withdrew inside herself. They would knock and knock, but Emma shook her head to Anna when she went to let them in.

The ladies would *tsk-tsk*, shaking their heads. "Doesn't she have family? What about *his* parents?" they whispered to each other, with their noses together on the other side of the door. Emma's parents and siblings were still in Germany, if they were even alive, and she had never met Thomas' parents. She had come to Chicago with the opera company from Munich almost six years ago. Though she had only a supporting role, Thomas had been adamant to meet her after the performance. She had been struck by his shy but ardent attention and they had eloped a week later. Thomas could never convince his parents back home in Peoria to see Emma as anything but a foreigner and a foolish mistake.

After a week of shunning the neighbor ladies' daily attempts, Emma unbolted the door and yelled, "*Was? Bitte...*go away. *Es tut mir leid, aber...*I am sorry, but I not needing your help." Then she shut the door on the shocked ladies and their covered dishes. Since then, Anna had to take care of herself and her mother. "Mutti?" she would whisper in her ear as she brushed her mother's hair. Then she would place a crusty piece of bread in her hand. Sometimes, Emma would eat it, but most often she would let it fall to the floor.

Emma's greatest fear was that she was to blame for Thomas' death, and this fear was paralyzing. When the Germans began their advance into France, Thomas had joined the Guard to show his patriotism. "Anyone wondering whose side you're on will see my uniform and know that you are a proud American wife," he had said whenever Emma looked worried. "Besides, I'll be home in a few months. President Wilson doesn't want us going to war anymore than you do."

It wasn't long after his enrollment that Emma realized he

had been wrong. Even as he trained at Camp Logan in his fatigues with the blue patch and white cross on his shoulder, the men in his unit still talked of staying stateside. When the "Prairie Division," as the 33rd became known, was sent in to clear the Argonne Forest, Thomas still wrote letters home reminding Anna that she was his good luck charm. His luck finally ran out on the banks of the Meuse River, just weeks before Armistice ended the fighting.

Now that May had rolled around after Thomas' death, the surviving men from his unit came pouring back into town. Emma went from debilitating grief to potent anger. From her seat this morning, she could look out the window of their apartment and see family and friends welcoming these boys back home. Crazed, she dragged herself from her chair to the bureau. Rifling through drawers, she found the package that the war department had sent to her. Tossing aside a bundle of letters and a military dog tag, she found the pocketknife. She opened it and placed the blade against her wrist. Anna ran to her and screamed, "Mutti! No!" Anna grabbed the blade from the weak hands of her mother, slashing her own hand across the palm. Anna wailed.

As if wakened from a dream, Emma squinted in an attempt to focus on her child, then she took the skirt of her dirty dress and pressed it against the wound. "*Still, Meine liebe. Keine Sorge.*" Emma cooed. She pulled the whimpering child up into her lap. Emma rocked her until the light coming in from the window turned a deep pink. Anna slept and Emma cried silently. She was suddenly aware of her daughter's gaunt frame—suddenly aware of her carelessness as a mother. She knew then what she must do.

"Anna, wake up. Wake up, *meine liebe...*" Emma jostled Anna slightly. She tried to lift her, but she realized she had no strength. Anna slid down and stood, rubbing her eyes. Emma rose slowly, then sat back down again. Grabbing Anna's hand, she tried once more. They left the apartment together for the first time in months. They walked up and down the Chicago streets, holding hands. People stopped and looked at them oddly, but Anna chattered constantly. Emma caught her reflection in a store window and almost tripped over herself in surprise. Who was this ragged creature? After weaving up and down—often re-tracing their route—they finally came to the steps of the Sisters of Saint Regina.

Emma knocked on the heavy wooden door. A matronly woman in a long black habit opened it. "Here is my daughter. I not want her..." Emma paused. She wanted to finish her sentence and explain *what* she didn't want for her daughter: For her to see her mother end her own life? To die of starvation? To be hurt any more by a mother who was unable to survive in a world full of killing and hate? She couldn't finish it—the words would not come. Instead, she pushed Anna forward and hoarsely barked, "Take her!"

Anna began to wail and grab at her mother's dress. "*Lass mich in Frieden!*" Emma screamed wildly at her daughter. Anna would not be subdued. The woman tried to pry Anna's tiny fingers from Emma's dress. Finally, Emma slapped Anna's face. Stunned, Anna stepped back and fell on the cement step with a small hand imprinted on her red cheek.

Emma was just as surprised by her own reaction. She had never struck her daughter before. A young Sister appeared on the stoop and lifted the limp child. Still crying, Anna curled up in the sister's warm embrace and laid her head on the woman's shoulder. Emma reached out her hand, her heart breaking to see another woman care for her precious Anna. Then she thought of the food and warmth waiting inside and dropped her hand to her side before the other woman noticed her possible change of mind.

As Emma turned to walk down the street, she heard the young woman humming a soft tune as she gently swayed Anna in her arms to soothe her. Emma heard the young nun say "Bath time, *ma petite princesse*" and then they were gone.

Chapter 19

Chicago & Morgan's Hat
1935 & 1937

I don't wanna ruminate on wars and fightin' anymore. It's not pleasant to think back on such things, 'specially when there's so many happier times to recall. And when you're old like me you can pretty well do whatever you want—with th'exception of drivin', apparently... at least according to my daughters and the DMV of Davis County! You know, sometimes I think folks forget that if they have a mind to, they can be happy in any situation. It's like my Daddy used to say to us kids when we'd have a duck fit over somethin' silly and act like we couldn't help our ugly ways: "Them's the same britches you're gonna get happy in so you might as well get started." He was the sweetest daddy to us kids you ever did see—so patient and lovin'. I always felt like I could go to him and tell him anythin'. I reckon I looked up to him in a lot of ways. He was a hard worker and an airtight Democrat. Oh, how he loved President Roosevelt! By and large, Daddy was happy to keep his opinions to himself, 'specially in a social setting, but when the fellas at Padgett's grocery store started in on FDR, Daddy wasn't afraid to tell 'em what he thought. I still remember layin' on the floor of the living room, listenin' to the president's speech when he took over for President Hoover. I was 'bout five years old and Daddy called us all in to hear what the president had to say. I still get gooseflesh when I hear a recordin' of FDR sayin': "This great nation will endure as it has endured" and "The only thing we have to fear is fear itself." I tell you, it was movin'! One of the first things FDR did was he passed a law sayin' it was all right to make and sell liquor again. I reckon he was tryin' to get all them bootleggers and gangsters to stop killin' people. I don't know that it helped much, though. A lotta folks was still mixed up with them rough fellas, 'specially in the big cities. They was kinda like heroes to the poor people who blamed the government for all their problems—we was in the Great Depression, you know. Everybody was lookin' for somebody to follow—some picked criminals and some folks, like my Daddy, picked FDR. I reckon Daddy picked right.

CHICAGO
APRIL 24, 1935

Ernest sat behind the desk in Willy Conrad's office on Twenty-Second Street—the fifth cramped one-room rental Willy had used since Ernest started working for him three years ago. He scanned the front page of the newspaper. A large picture in the center showed a man caught in a dust storm in Oklahoma. The man's thin frame was bent into a question mark as he fought the wind to enter his crooked house. Ernest evaluated his feelings as he studied the photograph. Did he pity the man? Did he scoff at the man's foolishness for staying in such an obviously hopeless situation? Or was Ernest just grateful that the man in the picture wasn't him? Before he could decide for sure, Willy entered the office.

"Hey, kid, outta my chair," Willy growled.

Ernest had noticed that Willy's demeanor was growing

steadily sourer with each week. He hopped up quickly and walked around to the opposite side of the desk, waiting a moment to let his boss start the conversation. Willy just chewed a tiny cigar stub.

"So what've I got today, boss?" Ernest said, sounding more upbeat than he felt. Willy hadn't given him a job in nearly two weeks.

Willy looked at Ernest through squinted slits. "Kid, I don't know what you're doing today, tomorrow, or next Thursday. The liquor racket just ain't got that same pizzazz it used to have. No more coppers running us down…the lawfulness of it may just put us outta business altogether." Willy ran his thick palm over the few oily pieces of hair left on his mostly bald head. The dozen or so thick, black hairs obediently lay down across the top of his shiny dome.

The black phone on the desk rang loudly. "Willy," he answered and then listened to the other end, scribbling frantically on the newspaper. After several "uh-huh" and "got it" replies, a smile crept across his face. He hung up the phone and beamed at Ernest.

"Well, kid, you got a job!"

"Where do I get the liquor?" Ernest asked, ready to make some money.

"No liquor. We're changing ballgames, kid."

Ernest didn't like the sound of this. "What do you mean?"

"Since Roosevelt had the bright idea to end Prohibition, the big players have moved into a new racket, but lucky for us stiffs, we're still gonna be their go-to delivery guys." Willy rubbed his pudgy fingers together, hungry for action. "You're gonna pick up a package…" Willy attempted to read his own writing. "On the corner of Columbus and Congress Parkway in Grant Park…in front of the Buckingham Fountain."

"Easy enough. What's the package?"

Willy looked up and gave Ernest an impish smile. "As a matter of fact, it's a dame."

"A dame?"

"That's right, kid. The lady's gotta get over to a gambling joint north of town...the Highland Park area."

"Well, why don't she just call a cab?"

"This dame is a valuable commodity and we're to..." Willy held up the paper and read the specific instructions: "Handle with care."

"I don't wanna be hauling hookers and gun molls all over town, Willy."

"Aw, kid. This is a job, plain and simple. We'll have calls for all manner of deliveries for the casinos coming in now—mostly booze and cash—but sometimes there'll be the occasional job that may seem a little nutty to us. Still, no matter what, we don't ask no questions about it. That's why we get paid top dollar, because we keep our heads on straight and our lips shut tight." Willy almost pushed Ernest out the door while he talked.

"How will I know it's her?"

"You'll know. If I know the Boss's taste in dames, she'll stand out like a firecracker. Now get going. She's supposed to be out there at twelve-thirty sharp."

"Does she know what I look like?" asked Ernest, still unsure how this exchange would work.

"Don't think so. The only description I got was she's a redhead and a knockout."

Ernest drove past the fountain and parked on the street. He was a few minutes early, but he got out of his truck anyway and made his way through the park. Although he had driven past it many times, this was the first time he had seen the fountain this close. The size of the pool was surprising, as was the deep color of the Georgia pink marble. Four seahorse statues sprayed out tall arcs of water toward the center. Ernest checked his pocket watch: 12:30 on the dot.

At that moment, Ernest saw a petite woman with red hair walking away from the fountain on the opposite side. He could only see her from behind, but her figure could definitely be described as attractive and she had the hair color to match the description. She wore a well-fitted organdy dress with cape sleeves and a large double tier collar. The dress was tan with black polka dots. The sheer fabric hugged her hips perfectly and fanned out six inches below her knees. Ernest felt instantly drawn to her. He was only afraid that the woman would get lost in the crowded Congress Parkway before he could reach her, nearly three hundred feet away on the other side of the pool.

Ernest cupped his hand to his mouth and shouted, "Ma'am. Ma'am." But the rushing of the fountain muted his cries and the woman continued walking away from him.

Just as he was about to break into a run, another woman crossed in front of Ernest. This woman had brilliant, unnaturally red hair, the color of his mother's homemade chokecherry jelly. She wore a black rayon evening dress trimmed with epaulettes of light brown fur. The front of the dress dipped far down into the valley of her chest with a rhinestone-encrusted clip at its upside-down apex, drawing the eye to her otherwise unremarkable cleavage. She was as tall as Ernest and impossibly slender. He was unsure of her age—probably in her late twenties like him, but she could have been younger. She looked as if she belonged on the cover of "Screen Romances" magazine. She was the epitome of glamour and beauty.

Ernest gave her a confused look. She smiled and deftly raised her left eyebrow, plucked to pencil-line thinness. "You lookin' for me?" she asked.

"Could be..." Ernest answered, hesitantly. He looked back toward the first woman, but she had disappeared into the mass of people.

The woman rolled her eyes. "Well, are you gonna give me a lift or not?"

"Yes, ma'am," he stammered. "My truck is right this way."

Ernest led her to his truck and opened the door for her. After checking that she was settled in, he walked to the driver's

Oh to Grace

side, took a deep breath, and got in.

"You got a light, fella?" she asked, with a cigarette between two fingers.

"Yes, ma'am," he answered and lit a match.

"What's with all this 'ma'am' stuff? You from down south or something?"

"Yes, ma'am. I'm from Tennessee."

"Well, don't stop yakking. I kinda like it." She took a long drag from her cigarette and blew the smoke out the window. Ernest glanced at her. She looked tired and slightly less glamorous up close. "My name's Rosie," she said.

"Ernest. Nice to meet you."

"You know, you remind me of somebody…"

"Oh, yeah?"

"Maybe a movie star…I know the one—it's Clark Gable! You seen *It Happened One Night*? That Claudette Colbert is one lucky bimbo," she sighed. "Now if Gable played a fella with your kinda accent—well, I'd be the first in line to see that picture."

Ernest was feeling pretty good about himself. He could see why Rosie was so valuable, with her keen understanding of men.

"Did you see *One Night of Love*?" she asked.

"Uh, I must've missed that one," said Ernest. He couldn't imagine going in a movie theater where the marquee above the door said: Now Showing—*One Night of Love*.

Rosie looked out the window as she talked. "It was full of singing—you know, fancy stuff like in an opera. The film stars was some Italian I never seen before and Grace Moore."

"Would you believe me if I told you my Momma knew Grace Moore when she was a girl?" Ernest asked proudly.

"No, really?" Rosie asked, perking up.

"No foolin'. Grace Moore grew up in the same little town in Tennessee as my Momma."

"Well, how about that!" Rosie sat back in the seat, resting

her head against the upholstery and looking up at the truck's ceiling. "You know, I'm going to Hollywood some day and be a star. I'm just waiting to meet the right people."

Ernest wondered if that's how stardom happened sometimes. Rosie had to be the mistress of somebody high up in the organization. Maybe he had connections and could give Rosie the big break she was waiting for. Maybe she really could be a star some day.

"I'll come see your first picture," said Ernest. "And that's a promise."

Rosie and Ernest drove the rest of the way to Highland Park in silence. When he delivered her safely to a trio of burly men in pinstriped suits, he was paid well and sent back to Willy. As he pulled away, Rosie blew him a kiss. *Maybe this won't be so bad after all*, he thought. *It sure beats getting shot at.*

As Ernest made his way back to town, Anna was returning to the insurance office where she worked. She had eaten her lunch at her favorite spot—the Buckingham Fountain. The day had been too nice to stay inside and listen to the catty gossip of the other secretaries. She liked the solitude she felt in the presence of so many strangers in Grant Park. Though there were a few occasions when a lonely businessman pestered Anna, trying to gain her attention, most often she was left alone with her thoughts and her lunch.

Anna was anxious for J.J. to comment on her new outfit—an airy organdy dress of tan and black that showed off her curvy figure. He hadn't called her in for a dictation yet this week, but today was Wednesday and he'd be coming over tonight. She felt a warm thrill at the thought of his weekly visit. Their relationship had become a balanced and logical part of Anna's life. She decided that this was the most reasonable way to have a romantic partner. J.J. met her needs for security—

he paid her rent and her salary—and she met his physical needs. That's not to say that she didn't enjoy their evenings together; J.J. was always attentive in pleasing her. But when he left her each Wednesday night at nine o'clock sharp and she stifled the urge to beg him to stay, she routinely told herself that this was how it must be. It was all part of their wonderfully modern and adult arrangement.

Just a few minutes after returning to work, J.J. called her for a dictation in his private office. Even before he said her name, Anna could feel his presence just behind her. It wasn't a particular sound or smell. She just knew he was there and he *needed* her.

Anna sat in the chair facing him, with her pencil and pad ready. J.J. perched on the edge of his desk, smiling down at her with his hands folded in his lap. For a second, they just focused on each other. Anna enjoyed the feeling of having someone need and want her. It gave her roots and purpose.

They left the door opened. There was nothing improper in their tête-à-tête. They would save hushed words and gestures of intimacy for tonight. "Miss Simmons, take a letter…"

When she finished with the dictation, Anna returned to her desk and typed the letter, eager to do a good job for J.J. When she pulled the paper out of the typewriter, she laid it on her desk and evaluated its level of perfection. She held a ruler to the margins to judge their straightness. She read and reread the copy. Everything must be just right. At last, Anna was pleased. This was her goal: to be useful to J.J. and to please him. It seemed an easily attainable goal. Anna truly thought life could go on like this indefinitely.

When the workday was over, Anna pulled her small black clutch from the bottom drawer of her desk. She would hurry home and freshen up before J.J. arrived at six-thirty.

At the same time, on the other side of downtown Chicago, Ernest was also leaving work. He had run several more errands for Willy, making it his busiest and most lucrative day in months.

As Ernest finished counting out the bills that Willy handed him, the phone rang. Willy answered it. His face showed alarm, then in a voice soaked in frustrated resignation, he said, "Yeah, I got it," and hung up.

"What happened?" Ernest asked.

"Well, it looks like we're moving again, kid," said Willy as he began pulling the drawers out of the battered desk and dumping the contents into a worn, leather briefcase.

"Why?"

"You know the casino out in Highland Park?"

"Sure. I was there today."

"The place just got raided," Willy said. "And we don't wanna be here if them thick-headed coppers connect the dots."

"How would they know about us?" Ernest asked nervously.

"Well, some of them got hauled into the slammer and we don't know if they'll sing."

"Did all of 'em get taken to jail?"

"Dunno. Probably." Willy was moving quickly, considering his roundness, entirely focused on getting out.

Ernest thought about Rosie and her dreams of being a Hollywood star. "What about the woman? The one I picked up today? Did they say anything about her?"

"That red-headed tramp? Why do you care? Them dames are a dime a dozen. What you need to worry about is us—you and me." Willy snapped the metal fasteners shut on his briefcase. "I'll let you know where I move the office to in a couple of days. Until then, lie low and relax."

Ernest slid his hands into his pockets, looking beaten and dejected.

"Don't look so glum, kid. Think of this as a vacation." Willy punched Ernest's shoulder. "Nobody's looking for the stiffs who pick up the goods and drive the cars. The feds want the big Boss—that's all. We just don't wanna give 'em any paper trail to follow." Willy placed his bowler on his head and tapped it down. "Believe me, kid. The Boss is gonna appreciate what we done. He don't forget the fellas who do him right…or the ones who do him wrong neither, come to think of it!" Willy laughed heartily at his joke as he walked out the door and hailed a cab. Ernest watched Willy nearly dive head first into the cab before it sped off.

Ernest worried about himself, but he couldn't help worrying about Rosie, too. She seemed smart enough. Maybe someone would come for her at the police station and she'd be all right. Thinking about Rosie made Ernest realize that he missed being around pretty girls who he could charm and impress. He'd been in Chicago for four years, and he hadn't had a date with a girl the entire time. All of the girls he'd met seemed too far above him. He wore his rural upbringing like an ill-fitting overcoat that he couldn't take off.

Ernest thought about the advice Napier Allen, his former schoolteacher, had given Matt in one of his letters. Mr. Allen said that when the right person came along he would know it and recognize her as his soul mate. Mr. Allen told Matt about Plato's theory that humans began life with four arms, four legs, and two heads. The mythological god Zeus had split them in half to diminish their power, thereby creating man and woman. Now the man would spend the rest of his life searching for the woman who would complete him, and vice versa. Ernest had laughed at the idea when Matt read it to him. Now he wondered if it could be at least partly true. Ernest definitely felt like only part of himself. Maybe the right girl would make him whole.

Chapter 20

FDR's speech was likely the first thing I remember listenin' to on the radio. After that I was hooked... we all was, really. We'd all gather together for Fibber McGee and Molly and the detective stories of Charlie Chan. We listened to the "National Barn Dance" radio show with the country music we all loved. George and Homer's favorite was Dick Tracy. They already liked the comic strips in the newspaper with them funny-lookin' criminals with the funny names. Daddy had a second cousin in Nashville that would cut 'em out of the Banner and mail 'em to the boys ever so often. Soon we started pickin' up the radio show. George and Homer both got so excited when they heard the announcer say, "Callin' all adventure fans! Callin' all Dick Tracy fans!" Then there was police siren sounds and a commercial for some sort of cereal. Quaker puffed wheat—that was it. Then the boys wouldn't say nothin' for fifteen minutes and if any of us tried to talk they'd shush us. They was just waitin' on pins and needles to hear the secret message at the end of the show. They thought Dick Tracy fightin' them criminals was the most excitin' thing there ever was. I'm not sure, but they mighta liked them mobsters better than the police. That was a lot of what we heard about for a while—

real mobsters and the police chasin' 'em down. There was some kinda story every day 'bout them nasty fellas durin' the Depression. I remember one story 'bout John Dillinger—he was a mob boss outta Chicago—he was married but he had a slew of lady friends. One of 'em was named Opal Long. I remember the name on account of opal is Dinah and Lou-Ella's birthstone. Anyhow, this Opal was different than all of th'other women that ran 'round with Dillinger's gang. She was a muscle-y tower of a woman who didn't get all doodied up in fur coats and paint her face like them trollops. They say she scrubbed and cleaned and worked her fingers to the bone for them fellas and when the police carted her off to prison, she wouldn't rat any of 'em out. Now I don't know if that was smart—I reckon times was hard and she was just grateful to have a roof over her head—but you gotta admire loyalty. Later she hooked up with one of the men in Dillinger's gang and settled down, I reckon. Some couples get together under the most peculiar circumstances.

Morgan's Hat, Tennessee
December 12, 1935

Of the four distinct seasons in Morgan's Hat, Matt liked winter the least. In the years since Ernest had moved away, Matt's feelings of melancholy had increased for every winter they'd been apart. It was true that Ernest's headstrong and foolish ways put Matt in the middle of many infuriating predicaments, but at least it was never dull.

Matt sighed heavily as he lifted another bag of seed corn and stacked it with the others in the barn loft. He stood and stretched out the muscles in his back, moving slowly as if he were walking under water and against the current. He leaned against the square window frame cut into the gable of the barn and looked out at the woods to the right and the vast fields just behind the barn and to the left. They looked like a neat patchwork of orange, yellow, and tan. The darkest section showed where Matt had planted the winter wheat he would harvest in the heat of the summer, though now all he could see was the rich brown of the upturned soil. It amused Matt that something could lie under ground for so long without any sign of growing, before miraculously bursting into tall stalks of wheat. He wished that he could wait out the winter so peacefully.

Matt sighed again. Maybe it wasn't his brother he was missing. Maybe what Matt needed was a girl. He chuckled. Now what would he do if a girl were dropped down right in front of him? Probably run and hide. Girls his age had made him a nervous mess ever since he first noticed a difference between him and them. Thinking back, he could probably pinpoint that moment of discovery to the first time Polly Clabo's chest lost its primary school flatness. Matt's mother had always been well-supplied in the chest area, but when girls he'd known his whole life began to change into new, mysterious creatures, it was a shock to his senses. It didn't help that with these newfound breasts, the owners also contracted a severe case of giggles and whispering.

Suddenly, Matt thought he heard a giggle from somewhere in the barn, followed by what sounded like a "hush."

"Who's in here?" Matt called out. No answer. Matt kicked around in the hay, but soon tired of the investigation and left to clean up for supper.

As soon as he was gone, Buddy emerged from under a mound of hay. Ida Mae Tipler, round and pink-faced, crawled out beside him.

"That was close, Ida," Buddy said. "You best get on home."

"Why should I do that? Matt's gone." She lovingly picked hay out of Buddy's black hair. "Now we're all alone," Ida Mae said huskily. She pushed down on his chest while wetly kissing his ear lobe.

"Get off, Ida! Don't you know when to quit?" exclaimed Buddy.

Ida Mae rolled over and sat up with a huff. She crossed her chubby arms in front of her and pouted out her lips. "You're nothin' but a coward, Buddy Watson. Who'd wanna neck with you anyhow?"

"Ah, come on, Ida. You don't have to get mad." He awkwardly put an arm around her. "I'm just lookin' out for you. If my Momma comes in here...she'll whip us both."

"I'd like to see her try! I'm nearly seventeen and you're already nineteen. If she tries to break us up, we'll run off together! We'd be just like Bonnie and Clyde!"

"I ain't robbin' no banks, Ida Mae!" Buddy was afraid of what Ida might talk him into.

"I know...I just ain't gonna let her take you away from me. That's all." Ida hugged Buddy tightly and buried her face in his flannel shirt.

Buddy wondered how he'd ever gotten into this situation. How had he let Ida Mae rope him into caring about her? He had escaped her ambushes and avoided her meaningful glances for years—until last spring. That was when saw her crying at the mouth of Drake's Cave. Any other time, he would have used her tears as a diversion to get away unseen, but something about her vulnerability tugged at him. He'd never seen her cry before.

He'd called out to her from a sufficient distance in case her tears had been a clever trick to lure him to her side. She had looked up and cursed him, then told him to go away. Buddy saw the sincerity in her misery. He had never been able to witness pain without feeling a portion of it in his own spirit.

"What's the matter, Ida Mae?" he asked.

"I hate you, Buddy Watson. I hate you and your brothers and your sisters and your ma and your pa! I hate all your clean livin' ways! I hope you all die and go straight to hell in your fancy church clothes!" She continued wailing, much to Buddy's dismay.

"What'd we do?"

"You hated me first...but I'll hate you more! I'll hate you 'til the day I die!" Then she threw a rock that barely missed hitting Buddy in the head. Usually her aim was much better, so he was grateful for her vision-blurring tears.

"I don't hate you, Ida Mae," he said quietly.

"Then why do you run away from me?"

"Well, why do you think? You're like a tornado, Ida Mae...I'm scared of you."

Ida had stopped crying and looked up at him. She smiled through her tears and started to get off of the large rock where she was sitting. Afraid that she would come after him, Buddy had taken off through the woods, running like a rabbit all the way home.

Stroking her straw-colored hair in the hayloft on this cold December afternoon, Buddy thought back on that warm spring day, amazed at the unlikely chain of events. Slowly, Ida Mae had fought her instincts of aggression and self-interest—the two most often-taught subjects in the Tipler home—to woo Buddy. She had spent her life watching the Watson family and wishing she had a group of people like them who she could depend on and work alongside. To Ida Mae, they seemed like the perfect family.

Generally speaking, Buddy would have agreed with Ida's evaluation of his family, but he had a hard time believing that he had much to offer to such a hard-working, strong-minded group. Buddy had struggled with mediocrity all his life. He lived in the shadows of his two older brothers and the untimely loss of his sister. This, combined with the fact that the Tiplers had been his ever-present adversaries all through grade school, made him appear whipped and overly submissive. The Tipler family had a child nearly the same age as every Watson child, but they were raised with entirely different ethics. Ida Mae was just as unkind and untidy as the other Tipler children, but she had been overlooked when the lazy trait was given out to her siblings. Buddy was highly pliable clay in her pudgy fingers, and she knew just what to make of him.

The smell of Burnetta's chicken and dumplings wafted into the barn loft and Ida's stomach began to growl. "I reckon I'll get home," she said reluctantly. "Ma's got beans with fat-back on the stove..." She got up and Buddy stood next to her. He pulled a piece of hay off her thick woolen sweater and gave her a peck on the lips. Then he walked her to the barn door.

"'Night, Ida."

"'Night, Buddy."

Ida Mae hugged Buddy again, holding him so tightly that a button on his shirt made a round impression on her cheek.

Buddy always dreaded saying good bye to Ida. He knew the thought of returning to her chaotic home where her mother would be weary beyond exhaustion, her father would be either mean drunk or asleep drunk, and her brothers and sisters would be fighting like a pack of wild dogs wasn't much of a motivation to leave. He let her hug him until she finally turned to go.

Buddy watched her walk into the setting sun before going home himself. Upon entering the kitchen, he caught the middle of one of his mother's lectures.

"All I wanna know is why you'd be askin' Clarence 'bout Fanny King." She pointed at Matt using a wooden spoon, blackened on the tip from frequent use on the stove. Matt stared at the floor, looking as if he'd rather be just about anywhere else at that moment. Clarence was carving a small piece of cedar into a fishing lure with the streamlined body of a minnow. There were microscopic shavings all over the checkered tablecloth. "Clarence, take that whittlin' outside. Just lookit that mess all over the supper table."

"Sorry, Momma," he said, and with a breath, Clarence blew the shavings onto the floor.

"Now, what's this 'bout Fanny King?" she asked. Clarence's handful of sawdust had not been enough to distract Burnetta.

"It's nothin', Momma," answered Matt.

"He asked me if I heard whether Fanny had someone to take her to the Christmas Pageant," Clarence said, wiping excess dust from his fishing lure with a handkerchief.

"Why'd Fanny need someone to take her?" asked Burnetta, as Buddy reached for a smallish dumpling that had bobbed to the top of the cavernous pot. Burnetta smacked his hand with her spoon without missing a beat in the conversation. "Ain't she got two good feet?"

"I reckon," muttered Matt, slightly sweating.

"Matt wanted to take her hisself, didn't you, Matt?" Clarence teased.

"Matthew Dingus Watson. What would you want with a brazen girl like Fanny? She's known all over town for...well, a Christian woman like myself wouldn't stoop so low as to repeat it. I cain't help but hear what they say and I tell you, it ain't good!"

"I was just makin' conversation with Clarence, Momma." Matt glared at his brother, to no effect. Clarence worked at his lure with the tip of an awl, fashioning eyes for it.

"Sometimes I think you got no sense, Matt. Girls like her will only bring you trouble. She got no kinda gentility, no careful upbringing. 'The meek shall inherit the earth.' That's what the Good Book says. That's the kind what you should be lookin' for."

Buddy listened to Burnetta's sermon and couldn't help but feel as if it was being directed to him somehow—just change out the name "Fanny" for "Ida Mae."

"I wouldn't ask Fanny King to walk to the end of the sidewalk, let alone to the Christmas Pageant, Momma," said Matt, still looking at the floor.

As with most people who think they sound more eloquent and convincing than they really are, Burnetta replied, "Well, that's that then."

After supper, Buddy sought out his father where he was reading the newspaper and smoking his pipe in the parlor. Buddy needed advice.

"Daddy, can I ask you somethin'?"

"What's on your mind, son?"

"How did you know that Momma was the one you oughtta marry?"

Frank set down his newspaper and puffed on his pipe a second. "Well, that's been many years ago. I don't rightly remember..."

"Was it her careful upbringing and her meek ways?"

Frank inhaled sharply and choked. He leaned forward with his hands on his knees and Buddy whacked him on the back a couple of times.

After he recovered, he answered, "No, son. I can't say it was meekness that drew me to your momma."

"Did Granny Dingus raise her real careful so she'd be a good wife and mother?"

"Granny Dingus was careful about raisin' your momma and her brothers and sisters, but not in a genteel way. They had to do much of the plowing and planting as soon as they were able—'specially after Granny Dingus lost her husband. Your momma was the oldest of twelve children and your Aunt Loreen was only a baby when her pappy died. Granny Dingus had no time for lookin' after household matters, so it all fell to your momma."

"How did Momma manage it?"

"Well, I reckon you never saw a more bull-headed woman than your momma...don't tell her I said that, Buddy."

"Oh, nosir."

"She is mighty determined and the hardest worker in all of Davis County. I don't know if that got handed down to her from a long line of Dingus relatives or if she became that way out of a bad situation. It's hard to tell."

"What kinda bad situation?"

"Well, Granny Dingus was a healer of sorts up in the Appalachian mountains. She would be gone for weeks at a time tending to poor, sick folks when your momma was young."

"I know it. I heard stories 'bout her remedies from Momma."

Frank looked around and pulled Buddy closer to him. "Once, after your momma's daddy passed, Granny Dingus went up into the mountains and stayed gone for a month. Your momma was left in charge of her younger brothers and sisters. It was late summer and she was full-up with cannin' and workin' in the garden. She put some of her brothers in charge of the hayin' and the little ones were playin' in the barn—swingin' on a rope from one pile of hay to the next." Frank's voice got quieter and Buddy had to lean in to hear. "One of 'em had the idea to make a loop in the rope so they could scoot their legs through and sit on it. Well, when the rope was passed to Momma's brother, John Jay—he was 'bout four years old at the time, he slipped his head through the loop by mistake. John Jay started to swing across to the other side, but he didn't make it and stayed right in the middle where no one was tall enough to reach him. His brothers and sisters in the barn with him came runnin' to find your momma but by the time she got there it was too late. John Jay had hung himself. Your momma had to get him down and make all the arrangements for his funeral..." Frank paused and puffed on his pipe again.

"How's it that we never heard of this before?"

"Your momma won't talk 'bout it. I got the story from Aunt Loreen and your granny. I reckon your momma never forgave herself for what happened to John Jay. Granny Dingus told me that she's always said it wasn't your momma's fault but it's no use. She can be as stubborn as a mule when she wants to...don't tell her I said that either, son."

"Yessir."

"So why're you askin' 'bout marriage, Buddy?"

"No reason. I just wanna know...if I ever meet the right

girl, I wanna be ready."

"Oh, you'll know. She'll stay with you like a head cold and you won't be able to shake her. Indeed, you'll know." Frank picked up his newspaper and began reading again.

Chapter 21

Take me and Ronnie-Boy, for instance. I knew he was a real special fella from our first date. He took me to Sully's—that's what everyone in town called Sullivan's Drug Store. We was sittin' at the counter and Ronnie-Boy ordered an ice cream soda for us to share. Zane Wilson, the soda jerk at the time, put the flavored syrup into an extra tall glass, added fizzy water and two dollops of ice cream. While we was talkin', Zane stuck two straws in the glass. I was so nervous—this bein' my first date an all—that when I turned round on my stool to face the soda, I was lookin' at Ronnie-Boy instead of at the soda so when I bent down for a drink the straw jammed right up my nose! Ronnie-Boy coulda teased me 'bout that, but he just looked real concerned. "You okay?" he asked me. When I said yes, he told Zane that he oughtta warn a girl before he sticks somethin' in her drink like that. Then he just kept up talkin' 'bout whatever he was sayin' before I done the stickin'. I felt like a million dollars. It didn't change his opinion of me one bit. Ronnie-Boy was always like that. You always knew where you stood with him.

Oh to Grace

CHICAGO
JANUARY 8, 1936

The past two and a half years had become a harmony of routines for Anna, mainly involving work and J.J. He still came over on Wednesday evenings. They had fallen into a rhythm that lacked some of the initial passion but made up for it with comfort and compatibility. They were like an old married couple on those evenings. He would lay his head in her lap, mostly reading silently, as she sat gazing out the window at the darkening sky. They would share a small box of sugar cookies or cakey brownies that J.J. picked up at the corner bakery, until he would yawn, stretch, and kiss Anna before leaving. Anna didn't mind this arrangement—it felt natural. There were still occasional times when J.J. would behave especially amorously, and they would go to bed together, but Anna didn't mind this, either. She enjoyed his attention, however it came.

This morning began just like most of the others. Anna woke up in her cold apartment, ate and dressed quickly, and walked the three blocks to her job. As she stomped through the snow piled up on the sidewalk, she thought about J.J. coming over that evening and let herself wonder briefly why he no longer brought gifts that weren't edible—no more bouquets of flowers or porcelain figurines. Granted, he had given her a lovely pin for Christmas, but she never wore it. It was of a large gold-plated peacock standing tall, with a pink Austrian crystal at the tip of each feather. It was a striking design—sure to generate notice. Anna was afraid someone would inquire about it and she wouldn't be able to lie adequately.

Suddenly, the wind picked up. She drew her scarf tighter around her face and neck and trudged on. *Maybe I'll wear the pin tonight*, she thought.

Once in the office, she hung her things on the community coat rack and sat at her desk. The other girls straggled in and began pounding away on their typewriters. Anna loved the constant clicking sound of the machines. She felt like a bee working in a cozy hive this morning. Suddenly, one of the girls jumped up and ran out of the office. She held her hand to her mouth as she flew out the door in the direction of the ladies' room.

"There goes Glory again," said Edna, turning around in her seat to face Anna.

"Oh," said Anna blankly. "Is she sick?"

"Are you fooling me, Anna? Some schlepper's got her in the family way," Edna dramatically whispered out one side of her face. "She's been running out to the crapper like that for weeks."

"Ladies," Miss Blum growled.

Anna realized she knew nothing about the girls in the office, just as in the orphanage. These were also empty faces that she carried on conversations with but cared little for. They could have been ghosts, for all the real they seemed to her. Anna thought of most of the other secretaries as mere caricatures of real people. To her, Glory was as a slightly perverse version of Shirley Temple. She was a petite blond with tight ringlets all over her head. She always wore low-cut dresses and blouses. Her favorite was a navy sailor dress. Some of the girls called her "Good Time Glory" behind her back.

Just as Glory returned, dabbing a handkerchief to her pale forehead, J.J. walked out of his office. Her back to him but still sensing his presence, Anna grabbed her pad and pencil and prepared to stand, assuming he would want her to come in for a dictation. She froze as she noticed how Glory stopped and looked at J.J. with intense familiarity. Quickly turning to her boss, she saw him mirroring the same expression. Thoughts swirled in Anna's mind. Her lungs felt as if they were filling with cement. She feared that the air could not reach her throat or her brain. That eternal second eventually passed and J.J. swiftly turned and re-entered his office, completely unaware of Anna. Glory sat down. No longer pale, she had flushed hotly. The clicking typewriters began again, but the once soothing sound now made Anna nauseated.

She stood shakily, blinking several times to clear her thoughts. Toward him or away? Did she even want the answer to her question?

"Miss Simmons, accompany me to the file room," barked Miss Blum before Anna could decide what to do.

Anna followed her out the door, past the file room, and into a small closet near the stairs. She didn't object or question where she was being led; she was just grateful for someone to follow. Miss Blum pulled the chain on the hanging bulb and shut the door behind them.

"Did you really think you were the only one?" Miss Blum spit out in staccato. The soft fur on the sides of her face bristled with the question.

"Miss Blum, I..."

"Don't try to lie to me, girl. I know everything that happens in this office. Who do you think authorizes the monthly expense for your rent? Mr. Griffith will be allowed his diversions because he is a man of wealth and importance. But you—you have no privileges, no rights. He is a married man, Miss Simmons."

"We didn't...that is...I never asked him to..."

"Leave his wife? Nor would he. Do you know how much she's worth? Her father owns most of the rail yards in Chicago. And this new little fling will end just like the rest." Miss Blum took a step back from Anna and breathed deeply through flared nostrils. "Collect yourself and return to your desk." Miss Blum placed her hand on the doorknob and paused. "By the way, this is your coffee break. You'll not be permitted another one later." Miss Blum shuffled away, leaving Anna to the hypnotic effect of the swinging light bulb.

Anna had to get outside. She flew down the stairs and burst out the door, taking gulps of freezing air with her hands on her stomach. The air rushed in too quickly and she attempted to slow her breathing, but anxiety rose inside her. She felt lightheaded and began to teeter backward, when a pair of strong arms reached out to grab her.

"Ma'am, are you alright?"

Vaguely, Anna thought the voice sounded familiar. She closed her eyes and saw silver spots flashing, then everything went black. When she opened her eyes again, she was sitting in a little diner. A large waitress was fanning her and someone was patting her hand. She moved her head slowly and saw a handsome man with a small moustache and dark, concerned eyes looking back at her.

"The poor dear," said the matronly waitress. "Out in this cold and without a coat. She's probably hungry, too. I'll go see if Al is done cooking her eggs." The waitress waddled off in the direction of the kitchen.

"I'm so sorry. I...I must be taking on a head cold," Anna muttered groggily.

"Here, ma'am, drink some of this coffee. Al can't boil water, so his eggs are runny at best, but Kate makes a respectable cup of coffee. This will warm you to your toes." He held the cup for her as she sipped. "My name is Ernest Watson."

Anna looked at him thoughtfully, then placed her fingers to her lips. "Why, you're the one who fixed my shoe!" She sat up abruptly, almost spilling the coffee. "But you didn't have a moustache before, though..."

"Well, I wondered if that was you! Yeah, I grew it a couple of months back." Ernest smiled self-consciously, showing off his dimple. "If I remember correctly, you were on your way to an interview back then—how'd it turn out?"

"Oh, I got the job—still have it, I think. I'd better get back to the office." Anna closed her eyes and shook her head, rising up slightly in her chair. "How can I thank you—again?"

"Well, you could start by telling me your name."

"Anna. My name is Anna Simmons." She blushed and looked down at her coffee cup.

"Okay, Anna. How about I take you to dinner? What about tonight?"

Anna was about to refuse and claim a prior commitment, when she felt a jolt of pride that made her sit up straight. "Yes, tonight. That would be wonderful."

"You ever heard of Rosa's, down by Lincoln Park? She's got some great spaghetti." Ernest ran a nervous hand through his hair, but a stray lock fell back across his forehead. Anna cocked her head to one side and thought how Ernest looked every bit like Clark Gable.

They finalized their plans for the evening and Anna returned to work. When she sat down at her desk, J.J. came out and called her to his office. She went in with her pad and pencil and sat in the chair. J.J. shut the door behind her and perched on the edge of his desk.

"I'm looking forward to tonight, Anna. What would you like for me to get from the bakery? Sweets for my sweet!" he said nervously. He tried to brush the back of his hand against her cheek, but she turned her head.

"I have plans tonight," she said, fighting back tears. She still melted at his touch and this infuriated her.

"Darling, what is it?" J.J. sat next to her, concern and fear written on his face.

Anna stood. "I think you should ask Glory to take dictation for you from now on."

J.J. grabbed her hand. "Anna, I've made a mistake. Please, you have to forgive me. You're all that matters to me." His eyes were round with panic. "I don't know what I'm going to do! You have to help me!"

Anna pulled her hand away, but sat back down. "Do you remember what you asked me that first day in your office? You asked me if I was happy. Are *you* happy?" Anna had never spoken to J.J. this way. She felt exhausted by the morning's revelation—not in the mood to play a scene with this dramatic man. She decided that directness was her only viable approach. "Whatever you're looking for, I want you to find it, but it won't be with me. I want out." Anna stood. "We're both selfish people, J.J. I just hope it's not too late to change."

That night, as Anna sat across from Ernest at Rosa's, she felt awkward and embarrassed. She had never been out with a man in public and she felt exposed —as if she were taking a bath on an elevator. The tablecloths were too bright a shade of red. The strolling musician's violin seemed out-of-tune. The burning candle in the center of the table was giving off too much smoke. Everything was whirring with a vibrant intensity that made Anna want to cover her eyes and ears. Ernest's easy-going manner kept her entertained, but she began to regret agreeing to dinner. She started chewing the skin on the side of her lower lip. What was she thinking, going out with a man so soon after breaking it off with J.J.? She wondered if she only wanted to punish J.J. for his sleeping around, but Miss Blum was right—she had no claim on him.

The violinist walked by just as thoughts of J.J. began to crowd out any other thoughts. Then a woman joined him and he introduced a song.

"From the opera *Carmen*," he said, skillfully pulling his bow along the strings of his violin.

Anna stared at the couple, lost in the song and her own thoughts of regret.

"Anna? I think you're about a million miles away," Ernest said.

"I'm sorry. I'm not very good company tonight, I'm afraid."

"Well, you couldn't look any prettier. I've always been kind of partial to redheads."

Anna turned away from Ernest to listen to the duet. The couple sang in turn with one asking and the other in reply.

Tu ne m'aimes donc plus?

Non, je ne t'aime plus.

Mais, moi, Carmen, je t'aime encore, Carmen, helas! Moi, je t'adore!

A quoi bon tout cela? Que do mots superflus!

Carmen, je t'aime, je t'adore!

"That's real nice, but I wish I knew what they were saying. I don't speak Italian," said Ernest in a polite whisper.

"It's not Italian. It's French. He's trying to make her love him," Anna replied, not taking her eyes off the couple.

"How's he doing? Do you think he'll win her over?"

Mais ne me quitte pas, O ma Carmen, Ah! Souviens-toi du passé!

Anna translated: "Still love me, Carmen. Remember that time."

Nous nous aimions, naguere! Ah! Ne me quitte pas, Carmen...

"We loved so well then. Don't leave me now, Carmen..."

As the couple began to walk to another table, Anna dabbed the corners of her eyes with her napkin. Ernest watched them stroll away and glanced back at Anna.

"Now why do you think that Carmen lady was giving him the run-around?" he asked.

"She wanted her freedom and she knew that men are nothing but trouble." Anna looked up after finishing her thought, aware that she had said too much, with too much feeling.

There was an uncomfortable silence, then Ernest asked, "How do you know French?"

"Oh...I learned it growing up..." she began.

"Probably one of them fancy boarding schools, huh?" Ernest looked down at his plate and twirled a long strand of spaghetti on his fork. "You must think a country fellow like me is pretty silly."

Anna patted Ernest's hand. "Of course not. How could I think my hero was silly?" Ernest beamed.

"Where are you from, Ernest?" she asked.

"Oh, a little town in Tennessee you've never heard of—Morgan's Hat."

"You must miss living in the country."

"Not by a long shot. Why would anybody want to live anywhere but in a big city with all the lights and sounds?

Nothing ever happens in Morgan's Hat. Although..." Ernest reached into his back pocket and pulled out a small cream-colored envelope, folded in half. "I just got a letter from my brother back home." He slid out the letter and scanned the contents. "There was a right amusing part about my younger brother Clarence. But you wouldn't want me to read it, would you?"

"Oh, yes. Please do."

Ernest read: 'Clarence was playing out on the hill past Floyd Meece's apple orchard. Clarence and Homer'—he's another one of my brothers—'and two of their friends were playing king of the mountain and throwing rotten apples at each other. Out of nowhere a bald eagle swooped down and grabbed Clarence by the straps of his overalls.'

"No! What happened to him?" Anna asked.

"'The eagle took him about ten feet in the air and dropped him like a sack of potatoes.'"

"Your brother made that up," Anna declared.

"Honest. Floyd Meece backed up the story himself and Matt said Clarence wet his pants and ran all the way home, crying for his momma." Ernest sat back in his chair, taking a deep, satisfied breath.

"What else does he say in the letter?" Anna tried not to sound nosy, but she was captivated by the idea of a letter from home. Something about having a family member write to you, even if the contents were commonplace, created a hunger deep inside.

"Well, there's a part in here about my brother Buddy..."

"Your brother's name is Buddy?"

"It's really Barnabas, but when I was little I couldn't say such a long name so we started in calling him Buddy."

"Go on..."

"All right." Ernest read on: 'Don't let on to Momma but it looks like Buddy's got a girl and you'll never guess who. That deceitful Ida Mae Tipler has finally won him over for good. I caught them necking in the hayloft yesterday evening. Apparently it's become a regular thing for them. I can't say what Buddy sees in her. She's meaner than a wet hen and has whipped him nearly as many times as her brothers have. I don't know what she's got in mind but it can't be good for Buddy. Since we're on the subject, you ought to be on the lookout for designing women like Ida.' Ernest stopped reading the letter. "So on and so forth. He goes on like that for a while."

Anna looked uncomfortable for a moment. "How many brothers have you got?" she asked.

"Well, let's see. There's my older brother Matt, my younger ones: Buddy, Clarence, Homer, and George, and my baby sisters Frankie Jane and Della Mae. My sisters were just three and one when I left town. What kind of kin have you got?"

"Oh, it was just me growing up."

"I don't know what I woulda done with no brothers...probably eat more, for one thing. Momma's a good cook but six boys can eat you right into the poorhouse."

Many of the couples had left the restaurant by now. Anna felt spent and ready to go. "I guess I better get home. I have work tomorrow," Anna said. "I had a really nice time, Ernest."

"I wonder why we keep crossing paths like we have." He reached out his hand to touch the tips of Anna's fingers. "I sure like you, Anna. Do you think I could see you again?" Anna felt her stomach lurch.

"I think that would be all right," she said, looking down at her plate but not at their fingers. He started to intertwine his fingers with hers, pulling them nearer. Then Anna remembered the old scar on the palm of her hand. She pulled away and began to stand. Ernest took this cue to jump up and pull out her chair for her. After he helped her with her coat, they walked out together and he opened the door for her. He walked her to the steps of her apartment and they said good night. Anna kissed him on the cheek before turning to unlock the building door.

Ernest tripped away, whistling "The Way You Look Tonight." Anna, too, was smiling after they left each other, so that she didn't see a figure standing just inside the door.

"Who's that, Anna? Didn't take you long to find a new man, did it?" J.J. grabbed her elbow tightly.

"J.J.! You scared me! What are you doing here?" Anna whispered, looking up the stairwell for any nosy neighbors' faces.

"This can't be over for us. You still work in *my* office. You still live in *my* apartment. You're mine, Anna." He tried to kiss her.

"J.J., stop! You're hurting me." Anna pulled away and slapped him.

"I'm sorry, Anna. I...I didn't know what to do..." he sputtered. Anna smelled alcohol on his breath.

"Go home, J.J. I'll move out as soon as I can find a new place. I'll start looking for a new job tomorrow. Just go home before this gets worse."

"No, don't look for a new job. I need you in the office. You're all that keeps me from going crazy!" J.J. was dialing up his drama and Anna could tell that this scene could last a while.

"Come upstairs for a cup of coffee," she said, warily, "But that's it. Then you go home. Do you understand?"

J.J. grinned broadly and followed Anna up the stairs to her apartment. Forty-five minutes later, she proved that she meant what she had said as Anna handed him his hat and firmly said good night.

When she finally got under the covers, Anna lay awake. Thoughts of Glory's rounding belly and J.J.'s rummy breath were peppered with flashes of Ernest's dark eyes and the light touch of his fingers across a checkered tablecloth. She wanted to break away from her life—the same way she had felt in Mrs. Sanders' woodshed so many years ago. It was as if she was back at square one. At that moment, the thought of keeping house for a kind, handsome truck driver seemed like the perfect

Oh to Grace

escape and a new start.

Chapter 22

Sully's was two doors down from my Daddy's shoe repair shop, and Daddy's shop was just two doors down from Mr. Padgett's general store. From the time I could walk, I was coursin' up and down those shops around the square. Most of them are gone now but it was a real handy situation for shoppin' back then. For a span of time, Mr. Padgett was the only one in town with a telephone. I still remember the day Western Electric put in the line—Mr. Padgett already had a telegraph line and they just added some more gizmos to turn it into a telephone. Boy, he was a stingy man—he wouldn't pay to see a pissant pull a freight train. O' course, I shouldn't speak badly of him—his daughter Adell was one of my dearest friends—but he wouldn't let anyone, not even Miss Joyce, answer that thing. He seemed proud and annoyed by it all at the same time. Anyway, one time Adell come runnin' down to Daddy's shop to tell him he had a phone call all the way from Chicago. Me and Momma and Della Mae was there, too, bringin' lunch to Daddy. Momma started hollerin' and wringin' her hands. "He's been run over by one of them street cars. I just know'd it! Oh, my poor Ernest!" My daddy said, "Hesh, Burnetta" and we ran all the way to Mr. Padgett's store. Miss Joyce was puttin'

up the red, white, and blue Independence Day ribbons all along the porch rails in front of the store when we got there. My Daddy went straight to the back and picked up the receiver. "Say something, Daddy," I says. He said, "Hullo" and soon he was all smiles—it was Ernest. Daddy shouted into the box: "You had a what? What did you say 'bout welding, son?" He looked over at Della Mae and Momma and me and said that Ernest must be learnin' a new trade up in Chicago which was a fittin' thing for a young fella to do and weldin' was 'bout as good as any. Then Daddy turned back to the telephone, listened a minute and shouted, "Who's Anna? Your wife?" Then he turned to Momma and said, "Oh, Burnetta, your baby boy just got hisself married!"

CHICAGO
JULY 3, 1936

Anna tiptoed around the dark apartment so as not to wake Elise and her roommate Sheila. She was grateful that her old friend had let her stay—no questions asked—for the past six months, but she was thrilled that this was the last morning she would have to dodge elbows with the girls in front of the mirror as they all tried to get ready for work. Elise had also helped Anna find a job at Marshall Field's. All three of the girls worked in the block-long South Street Aisle, the bottom floor of the enormous department store. Elise and Sheila both pushed fragrances at the perfume counter and Anna sold ladies' scarves and gloves a little farther from the main entrance. When she wasn't waiting on customers with plumed hats perched atop their heads and fur stoles draped across their shoulders, Anna loved to look up above the five floors of the store, at the Tiffany glass ceiling made of more than a million tiny pieces of iridescent favrile glass tiles. The muted tans, yellows, ivories and sky blues used in the design gave the illusion that every day was sunny and bright outside. As she looked up, Anna often found herself breathing deeply, as one would do on the first warm day of spring.

Her job was simple. Mostly it was a mindless exercise of fanning gloves behind the glass cases, draping silk scarves over metal stands, and an occasional trip to the stock room. It gave Anna entirely too much time to think about J.J. She hadn't seen him again since the day in January when she had returned to the office to pack up her desk. J.J. had stood motionless at the door to his private office with his arms folded across his chest, watching Anna pack up her belongings. His cold demeanor and menacing glare led his secretaries to assume that Anna had been let go for some breach of ethics or incompetence. She tried to act untouched by any of the office gossip as she exited past the rows of confused expressions. She had wanted to avoid Glory most of all, but Glory, with perfect timing, had walked across the office so that she could hold the door for Anna as she left. "I'll get that for you, honey," Glory said with a thinly veiled triumph in her voice. Anna only nodded her head in thanks. Who knows what lies about her J.J. had spun for this woman who was carrying his child? Anna was humiliated.

The bright light for Anna in the last six months had been Ernest. He was J.J.'s opposite in so many ways. Ernest was so proud to show Anna off all over town. He was smooth in his wooing of her—similar to J.J.—but it was obvious that Ernest always had Anna's best interests at the forefront of his mind. "Are you warm enough? Was the food to your liking? If you're too tired to walk, we could get a taxi." At first Anna had felt overwhelmed by his attention, but she had become so accustomed to it that if twenty-four hours passed and they weren't together, Anna would feel a hole in her day as she went to sleep that night.

When Ernest first mentioned marriage to Anna, she resisted the idea. Ernest knew nothing about her past but the few carefully crafted facts she offered him. Anna assumed her mistakes with J.J. would prevent her from having any kind of normal, decent family life. She didn't even dare to wish for the dream of hearth and home—something she knew mainly from books and movies. But eventually, Ernest wore her resistance down. He made anything seem possible, even happiness, and Anna had just enough optimism left to be convinced.

Anna took extra care in her preparations this morning, squinting at herself in the small, square mirror in the dark bathroom. She parted her hair on the side and smoothed down the top until there were no stray strands, then brushed out her red curls and pinned up coiled sections with narrow hairpins. As she concentrated on her hairstyling, Anna reflected on Ernest's final winning proposal. He had said, "Anna, you know I love you. I've told you nearly every day for the past few months. I've told you and now I wanna show you. I wanna marry you and take care of you. I wanna be your fella forever and ever." Anna had stared into his eyes. She waited for a voice that would warn her to run from Ernest. She wanted to hear: *Don't do it. He's just like J.J.* But nothing came. She told Ernest *yes*, and now the day had come.

A snort erupted from the bedroom where Elise and Sheila slept in their twin beds. Anna felt guilty that she hadn't told them about her plans today. She wondered why. She wasn't embarrassed by Ernest. Any woman would approve of his looks and pleasant ways. Anna had to admit that she was still afraid the wedding wouldn't come off. Somehow, Ernest would change his mind at the last moment. Ignoring a feeling of inevitable disaster, Anna returned to the living room. She pulled a small box out from under the sofa where she slept. It held a few of the belongings from her old apartment. She untied the twine and opened the box. Among the items were the peacock pin and the shepherdess figurine J.J. had given her. She pulled them out quickly—afraid that Elise or Sheila would come out and see what she was doing—and put them in her purse.

Anna took one last look at herself. She was wearing a new

dress she had bought at Marshall Field's just for today. It was made of a light and airy, ivory eyelet batiste, with a narrow matching belt and a wide cape collar that extended past her shoulders. Centered on her chest was a large, ivory organdy flower. The dress was perfect. It had cost her almost a month's wages, but staring at herself this morning, she knew it was worth it. Ernest would be so pleased. Anna pinned on her small, cream-colored hat with flipped-up brim and blue and pink flowers on top. She pulled the loosely woven net veil down partially over eyes. She was almost ready to meet her groom.

The traffic was already heavy this morning. Anna walked briskly but carefully as she tried to avoid the dirt and grime that might spoil her dress. At the intersection of State and Washington, she glanced at the clock outside Marshall Field's. Eight twenty-five. She was supposed to meet Ernest at ten o'clock. Anna chewed her lip. She knew she couldn't be late. She turned right onto Madison and found the store quickly. The sign above the door read *Schmidt's Pawn Shop*. The elderly owner was standing outside the door, looking through his pockets for his keys. He finally pulled out a large ring with twenty or so keys hanging from it. Anna waited impatiently behind him as he tried each one, with shaking hands and fingers severely misshapen from arthritis.

"Sir..." Anna said quietly.

The man made no response. Cars honked and passed by behind them.

"Sir..." she repeated a little louder. The owner turned swiftly, surprised by Anna's presence.

"You startled me, *Fräulein*," he said.

"I'm sorry. It's just that I'm in a terrible hurry..."

Unsympathetic, the man returned to his slow progress with the keys. "Hurrying these hands never has done a bit of good. *Einen moment, bitte.*" Then the key turned in the lock with a loud click. "Aha!" The owner opened the door and walked in without holding it open for Anna or even looking back at her.

Oh to Grace

Anna stepped in and approached the counter.

"Are you Mr. Schmidt?" Anna asked.

"Yes, *Fräulein*. Did you think maybe I was Errol Flynn?" he asked grumpily. Mr. Schmidt walked to the back of the store and re-emerged in a few minutes wearing a brown smock over his suit. He perched on his tall stool, pulled out a velvet-lined box full of jewelry and loose gems, and set it on top of the glass counter. He quickly became engrossed in studying the items with his jeweler's loupe, forgetting that Anna was even there.

Anna cleared her throat. "Mr. Schmidt?"

"We don't open until nine o'clock, *Fräulein*." Mr. Schmidt pointed to the wall of clocks behind him. "It is now ten minutes until nine."

Anna's shoulders slumped. For the next ten minutes, she paced the length of the small shop, barely looking at the merchandise. She was more interested in unloading her items than getting anything new. The gifts from J.J. made Anna feel ashamed, and yet she had kept them until today—the last possible moment before she would share a home with her new husband. Why had she held on to them, if her feelings for J.J. were so changed?

Now that she was here, she might as well think about getting Ernest a gift for their wedding day, although buying a gift for him with money she'd raise by selling off things from an old tryst felt immoral. Was it wrong to profit from adultery? Anna reasoned that she was paying enough with her constant, nagging guilt and the ever-present worry that Ernest would reject her if he found out the truth. The amount she might make from these two gifts was nothing in comparison. As she looked down into the overcrowded display cases, Anna ran her finger along the cold metal strip on the top corner of the case. She saw a Buck Rodgers pocket watch, a belt buckle with a carved likeness of President Roosevelt and the Capitol building, and an electric blue tie with a picture of Popeye, the Sailor Man. None seemed to say "I love you, Ernest. Happy wedding day."

She was looking at a slim silver cigarette case next to a lovely set of tortoise-shell hair combs when the thirty or so clocks in the room begin to toll out the hour. Mr. Schmidt said, "*Fräulein*, how may I help you?" in a tone that implied he was speaking to her for the first time this morning. So jovial was his manner that Anna glanced behind her to be sure he was actually addressing her and not a new customer just entering the tiny shop.

"I have two things I'd like to sell," Anna said as she opened the front flap of her braided leather purse.

"Always to sell..." muttered Mr. Schmidt. "Never to buy..."

"Pardon me?" asked Anna.

"Never mind. Let's see what you have." Mr. Schmidt's jovial manner had disappeared. Anna placed the peacock pin and the figurine on the counter. "Hmmm...the girl is French...a Meissin, and not a nice one at that...I'll give you ten for her. The pin is Austrian...uh...five dollars." He pushed them away, unimpressed. "So that's fifteen, *Fräulein*."

"Fifteen. Thank you, Mr. Schmidt." Anna was relieved to get rid of the artifacts from a low point in her life. She would have paid far more than fifteen dollars to remove the memories, too.

"Is there anything else?" asked Mr. Schmidt as he counted out fifteen one-dollar bills, licking his thumb after laying each one down on the counter.

"How much is this cigarette case?" Anna asked, walking back to the counter in the opposite corner of the shop.

"That case? Oh, that is $14.50. For another fifty cents I engrave it with initials."

Anna looked at the money sitting in a tidy stack on the counter. "Engrave it?"

"Twenty-five cents per letter, *Fräulein*."

"Yes. That would be fine." Anna watched him open his cash drawer and replace all the bills as if he was welcoming long-lost children. "How quickly could it be done?" she asked.

"I can do it now, if you can wait a few minutes."

Anna looked back at the clocks: ten minutes past nine. "Yes. If you'll hurry, I'll wait."

Mr. Schmidt had Anna out the door with fifteen minutes to get to the courthouse. She nearly ran down Madison, pausing only briefly for the oncoming cars as she crossed the through-streets. After she crossed Clark Street, Anna stopped in front of a black metal fence that surrounded an old church tucked between two towering skyscrapers. Organ music pulsed from inside, competing with the car horns and squealing brakes on the street. On one long wall, presumably a side to the chapel, was hidden an intricately constructed stained glass window. The building that stood beside the church cast a dark shadow on it. The window showed a picture of Christ hanging on the cross, with a group of his followers kneeling beneath him. As Anna stared up at the dingy pieces of colored glass, she thought about the marvelous ceiling at Marshall Field's. She wondered at the inequitable treatment of the two pieces of art—one for all to enjoy, and the other reserved for the wealthy patrons of a department store.

A pedestrian bumped into Anna and she was transported back to reality. As she continued on her flustered way, Anna thought what it might be like to get married in a beautiful old church like the one she saw. Ernest had told her that he didn't care where they had the ceremony, but she wanted it done quickly and quietly. Besides, Anna hadn't set foot in a church since she left St. Regina's.

She turned right onto La Salle Street and hastily made her way to the City Hall building. As she approached, she looked up at the massive gray stone structure, standing eleven stories high and covering an entire city block. The first few floors had little ornamentation, but the upper two-thirds of the building were wrapped in lines of intimidating stone columns—more Greek temple than clerk's offices. Anna always thought it looked as if the lower third of the building was meant to be underground, but—by misfortune or mistake—the building was revealing its basement. This morning, it made her think of a girl showing off her bloomers. Anna wondered at her ability to imagine such ludicrous things just minutes before her wedding and subsequent entry into adulthood. She had tried to tamp down her wild imaginings, but as her nervousness grew, she lost her grip on rational thought. Anna shook her head a little to focus her mind, and began searching for the entrance to the county building.

Following Ernest's instructions, she went around to the east side and entered. She was greeted by a polished marble stairway, but no Ernest. She stopped a man in a dark business suit who was leaving the building and asked him for the time.

"It's twenty-five past ten, ma'am," he said.

She glanced up and down the long corridor again and tried not to cry. Feeling as if she had lost Ernest, she went to lean against one of the curved stone pillars that supported the domed ceiling sections of the corridor. As she rubbed her forehead, Anna watched the gilded hanging light fixtures sway slightly from footfalls on the floors above. Anna bit her lip hard, hoping the pain would stop the tears that sat hot in the corners of her eyes.

"There's my girl," said a voice from behind her. Ernest walked closer, with one hand reaching out.

"Oh, Ernest…" Anna said as she hugged him close to her.

"What's the matter?" Ernest asked, as the smile on his face was replaced by a look of concern.

"I'm so sorry I was late!"

"It's nothing, honey. I got most of the papers filled out while I was waiting." Ernest slapped a small stack of paper in his hands.

"So you didn't think I had…" Anna was all wonder. Her original feelings that her marriage would never happen began to ebb away.

"Didn't think you had what? Jilted me? No, honey. I know how women can take a while to get ready in the morning what with fixing their face and hair and all other manner of preparations." Ernest held her hand and took a step back to look at her. "Lemme tell you, Anna, it was worth it. I never saw a girl as pretty as you are right now."

"Oh, thank you," Anna sighed. "You're so sweet..."

"Alright," he interrupted. "The judge is waiting for us down the hall. I just need to get a few things on the application. I know you don't have any folks living, but do you know your mother and daddy's names and birthplaces? Oh, and also there's a place for your mother's maiden name."

Anna's feelings of disaster flowed back in. "Well, Ernest, I don't know..."

"Don't know which one, honey?"

"I didn't live with my parents after I was four, you see."

"Well, is there somebody we can call? Maybe the school where you went—maybe they could tell us some of this?" Ernest rummaged through his pockets, looking for change for a pay telephone.

"How about if we put what I do know and then we can see what the judge says," Anna replied quickly.

"Alright...what've you got?"

Anna searched her memory to recall the times she had overheard the Sisters' hushed conversations about her. They said that Anna's mother had been asked to fill out some forms before she left Anna, but Emma had refused. All she would give was the name of Anna's father and her own first name. "My father's name was Thomas...Simmons, of course. And my mother was Emma." Anna had always assumed they both came from Chicago, but she had no idea if this was true.

"Is that all?"

"I think so..." Anna said tentatively. "Do you think it's enough?"

"Well, we won't know 'til we try." Ernest filled out the

application without looking up at Anna. When he did glance at her, he saw that her face was full of distress. "Don't worry, honey! We'll be married today, come hell or high water. When you agreed to marry me, I promised to take care of you and that's just exactly what I'm gonna do." Ernest kissed her forehead and she felt some glimmer of hope.

They chose one of the lines queued up outside the row of clerk windows. When their turn arrived, Ernest showed the clerk their application.

"There is some information missing," said the woman behind the half glass window.

"Well, here's the thing," Ernest began. "My wife-to-be is an orphan, you see, and she just doesn't know some of the answers."

"Well, we can't process your application without proof of her background, sir. That's the rules." The woman pulled out another sheet of paper from one of the many stacks behind her. "Fill this out and come back on Monday. You can take your case to Orphans' Court. Next?"

Anna squeezed Ernest's hand to pull him away from the window, but he looked back at her and winked. "I appreciate your advice, you seem to have a real good handle on your job here, but I was wondering if there was some other way of doing this." Ernest flashed a smile. "You see, the little lady has just got her heart set on getting married today. I hate to let her down. Imagine how her life's been." He leaned forward and whispered. "She lost both her parents to the diphtheria, had to live in an orphanage where she ate nothing but raw cabbage. When that place got burnt to the ground, she got kicked to the curb and had to get a job selling fruit on the street...It's about time this girl catches a break, don't you think?"

The clerk glanced at Anna with her dainty white gloves and delicately trimmed hat. She rolled her eyes, but smiled at Ernest. "I suppose I could run your application through, but there can't be any empty blanks." She said the last few words with emphasis and gave him a look that implied what he should do next. Ernest wrote *Chicago* in both spots where it asked for parents' birthplace and *Smith* for Anna's mother's maiden name. The clerk took the application and intentionally smeared Ernest's pencil marks with her thumb. Then she pressed it with a large red stamp showing the city seal.

"Congratulations, Mr. Watson. Step back to Judge Handford's office, please."

Ernest took Anna by the elbow and led her to the judge's office. "Ernest...how did you...why did you..."

"Didn't I say I'd take care of everything? So I had to tell some whoppers to a clerk behind a window that we're never gonna see again. What's it really matter?" Ernest gently adjusted Anna's net veil before opening the door for her. "I know none of that stuff is true—thank goodness for you it's not—but everybody loves a good sob story. If the only way that lady was gonna stamp our papers was to get her to feel sorry for us...well I woulda started bawling right then and there if I needed to." Anna kissed Ernest's cheek and they both crossed the threshold of the judge's office.

After the brief ceremony, Ernest ran into a drugstore to call his family back in Tennessee. He especially wanted to speak to Matt, but his brother was at home on the farm. Ernest thought it was a long shot to expect Matt to be at his father's store at this time of day, but it had been almost three years since his last visit home. He wasn't sure of anyone's daily routines anymore. His father was the only member of the Watson family that Silas Padgett would allow on his store phone, and Frank's hearing made it difficult to say much about their big news. Burnetta was too hysterical to speak to anyone, so the conversation was short.

After the call ended, Anna and Ernest boarded a streetcar. "I've got something to show you," Ernest said as they found their seats. He could hardly stay seated during the half-hour trip to the northwest section of Chicago called Portage Park.

Anna's curiosity grew as they passed one two-story brownstone flat after another with cozy front porches and tree-lined sidewalks. "Here's our stop," Ernest said, finally.

They stepped off the streetcar, walked one block, and stopped in front of a pale yellow brick house. It was tall and trim, two stories with a narrow front. There was a porch made of two fat brick columns in matching pale yellow, and a dark green awning. On the left, stairs led to an underground entrance to the lower floor. "Here we are," Ernest said, now sounding more nervous than excited. "Honey, this is our new house."

Anna didn't understand at first what he meant. "Our house?"

"I couldn't decide what to get you for a wedding present, so..." Ernest's eyes pleaded with Anna. "Do you wanna go inside?"

He unlocked the front door and opened it wide. "I suppose we oughta do this right," he said, as he lifted Anna up and carried her inside to a tiny, tiled entryway. Ernest set her down and they climbed the steep staircase to another door that entered into a cheerful living room. The walls were papered with a charming design of baskets holding yellow, orange, and red flowers on a cream background. Two pumpkin-orange armchairs faced a stone fireplace. An arched doorway led to the bright green kitchen with green and white checkerboard tile floor.

"Well, what do you think?" Ernest asked as he ran his fingers through his hair.

Anna reached up to sweep back a stray lock on his forward. "I love it, Ernest."

He exhaled. "The top floor's all ours. There's a fellow who lives in the downstairs part. I met him. He's real nice." He held her hand and drew her through the other arched doorway that led down the hall to the bedroom and bathroom. "I got most of the furniture already, but I know it needs a woman's touch here and there." Anna walked into the bedroom and surveyed Ernest's purchases. He had bought two mahogany dressers—one fat and squat and the other tall and slim—and a full-sized bed with a matching mahogany headboard. There was a white chenille bedspread with a large medallion design in the center laid out on the bed.

"Everything's perfect. I wouldn't change a thing."

"With all that's been going on this morning, I bet you're mighty hungry." Ernest pulled Anna back out of the room and into the kitchen. "I got us some fixings for a wedding lunch. It's all in the icebox," he said with a boyish giddiness to his voice.

Ernest tied a white dishcloth around his waist as he instructed Anna to sit in one of the two wooden chairs pushed under the small kitchen table. As she sat, Anna watched him pull out a plate of deli meats and cheese and a bottle of milk from the small refrigerator. He set them on the table and retrieved plates and drinking glasses from the cabinets and a loaf of bread from the counter. Ernest finally sat in the opposite chair.

"Oh, I forgot the mustard," Ernest said and stood to get it from the icebox.

"Let me..." Anna said.

"No, Anna. I wanna wait on you today," said Ernest with a wink. "It's part of my wedding gift."

"You've done so much already," Anna said. "I have a gift for you, too." She opened her purse and pulled out the cigarette case wrapped in tissue paper. "It doesn't seem like much of anything..." She regretted that she hadn't spent more effort and money on his gift. Ernest unwrapped it.

"Would you look at that? I needed just such a thing for my smokes!" He kissed her on the forehead and sat down to make his sandwich.

They ate their lunch together in relative silence, unusual for Ernest. When Anna finished the last bite of her sandwich, Ernest jumped up. "There's one more thing," he said. He brought a small round layer cake to the table. The entire cake was frosted with fluffy white icing and the sides were covered in chopped nuts. There were a dozen cherry halves placed around the edge. "I got it at that Italian bakery around the corner. The lady said it was a wedding cake."

"Oh, Ernest, you thought of everything!" At that moment, Anna wanted Ernest to hold her in his arms more than anything in the world. She wanted to show how grateful she was for his thoughtfulness. "Can we save the cake for later?" she said shyly.

"I s'ppose so," Ernest said, pouting slightly. Then he saw the shining look in Anna's eyes and raised his eyebrows in recognition. They walked to the bedroom and turned back the bedspread.

Their first time together was brief and reserved. In their shy intimacy, Anna realized how little they really knew each other. After the new couple had made love, Anna laid her head on Ernest's bare chest and listened to his even breathing. He was soon asleep, but she continued to lie against him, tuning her ear to listen and measure his heartbeat. It sounded strong and confident. Suddenly, the thought of his heart ceasing to beat caused a wave of panic to pass over her. How could something so small and commonplace as a heartbeat mean life or death for an entire person's body? Now his heartbeat seemed to throb only because she willed it to happen. She wished that the rhythm of their hearts could beat in unison. She reasoned that then they could stop at the same time, too. Anna knew she would do anything for Ernest—his regard for her was all that mattered to her now.

Oh to Grace

Momma and Daddy didn't get a phone line at the house until after I was married. Daddy held off as long as he could. Said he didn't need it as long as he had the radio and his nose. My daddy was what some people called a weather prophet. He could stand outside of an evenin' and tell you what the weather would be like the next day. He knew all about the clouds and the wind and the smells. Sometimes he could just feel a storm comin'. Said he could feel it in his ears like they was 'bout to bust. One night he stood out in front of our house and started sniffin' the air like he always did. Then he called to Matt, "Go hitch up the cart. They'll be needin' us in town." We asked him what was the matter and he said, real calm-like, the courthouse was on fire. Now we lived a good five or six miles from the square, but sure 'nough he was right. He saw just the faintest glow on the horizon. Judgin' from that and the smell he figured there was a fire. Seein' that the courthouse was the biggest building over there, he knew that must be it. By the time he and Matt got out there it was aflame. It took all the men from 'round Morgan's Hat most of the night to get the fire put out but they were able to contain it. I reckon my daddy wasn't a real prophet but it'd be somethin' to be able to tell the future, wouldn't it? Maybe like one of them gypsies with the crystal ball and long red fingernails? I reckon that's all pagan voodoo, but it still gets some folks' minds a-whirlin'.

MORGAN'S HAT, TENNESSEE
JUNE 27, 1937

On their second visit to Morgan's Hat as a married couple, Ernest and Anna took the train into Clarksville. Matt waited for them at the depot in a navy Chevy sports coup he borrowed from Silas Padgett, the local grocer. His momma wanted her beloved daughter-in-law to arrive in style and insisted that Matt find a better vehicle than his old Dodge truck. Matt protested the use of the car. The two-seater sports car had a rumble seat in the back and he knew just who'd be sitting in it all the way home from the depot. He tried to paint grotesque pictures of the dangers of the rumble seat for his mother, but she weighed the odds of decapitation for the unlucky backseat passenger and decided it was in her favor.

"It's a real smart looking automobile," she said. "Anyhow, I ain't heard of no one gettin' their heads lopped off 'round here just by sittin' in the dickie seat. You'uns just be extra careful, ya hear?" And that was that for the sports car. Matt picked them up as arranged and rode all the way back home in the rumble seat. He was picking out bugs from his teeth all evening after they got home.

Now it was Sunday afternoon, and the Watson family members gathered for a post-church dinner. With stomachs full of fried chicken and three kinds of pie, they spread out like lazy dogs on the back porch. Burnetta sat in her usual place on the porch swing, with Frankie Jane and Della Mae on either side. She tried in vain to cool herself with a rounded fan made of waxy yellow paper, with "Palmer Funeral Home" printed on the front in a slanted script. Ernest and Anna sat together on a wooden bench and Frank and Matt sat in rockers nearby. Clarence opted for the shade of the giant oak just down from the porch steps. He was already dozing with a hat over his face to keep the flies away from his open mouth. Homer and George found their preferred place on the porch floor, lying on their stomachs flipping through the pages of an old National Geographic magazine.

"What're you looking at there, boys?" asked Frank.

Homer and George stared at the glossy, colored photos of a coronation in Ethiopia. The seated king and queen were dressed in red velvet robes with gold trim down the front. The king held a scepter, and they both wore tall golden crowns. Another photo showed a soldier in what looked like a striped pajama shirt of blue ticking, a crudely skinned fur pelt across his shoulders, and a wild-looking helmet with tall shoots of weeds poking out the top. He wore no shoes and carried a rifle in one hand and a black metal shield in the other. The pictures might have been from another planet—the boys were so unaccustomed to such a mixture of grandeur and absurdity.

"It looks to be a party where they was gettin' a new king," answered Homer.

"Is that so? Whereabouts?" Frank asked, his pipe between clenched teeth.

"Ethiopia... Matt, where's that?" asked George.

"That's in Africa—somewhere on the east side," Matt answered.

"I reckon I'm gonna go there one of these days," Homer said, matter-of-factly.

"Pig's eye!" George replied. This was the boys' favorite phrase for calling each other out. It was shortened from "pig's eye—you lie!" Their other favorites included: "pig's feet—you cheat, pig's snout—you're out, pig's chin—you win" and the very useful "pig's pinky—you're stinky."

"Aw, what do you know?" Homer countered.

"I know you ain't never gonna leave this town."

"Why not? Ernest did it and plenty of other people besides."

"Well, goin' to Chicago is one thing, but leavin' the country is somethin' else entirely," George said.

"Well...what about Harley Dickson?"

"Movin' to Memphis ain't world travel. That's not even leavin' the state!"

"Pig's thumb! I know that! Don't you remember last year Carmine Baker tellin' everybody at Padgett's 'bout the letter he got from Harley Dickson? He went all the way up to Canada for his uncle's cotton business," Homer said with finality.

"Ooh, that reminds me," said Frankie Jane, perking up. "I heard Harley Dickson's lost his job. Now he's as poor as a pauper."

"Frankie Jane," rumbled her father, "you know gossip is a sin."

"What's this?" asked Burnetta, ignoring her husband's rebuke. "What's happened to Harley and Doris?"

Frank sighed deeply. He decided it would be better if the facts were laid out straight. Maybe that would keep the stories from changing too much through the re-tellings.

"It seems as though Harley's uncle lost his membership in the Memphis Cotton Exchange," Frank began. "Caffey Roberston, the Exchange's president, claims Harley's Uncle Mather reneged on too many verbal agreements with his suppliers, tarnishing his reputation. Without the membership, Mather has no voice in the cotton industry, and the Mather Dickson Cotton Company is going bust."

"Lands-o-Goshen! Who ever heard of such a thing?" Burnetta did little to hide the triumph in her voice. Harley and Doris both canvassed the town with boasts of their new financial venture before leaving town nine years ago. It would be a treat for her to see them back in Morgan's Hat with a transformed humility.

Before another word could be said for or against the Dickson family, Buddy and his wife walked around the corner of the house to join them. Buddy's wife, Ida Mae, carried their four-month old baby boy in her arms. As soon as Frank—the wise *pater familias* of the Watson clan—saw them coming, he hopped out of his old rocker and sprinted off inside the house. He knew his wife well enough to see that a storm was about to erupt.

Buddy married Ida Mae Tipler only a few weeks after she broke the news to her father about the child she was expecting. This was a blow to all of the Watson clan, but especially to Burnetta. She despised Ida Mae for luring her gullible son into "sinful lust," and she made sure everyone knew where the fault for the pregnancy should lie.

Sensing his mother tense up at their arrival this Sunday afternoon, Matt watched Buddy and Ida as they approached the group. He imagined that they were a couple of unsuspecting zebras approaching the watering hole where a family of ferocious lions laid in wait. Matt had spent half the night reading an article entitled "Travels to the Serengeti" from one of the National Geographic magazines. Suddenly, every interaction within his family had an animalistic quality to it, and Buddy and Ida Mae were just fortunate to encounter such a sated pride. *They seem happy enough*, thought Matt, as he saw the grins spread across Buddy and Ida Mae's faces. But he couldn't help but wonder why Buddy would want to get tangled up with the family that had given him so much grief in the school yard over the years. Granted, Buddy had not often been one to fight the prevailing power. Matt guessed that Ida Mae determined early on that Buddy was worth chasing and she didn't give up until he gave in. Matt had witnessed Buddy fighting back with an uncharacteristic enthusiasm, but he eventually decided it was his fate to let this round, bossy girl love him.

Ida Mae bounced her son on her hip as they made their way up the porch steps. Burnetta held back her desire to return the smile Barney Jr. presented to her. She was becoming more attached every day to her new grandbaby boy. It was Barney's supreme good fortune that he favored the Watson side instead of looking blond, pink-faced, and chubby like every person in the Tipler family. Barney had dark hair, eyes, and lashes like Buddy and Ernest, and he smiled easily. As far as his grandmother was concerned, there was no Tipler blood in him at all.

Burnetta snatched him from his mother as soon as they stepped foot on the porch. She pressed him into her wide bosom and it wasn't long before the baby was sleeping peacefully. Ida Mae plopped down in a rocker and started vigorously fanning herself. "Lands, it's hot today! I don't know how ya'll can stand it out here!" she proclaimed.

"Ah, it ain't too bad, hon," answered Buddy after a pause. Most of his family rarely acknowledged anything she said, so when her remarks fell on deaf ears, Buddy felt it was his obligation to fill the quiet.

"No, Buddy, it's good and hot, like the devil hisself ordered it up for church day!" More silence. "I reckon it's the hottest day we had all year." Still no answer. "My pa always says it's days like this that'll make a sinner go to Sunday meetin', though it didn't much work on us today, did it, Buddy?"

Burnetta inhaled and exhaled loudly through her flared nostrils. "Anna, honey," cooed Burnetta softly, all the while wearing an insincere smile, "Do you wanna hold Buddy's baby?" Anna felt an infusion of terror. She had never held a baby before. She also had an itching suspicion that Burnetta was more interested in vilifying Ida Mae than showing off little Barney.

"No, I couldn't..." Anna began. Then she looked at her splayed out sister-in-law—trying to cool off from the summer heat—and saw that her blouse was sporting two wet circles right across the front. "Well, maybe I will, Mrs. Watson." She lifted the sleeping baby gingerly, surprised at how heavy he was. "Ida Mae, why don't you come in the house with me for a minute?" Anna whispered. "It'll be a little cooler inside, I suspect."

Most of the family was lightly dozing, but Matt had been watching all of the subtle drama on the porch. Just as Anna suggested they go inside, he too noticed the milk rings on Ida Mae's blouse. Realizing what Anna had just done for the outcast in-law, Matt smiled.

"I believe I may walk out and take a look at your new truck, Matt," said Ernest, stretching his legs. "Homer, George, how 'bout you walk with me a bit?" The younger brothers, sixteen and thirteen years old, jumped at the chance to spend time with their stylish older brother. "Matt, you coming?"

Matt looked at the two boys, who were almost panting from the excitement of the invitation from Ernest. "Nah, I'll just stay here and fiddle with my guitar a while, I reckon," answered Matt. He pulled his Gibson out from behind his chair. He always gave it a visual inspection before playing it—strings in good condition, still shiny black around the edge—but the blond-brown section near and below the sound hole had lightened over the years from faithful playing. *Strum*—still perfect. It was one of Matt's most prized possessions.

He began to pluck the strings, twisting the knobs to tune it. He played lightly and hummed along to his own tune for a while. Then he played a few hymns—soft ones like "Come Thou Fount of Every Blessing" and upbeat ones like "Bringing in the Sheaves." He patted his guitar's soundboard in appropriate places during "He Keeps Me Singing." *Jesus, Jesus, Jesus, sweetest name I know*—pat, pat, pat—*Fills my every longing; Keeps me singing as I go.*

He finished with the melodramatic "Up From the Grave He Arose." During the verses, he plucked each individual note with a reserved intensity, as if he was holding back until just the last second: *Vainly they watch His bed, Jesus my Savior. Vainly they seal the dead, Jesus my Lord!* Then he strummed the chords with spirit:

Up from the grave He arose with a mighty triumph o'er His

foes.

He arose a Victor from the dark domain
And He lives forever, with His saints to reign.
He arose! He arose! Hallelujah! Christ arose!

While Matt played, Anna and Ida Mae returned to the porch. Ida Mae was wearing a different blouse now and little Barney wore the satisfied expression of a baby who has just eaten. He happily sucked the side of his fist. Anna resumed her seat on the porch swing next to Burnetta. A look of relief spread across Anna's face.

When Matt's final chorus ended, Buddy looked up from his nap and asked, "Where'd you get that shirt, Ida?" Matt interrupted by asking Anna if she had a request.

"What was that first one you played, Matt? The one with that says 'Oh to grace...something...something...I can't remember...'" Anna stammered. She was working hard to keep the conversation away from Ida Mae's milk leakage.

"This here thing belongs to Anna. Ain't it pretty?" said Ida Mae, with obvious pride. "My hooters was leakin' like a sow with fifty teats, so she let me borrow it."

Anna blushed from her chin up into her scalp. "I reckon I'll go see what the fellas are doin'," said Matt, stifling a laugh. "Anna, would you like to walk with me?" She nodded her head quickly. The tension growing from Burnetta's ever-mounting disappointment shivered like a wave of heat across the porch railing as they descended the steps.

When they were out of earshot from the group, Matt said, "It was awful nice of you to help out Ida Mae. She wasn't raised to have much sense of what's right in mixed company."

"Well, it didn't do much good, I'm afraid," said Anna. "She's pretty determined to look like a fool in front of your mother. Doesn't Ida Mae know how much your mother... well... how much she..."

"Can't stand the sight of her? I reckon I can't tell. If Ida Mae knows, she either covers her disappointment real well or don't care."

Soon they were near enough to hear Ernest, George, and Homer talking. "Does she have a crystal ball and big gold earrings like you see in the picture shows?" Ernest was asking.

"Nah, she just takes a-hold of your hands, rolls her eyeballs way back, and tells you things that'll happen to you," said George, the younger and more naïve of the two boys.

"What are you boys talkin' 'bout?" asked Matt when they had reached the side of the barn. Ernest was smoking a cigarette.

"Homer and George went to the circus yesterday and saw a fortune-teller," answered Ernest.

"You know how the folks feel 'bout you wastin' your money on that nonsense. Momma'll skin you alive if she finds out," Matt said to Homer and George. Any of the four boys standing in the barnyard were nearly twice as tall as their mother, but they all possessed a healthy fear for Burnetta's wrath.

"I say we look into this Madame Desiree," said Ernest as he ground his toe into the cigarette butt he had just thrown into the grass. "It sounds mighty interesting." Ernest turned to Anna. "What do you think, my sweet?"

"Well, if you think your mother would be mad..." she began.

"No, she won't be mad. She's still too mad at Buddy right now to pay us much mind." Ernest replied. "That does it, then..."

Ernest, Anna, Homer, and George started toward Matt's truck, parked under the open shed next to the barn. "How 'bout you, Matt?"

Matt tossed Ernest the keys. "I learned my lesson the last time you talked me into goin' with you to a freak show. You're on your own this time, buddyroe."

The group piled into the truck and drove toward town. Matt watched them for a minute before walking to his favorite spot behind the barn. He pulled out the letter that had come with the package of National Geographics from Mr. Allen and sat down on a log. Matt had already read the letter twice but was glad for a moment of solitude to read the news from his former teacher again.

Matt,

I hope these editions of National Geographic find you well and happy. Though as Aristotle said, "Men are what they are because of their characters, but it is in action that they find happiness or the reverse." In other words, you have to make your own happiness. At any rate, that's what I've found.

It's hard to believe that August will mark fifteen years since I left Morgan's Hat. Though we've never spoken of it in our letters, I know you were well aware (as was most of the town, I'd wager) of the circumstances surrounding my departure. To put it plainly, I made a fool of myself in the name of young love. For a great portion of the past fifteen years, I lamented my actions and sentiments, just as I resented that they were not fully reciprocated. You know that I now have Alice and our two boys to erase past mistakes, but that is not what set things right. No, it happened before that cloudy day that I stepped off a Nashville streetcar into a sudden spring shower and an angel shared her umbrella with me.

The moment of clarity came one afternoon as I sat in my classroom after the dismissal bell had rung. My landlady, the formidable Mrs. Grimes, had handed me a letter from you as I walked out the door that morning. I found no time to read it until the end of the day. In it you recounted a story of Ernest and his nearly fatal experience with one Dorcas Hogg (possibly the worst speller in the history of the Granny Silas School) and her jealous boyfriend, Charlie Duncan. You said something in that letter that hit me with such force, I knew it was time for me to move forward. You wrote that Ernest was always looking for romance but getting trouble instead. You said that he should search out life and get what came with it—be it romance or not. You said it was like looking for stick bugs out in the woods.

You never seem to find them when you're looking for them, but when you just ramble through the woods, letting your mind wander but keeping your eyes open for the wider view, you see them by the dozens.

You can't know what effect that had on me that afternoon in my empty classroom. It was just the shove I needed and I don't think I've ever thanked you properly for it. If I hadn't decided to change my approach at life, perhaps my first encounter with Alice would not have come off so well. I'm indebted to you, Matt.

I've been asked to send a word of thanks to you from Will and Tom. They were thrilled with the set of wooden cars you made for them. They have raced them all over the sitting room. Every volume of poetry I own has been converted into some type of ramp or abutment. Coleridge and Wordsworth haven't seen this much fun in a century!

Your faithful friend,
Napier Allen

As he laid the letter down, Matt felt the muscles in his cheeks twitch. He hadn't realized that he'd held a tight, closed-lip smile throughout his reading of the letter. As he massaged his cheeks, he basked in the tremendous joy of knowing that he'd helped the man who taught him so much. He scanned the row of pine trees opposite his seat, noticing the slender beginnings of the fall's coming pinecones. Soon his eye fell on a long stick bug, lying splay-legged on the side of the tree. It was a shade lighter than the bark, but perfectly camouflaged until that moment.

By the time Matt finished his letter, Ernest and his group arrived at the imitation circus. As they approached the ring of covered wagons, a smile crept across Ernest's face. "Did you happen to notice if Madame Desiree had an unusual number of legs?" he asked.

"No, why?" asked George.

"No reason. Just wondering."

Ernest paid everyone's admission. They ignored the large tent in the center, where sounds of neighing horses and barking dogs could be heard. Instead, they walked along the circle of wagons until they came to one with a large eye painted on a sign just outside the door.

Anna laid a hand on Ernest's wrist. "Do you think this is a good idea?" she asked.

"Sure, sweetheart. What could happen?"

George said, "We went to see her yesterday and she said I'd be a farmer with a passel of kids to raise. I reckon she figured that out just by lookin' at me."

"She told me a whole lotta hogwash 'bout seein' me in battle and my chest gettin' pinned up with silver stars and the like," said Homer. "It weren't too bad of a thing at that…better than havin' a bunch of mealy-mouth kids." George kicked Homer in the shins.

Anna wanted very much to know at least a piece of her future, but she was afraid to ask about what weighed most heavily on her mind. "I'll go," she said, surprising her husband.

"All right! That's my girl!" Ernest gave her a side hug and watched her step cautiously up the two metal steps that had been unfolded to the ground from the entrance of the wagon.

Inside the wagon, the air hung thickly with fragrant smoke. The walls were covered with dark drapes that Anna squinted to examine more clearly in the shadowy room. "Sit here," a voice creaked. Madame Desiree was so still that Anna hadn't noticed her sitting on the floor. The woman had skin the color of rich mahogany. Her face was lined with as many wrinkles as the folds of the brocade draped from her head to the floor. All of the fabric in the wagon seemed to have come from the same bolt. Anna thought the fortune-teller looked as if she was drowning in it. "One dollah," said Madame Desiree.

Anna sat on the opposite side of a low wooden table from the woman and slid the dollar across to her. "You hands," said Madame Desiree. Anna held out her hands. The fortuneteller grabbed them tightly in her own thin, dry hands. Anna looked down at the woman's impossibly long red fingernails, each one curling slightly at the ends. Madame Desiree threw her head back for only a moment before snapping it back sharply, locking eyes, and holding Anna's left hand, palm up. She rubbed it gently with her own left hand. The fortune-teller murmured something that sounded like *"C'est grave..."* then she resumed her position, holding both hands and pointing eyes skyward.

"Ask you question," said Madame Desiree. Anna had not anticipated her part in the proceedings, but her question leapt forward without any thought.

"Will I give Ernest a child?" she said quickly.

Madame Desiree made a buzzing sound with her clenched teeth and swayed from the waist up in a slow circle. Then she chanted: *"Un bébé. Un bébé. Un bébé."* Anna's head felt heavy in the hot room, and the blanketed walls seemed to close in on her. She blinked repeatedly to stay focused, afraid she would faint. Suddenly, Madame Desiree stopped. "No. No *bébé* for Air-nest. Dat is da word day send me. You done."

Anna was shocked by the fortune teller's abruptness. When she stumbled out of the wagon, fear was written all over Ernest's face. "Honey, what is it?" He grabbed her in his arms and helped her to a nearby tree. "Go get her some water," said Ernest to George, with a little panic in his voice. Anna's color returned to her face after a few deep breaths.

"What happened?" asked Homer.

"Leave her be," snapped Ernest. "I should've gone in first—that crazy voodoo witch."

"I'm fine," said Anna, weakly. "I just wasn't expecting it to be so hot in there." She smiled at Ernest, who gave a half-hearted chuckle and scratched the back of his head. He bent down to kiss her forehead and helped her to her feet.

"You next?" Homer asked Ernest.

"Nah," said Ernest. "We better get back."

"Yeah, I'm hungry," said George. "Let's go see if Momma's got some 'o dat blueberry buckle left over from dinner."

Homer and George jumped in the bed of the truck while Ernest opened the passenger's side door for Anna. Anna looked back towards the fortune-teller's wagon and saw Madame Desiree ducking her head to exit the draped doorway and walk out into the sunshine. She stood with her hands on her hips—metal and wooden bangles in stacks on her thin arms—staring at Anna. Madame Desiree's face was void of any malice or boasting. Anna wasn't sure, but she thought she read pity in the black eyes of the prophetess.

Chapter 24

Morgan's Hat & Chicago
1939-1941

Personally, I tend to prefer the attractions you see at one of them music and arts festivals over seein' somethin' odd and unnatural like a gypsy fortune teller at a freak show. A few years back, me and Della made a trip to the Mountaineer Days Festival in Tracy City. Besides their hillbilly church service, they also had a greasy pig contest, a horseshoe tournament and a toilet seat toss. Della's boy Dillon told us to stop over in Monteagle on the way. You ever been to Monteagle? It's just a ways up the road from Chattanooga. Well, anyhow, Dillon said we had to eat at this real nice restaurant called the High Point. He lives in California and he's forever saying nonsense like "food is art" and "savor the local Q-zine." So we went in and I knew somethin' was funny when they laid out heaps of flatware for us to use, but we ordered something too 'spensive anyway...I cain't remember what... and the waiter told us that Capone used the restaurant for a hideout on his way from Chicago to Miami and visey-versey. Imagine that! Al "Scarface" Capone comin' through Tennessee with his whiskey and criminal friends! Who ever heard of such? And do you know that Della made me eat snails? O' course, we used to eat baked raccoon and fried dandelion flowers growin' up, so once I got past the sliminess, it weren't half bad. I reckon I've got some pictures from the festival in that other shoebox over yonder—the one that says Aerosoles on it. Not that one—it's still got shoes in it. The one under it, Amelia-honey, there it is. Lemme see if I can't find the one where Della won the watermelon-eating contest.

JULY 14, 1939
MORGAN'S HAT, TENNESSEE

"Now here's a peachy little tune that came out a couple-a years back outta Fort Worth. It's the Pillman Sisters singing their biggest hit yet 'Just Thought You Oughtta Know...'" As the radio announcer's voice trailed off, fiddles, guitars and a banjo opened up.

You done me wrong for the last time, fella
I'm at the end of my row
You done me wrong for the last time, fella
I just thought you oughtta know
If I see you again a-wearin' that grin
A-wearin' that grin and a-drinkin' that gin
You'll be sleepin' with the hounds again
Just thought you oughtta know...

The rolled-up sleeve of Ernest's tanned left arm flapped in the breeze as he drove with the window rolled down. He tapped his hand on the outer door of the truck in time with the song. Installing a radio in his truck was a stroke of genius. Now that he had entered the range of the radio stations near Morgan's Hat, he could pick up the music that made him recall his youth with fondness.

He needed to make it to Monteagle to pick up some items for Detroit Will and the boys back at the gambling saloons and return by Monday. Why not cut through Morgan's Hat and see the family on the way? He had a truck full of yellow Sundance corn to provide a cover for his actual mission. He would run over to Padgett's Grocery Store and see if he could unload some of it.

Ernest had kept the details of his trip from Anna that morning. He kissed her while she slept in the dark hours before dawn, and then slipped out. He would have loved the company of his pretty wife on the long car ride, but he wouldn't expose her to the dangers of his job. In the more than seven years that he had been working for Will, there had been too many close calls with police officers and rival gangs. Anna sometimes wondered how a truck driver could bring home the kind of paychecks that Ernest earned, but she was grateful to have a loving husband who made it possible for her to quit her job and live in a comfortable home.

Ernest was unaware of the true reasons for their rushed wedding. Always willing to believe the best of others, especially when this belief coincided with his own desires, he took Anna's *yes* as a compliment. Throughout their three years of marriage, he had elevated Anna to a peak of perfection in his mind and she took no pains to contradict him. He hired someone to clean their house and wash his shirts so that she could live a life of leisure. He tried to take her out to restaurants as much as possible so she wouldn't have to cook, either. She meekly attempted to refuse, but always gave in to him.

Last night, Ernest had told Anna how he hated to leave her for a few days. He never mentioned that he would stop by Morgan's Hat; he just said that he had to travel pretty far south. He held her tightly in their little bed in the darkness of their room, both facing the same wall with his arms wrapped around her waist and his face buried in her neck. He loved falling asleep this way.

This morning, Ernest had left a quick note on the nightstand table. It read: "Darling, I love you so. Until Monday, Ernest."

Oh to Grace

Late in the afternoon, Ernest pulled up in front of Padgett's store and got out of the cab. He stretched a minute, considering what to do first. Should he stop by his father's store or try to sell the corn? He decided to get his business out of the way. He looked around at the familiar town square. Very little had changed since he left for his chance at a different life in the big city. The courthouse sat in the center, with its large round clock at the top and a circle of sidewalks and parking spaces around it. All four sides of the square had a barbershop or beauty salon. Then there was Gordon's Hardware, the Post Office, Ned Pilson's Law office, Rose of Sharon Flower Shop and Doctor Jameson's office. Frank Watson's shoe repair shop sat conveniently next to Joppa Shoes. Then came Bread of Heaven Bakery, Sullivan's Drug Store, and Padgett's General Store. The two newest stores—the bakery and the florist shop—were run by sisters who, when naming their businesses, bucked the conventional trend of using the proprietor's name and turned to the Bible for inspiration instead.

There were benches at every corner, but few people were out in the afternoon heat. Ernest saw two boys, about the age of George or Homer, standing outside the store, taking turns spitting squirts of brown tobacco juice on the sidewalk.

"Afternoon, boys," Ernest said with a tip of his hat.

They returned his greeting with a slight nod as Ernest reached for the door. A woman holding a cumbersome sack of full of groceries was leaving and he held the door open for her.

"What a nice boy," she said before looking up. "Well, if it isn't Ernest Watson! How fine you look."

"Thank you, ma'am." He recognized her as Daphne Perkins, a woman who quilted alongside his mother at the weekly sewing bee.

"I'd love to visit with you and hear about all your people but I s'ppose I should get this food home and outta this heat. I fear I'll be late in gettin' supper on the table. Do you know the time, son?" she asked him.

Ernest pulled out his watch and answered, "A quarter to five, ma'am."

The top-heavy bag shifted and she juggled it slightly. Ernest kicked his foot against the door to keep it open and grabbed for the bag, dropping his watch as a sacrifice for the groceries. Once steadied, she tried to take the bag back from him, but he insisted on carrying it to her car.

As they began to walk away, Mrs. Perkins called out to Ernest. "Is that your watch, son?" she asked, pointing to the ground.

"Oh, yes. Thank you, ma'am," he said as he balanced the bag on his right hip. He bent down to pick up the watch with his left hand and slid it into his pants pocket. Once at the car, she thanked him warmly. After refusing to take her offered dime, they parted ways. Unbeknownst to Ernest, during this exchange, one of the boys loitering outside the store jabbed his companion in the arm and they quickly walked away.

The bell on the grocery store door announced his arrival. Without looking up, Adell Padgett said, "I'll be with you in a jiff." Ernest walked to the back of the store and placed both elbows on the counter with his chin resting in his hands, just as he had a lifetime ago—only now he had to compensate for his height by bending at the waist considerably. Had the counter always been so low?

Adell turned around to assist her customer and saw her best friend's handsome older brother. "Why, Ernest Watson! This just takes the cake! Frankie Jane and me was just talkin' 'bout you only yesterday! What in God's green earth has brung you to Morgan's Hat?"

"Just a truck full of corn. Your daddy here?" said Ernest as he stood up and flashed his winning smile.

"Nah, daddy went to make a delivery to Mrs. Henderson, but he said he'd be back to close the store. You know, I been workin' for him since I was knee-high to a grasshopper but he says, 'No girl of twelve is gonna count my cash drawer.'"

"I can wait." Ernest pulled his handkerchief out of his back pocket to wipe his brow. "It's mighty hot today."

"Daddy says August is gonna be hot as floogies this year. What's it like in Chicago? Is it real hot there?"

"Oh, sure, it's hot, but we go and catch a movie at the Gateway Theater and stay pretty cool," he said nonchalantly.

"Ernest, tell me more about livin' in Chicago…" Adell continued to interrogate him in this way while they waited for her father to return.

Bo Dickson, Jr. and Zeke Clabo left their loitering post outside Padgett's Store and jumped into Zeke's old pick-up. "Hellfire, Bo! Why you in sech a gall-durn hurry?" bellowed Zeke.

"My daddy's been a-lookin' for somebody for a long time and I jest seen him," Bo said with mounting satisfaction.

When they reached the old Dickson farm, Bo started yelling for his father before he even saw him. Harley was stretched out on a threadbare pink loveseat in what was once a fashionable parlor. Harley's mother, Viola Dickson, had strutted in front of her company when showing them into "The Parlah," as she called it in her best Southern deb accent. She always made sure to point out the Dutch paintings, plush French furniture, and the required number of doilies and curios strategically placed around the room. But now, lacking the necessary funds, Harley could not bring it back to its original splendor. He had tried to stay in Memphis and find another job after his uncle's cotton business went under, but times were difficult in the Bluff City. When he delivered the news to Doris that they would have to move back to Morgan's Hat, she ran away with a vibraphonist who played with a local swing band. Completely dejected, Harley and Bo Jr. returned to the old homestead. Harley had bragged too much before he left, and he knew it. He imagined the whole town was laughing at him behind his back, so he became a recluse from society. He had nothing to be proud of anymore.

"Daddy! You ain't never gonna guess what I jest seen!" Bo called.

After settling matters with Silas Padgett and unloading the corn, Ernest dusted off his pants and began to walk over to his father's shop. Just as he stepped onto the sidewalk, Harley and Bo pulled up in Zeke's truck. They sped into a parking spot and rolled both front tires over the curb, with the bumper hanging over the sidewalk. Harley jumped out of the passenger's side, looking wild-eyed and ready for a fight. He had brought his father's revolver, and it hung at his side as he approached Ernest.

"Give it here, Watson," Harley barked.

"Harley? What are you hollerin' about?" Caught by surprise, Ernest's country dialect returned.

Harley grabbed Ernest's collar and dragged him to the side of the store, with Bo following along behind. "You got my daddy's watch, you thievin' snake!"

"Alright, Harley. I don't want no trouble with you." Ernest slowly reached his right hand into his pocket to retrieve the watch, forgetting that he had put the watch in his left pocket. He mistakenly pulled out the top of his small pocket pistol instead.

"Watch-it, daddy! He's got a gun!" shouted Bo.

Harley instantly aimed his gun at Ernest with the tip of the barrel pressed against his chest. He fired. Unprepared for the recoil, Harley fell back against the wall of the store. Like a gruesome mirror image, Ernest fell back in the opposite direction.

"Lord-a-mercy! No!" Harley screamed as he dropped the revolver and stumbled toward the truck. Adell came out the side door with her father after hearing the gunshot. They ran to Ernest's side and saw blood pouring from his chest. Silas Padgett had spent a year and a half of World War One in France as a medic. He assessed the situation and saw no hope for Ernest—he was most likely already dead.

"Adell, get Doc Jameson...now!" Silas yelled. She ran toward Dr. Jameson's office.

Ernest made no sound. The effect of the bullet had been instant, and his face still wore the shocked look of a man about to be shot. "Don't leave us, son," Silas begged, pressing on the wound with a handkerchief. Blood flowed freely in an ever-growing pool around his body. The same helpless feeling Silas had endured in the war came swiftly back upon him. Just as he had on the battlefields in France, he desperately wanted to do something for this young man. Then Silas spied six-year old L.J. Freeman standing on the sidewalk, peeking around the corner. "L.J., you know where Mr. Watson's shop is? Well, go and get him quick. Tell him his son's dead!"

With Bo at the wheel, Harley talked madly all the way back to the farm. "What am I gonna do? What am I gonna do? I'll have to ask Doris. She'll know what to do," he babbled.

"Ask momma? Daddy, momma's not here..."

"Shut up, Bo! You just get us on home!"

As soon as the house was in view, Harley jumped out of the moving truck and ran inside. He stumbled past furniture, upending a kitchen chair, and went straight to his childhood bedroom. Harley crawled under his bed. Mumbling to himself for almost half an hour, he stayed there until the sheriff and his deputy came in and pulled him out by his boots. Harley's outstretched fingers left streaks on the dusty floor as he swore at the men.

Chapter 25

Lemme see here... This box is just full of all manner of photos and clippings... Would you look at that? I haven't laid eyes on this in years. This here is Ernest's obituary that was in the Davis Gazette. Anna wrote this a couple days after Ernest died and I cut it out to keep it. It says:

You were so far from me the day I lost my love/ No one knows my pain but heaven up above/ I did not hear your last breath or hold your dying hand/ You were all alone, my brave and gallant man/ You will be greatly missed by women and by men/ My sweet and loving husband— kind and faithful friend/ Seas of tears will I forever weep/ While you in death remain asleep/ From your loving wife and family.

It still touches me every time I read it. No wonder Anna went back to Chicago right after the funeral. I reckon it seems odd to keep somethin' so sad. Maybe George weren't the only one to collect queer things. But we always clipped obituaries and stories from the paper if they named one of our kin—it was like we had to prove it to ourselves that it ever happened— that they ever lived at all. That was sure true with Ernest's death. No one would've guessed he'd die like he did—'specially Anna.

June 24, 1940
Chicago

Anna fidgeted in her armchair, trying to read. Her flat in northwest Chicago's Portage Park neighborhood was too quiet and the lack of sounds distracted her. While Ernest was alive, afternoons spent reading had been nearly impossible. He always wanted to talk or listen to gramophone records or just go out. Sitting still had never held much interest for him. Anna missed so much about Ernest, but she missed his energetic presence most of all. He was all life; something Anna never noticed until he died. She was determined to revive her earlier reading habits, but her heart wasn't in it this afternoon.

When she first heard of Ernest's death, Anna felt completely numb. For someone who was always expecting bad news, Anna was thoroughly caught off guard. It was like walking under a cluster of trees with low hanging branches and passing through a spider's web—the silver threads dropping a net on the unsuspecting individual, leaving slender trailing strands on the arms and face of the unfortunate passerby. Hours after the incident, the ghostly threads still tickle and unnerve.

A telegram from Ernest's father had been delivered to her door the afternoon that Ernest was shot. It said only: "Ernest is dead. Coming to fetch you. Frank Watson." When Frank and Matt arrived at her door the next day, Anna was still wearing the same clothes she had worn when the telegram arrived. She had nothing packed for the trip, so Frank quickly chose a few items and stacked them in a red cardboard suitcase. It seemed improper to Frank for him to even see the undergarments belonging to his daughter-in-law—let alone handle them—but Frank deemed it a worse sin for Matt to do the packing. Matt sat in the armchair next to Anna, soothingly patting her hand. He explained the circumstances of Ernest's death and Anna asked no questions. She only nodded her head without remark.

Anna tried to remember the events before and after her father-in-law and brother-in-law arrived to collect her. How strange the memory was to her now; she blushed at the thought of Frank rifling through her drawers to find her slips and underwear.

She looked down at her book again. It was *Cold Comfort Farm*, a book she had borrowed from the library. Just from the first chapter, Anna learned that Flora, the main character, was an orphan. Twenty years old and nearly broke, Flora was looking for a family who would take her in. Anna stopped reading before starting the second chapter to consider the similarities between her own life and Flora's. Anna was almost six years older than the character in the story, and also an orphan. Not quite as financially destitute—Ernest had left Anna a small sum of money—but she knew it wouldn't last forever. Anna considered her options. She could save rent money by moving to a smaller apartment. The pale yellow brick house had much more room than she needed, but she loved the little front porch and the bright green kitchen. This house felt more like home than any other place she'd ever lived.

Anna absentmindedly flipped the pages of her book, absorbed in her own problems. Then she read an exhortation given to Flora by her friend, Mrs. Smiling. The older woman suggested that Flora find some kind of job so that she could afford a flat of her own. *Was this a sign?* Anna shut the book. She decided to take Mrs. Smiling's advice and look for a job.

She opened the door to the coat closet and found her hat and purse. Looking at herself in the small mirror hanging by the door, Anna re-tied the large red plaid bow on her taffeta shirt. She smoothed the crepe fabric of her black skirt and matching short-sleeve jacket. Placing her black straw braid hat on her head, Anna descended the stairs and walked a short block to board the streetcar. After a half-hour ride, she joined the heavy bustle of traffic on Milwaukee Avenue. Anna knew that the Six Corners shopping district housed a variety of stores. Not wanting to return to Marshall Field's, this seemed like the most realistic option.

The first shop Anna entered was Foster Music Company. It was a beautiful store with polished hardwood counters, shelves full of sheet music and records, and two large grand pianos. There were rooms in the back of the store with glass walls where patrons could listen to records before buying them. Anna had always loved to look inside the windows of this store as she passed by. She admired the gracefulness of the pianos with their raised lids tinkling music.

When she entered, Anna noticed a middle-aged woman in one of the back rooms, listening to a gramophone record with her back to the door. Anna approached the counter and waited. After several minutes, a salesman eventually emerged from the stock room.

"May I help you, madam?" he asked.

"Yes. I'm looking for a job." Anna attempted to mask her nervousness.

The salesman's smile faded. "There are no positions available." He wore a sour expression. "Is there anything else?"

Anna was too humiliated by the salesman's abrupt and pompous demeanor to leave right away. If she left now, she'd look defeated and desperate. The woman from the listening room had exited and was re-shelving her selection. Anna noticed the woman's actions and said, "I'd like to buy a new record for my gramophone."

"Miss Bäcker, please see to this...customer," said the salesman.

The middle-aged woman stepped forward and smiled. "Yes? Can I play a recording for you?" she asked in a soft, lilting voice. "What would you like to hear?" Anna detected a slight but unidentifiable European accent.

She paused for a moment. Ernest had always been the one to pick out records for them. She didn't know where to begin.

"Do you have anything to recommend?" asked Anna.

The woman selected four records and directed Anna to follow her to the listening room. When they were alone, Miss Bäcker laid a hand on Anna's gloved one and said, "I heard you talking to my employer. I am sorry you are looking for work. This world can be a harsh place."

Anna was startled by the woman's sympathy. "Thank you," she murmured, as she removed her gloves and laid them on a small table.

"Do not give up," continued the saleswoman. "Maybe your husband has a job?" She gestured toward Anna's wedding ring.

"I don't have a husband. He died last July," Anna replied. She had trained herself to show no emotion when the topic arose, but there was the smallest catch in her throat this time.

"*Das ist schade,*" said Miss Bäcker. Aware of her lapse of English, she translated. "That is sad!"

"May I listen to the records?" Anna asked, brusquely changing the subject.

"Of course. Let us see...I have a show tune you may like called 'I Could Write a Book.' There's also 'You are My Sunshine' and 'Back in the Saddle Again.' Or if you prefer opera...there's a new recording of Puccini's 'Madama Butterfly.'" It was obvious which record the saleswoman hoped Anna would choose, but Anna was too distracted with her own thoughts to notice.

"Oh, I suppose you could play them all," Anna replied.

"I think you will enjoy '*Ancora un passo*' from 'Madama Butterfly,'" the saleswoman said with enthusiasm. As she set the record on the player and it began its rotation, pure joy spread across her face. Anna watched the woman as she listened to the soprano sing the impossibly high notes. Her features softened and Anna realized that behind the mundane clothes and indifferent appearance, the saleswoman was quite lovely. Her graying hair was smoothed down on the top and sides until it gathered at the nape of her neck in a tight chignon. She wore small wire-rimmed glasses perched atop the bridge of her nose, partially obscuring the brilliant green eyes behind them.

When the song ended, Miss Bäcker turned to face Anna again. She wore a look of stillness and relieved satisfaction. "I have heard it many times, but it enchants me still."

"I don't know the story," Anna said, apologetically. "What's it about?"

"It is a tale of a woman who falls in love with a foreign man, despite her family's objections. The man leaves her. She waits for him to return, with only their child to comfort her. As with most operas, the final curtain brings on death. Cio-Cio San, the woman in the story, kills herself and gives up her child to the man and his new wife." The two women stood in the glass room, silently contemplating the tragedy of the story as the record slowed its spinning.

"How terrible..." Anna said. "How can such a sad story sound so beautiful?"

"Sadness comes to everyone. I know this as well as you," Miss Bäcker said. "I too lost my husband very young...too soon...but maybe you are fortunate where I was not. Maybe you have family?"

"I have no one...no family to speak of." Anna chewed the inside of her lip, trying to press down the anxious thoughts rising inside.

"Do not go through this alone, *meine leibe*." The wistful look on the saleswoman's face disappeared. She looked stern as she advised Anna. "You have lost him. He is gone. But *you* are not dead. You cannot feel alive if you are alone. You will go mad with your selfish, lonely thoughts."

At first, Anna felt offended by the woman's rebuke. But there was something in the saleswoman's eyes that showed her expertise on the subject. "Thank you for your help," Anna said. She suddenly had to leave the closeness of this small glass room where she and the saleswoman, two lonely widows, ran the risk of suffocating in the remorse and regret of what might have been. "I don't believe I'll make a purchase today."

"Good day, madam," said the saleswoman.

As Anna left the store, Miss Bäcker sat down at one of the pianos and played the introduction to a dissonant piece. Back on Milwaukee Avenue, Anna heard the saleswoman singing in perfect operatic German. Anna glanced down at the scar on her hand as she slid her glove back in place. She rubbed the raised line that seemed to throb in time with the swelling chords of the song.

Anna turned and watched the woman through the store window as she played and sang. She stared until the outline of the woman grew blurry and the noisy traffic behind her softened as if she had cupped her hands over her ears. Her mind dug into its deepest recesses, looking for some past memory or connection to this woman and this moment. A spinning vision of a phonograph playing in a modest living room and a woman with soft golden hair rippled on the edge of Anna's mind. Just as the vision began to clear, like a cork bobbing slowly to the surface of a deep pool, a man on the street bumped Anna's arm.

"Excuse me," he said with a tip of his hat before continuing on his way to catch a streetcar.

Anna looked back through the store window, but the woman had finished playing. Eventually, Anna walked back to her flat. Upon entering, she walked directly to her bedroom. Pausing by her bureau, she glanced at herself in the mirror. She took off her hat and gloves and looked down at her gold wedding band, then gently slid it off. Feeling equal parts determination and fear, Anna dropped the ring in a china saucer with a tiny *clink*.

Oh to Grace

Chapter 26

You know, memory is a peculiar thing. I cain't remember what I ate for breakfast this morning, but I do remember mighty clear about things that happened years and years ago. Like what I was wearin' the day I met Ronnie-Boy; it was a short-sleeved dress printed all over in little bunches of cherries. That's a nice memory but there's memories that bring on sufferin' too, like the days 'round Ernest's death. I remember the exact shade of gray the suit Harley Dickson wore for his trial was, and how twitchy he was during the whole thing. You know, he only got two years in prison for killin' Ernest because they called it self-defense. After he got out, he went crazy—stoppin' folks on the street askin' if they ever killed a man—he weren't never the same. I can also remember how Anna looked when Daddy and me took her to the station to go back to Chicago after it was all over with. She was wearing the prettiest blue and white-checkered dress. She had on a navy belt with a little circle on the buckle made of tiny pearls and she had on a pair of little white gloves with a pearl on the back of each. She was so pretty but she looked sadder than the last pea in a pea pod. When she found her seat on the train, she looked out the window and waved to us. Daddy and me just stood there and

watched the train pull out. He tried to talk her outta leavin' but she was bound and determined to get back to Chicago.

September 4, 1940
Morgan's Hat, Tennessee

Burnetta Watson buzzed around her kitchen like a bumblebee—or at sixty, she was swiftly shuffling in her laced oxfords like a queen bee that had given up her yellow-black stripes for a checked apron in a colorful percale. She had made the apron last winter, styled from a picture in the Sears catalog. Not correctly accounting for her girth, she made the two ribbon-trimmed pockets too far apart to be of any real use. The model in the catalog had her hands shoved happily in her pockets, obviously enjoying all of her daily domesticities. This had convinced Burnetta that the pockets were essential.

Burnetta muttered to herself as she tasted the simmering applesauce, then she walked to the pie safe for the tenth time that morning. She opened the drawer and pulled out two letters. The first one was dated June 24, 1940. Burnetta skimmed to the end of the letter:

...I have no other family now but you. If I could be of some help to you and Mr. Watson, I would like to come to Morgan's Hat to live. I'll understand if you say no to this right now. I know that our loss is still unbearable at times and I do not want to remind you of anything unpleasant.

Please give my love to Frankie and Della.

Sincerely,
Anna Simmons Watson

Burnetta sniffled and wiped her nose on her apron. "That dear, dear girl..." she sighed. Then she unfolded the second letter, sent in late August. It was much shorter than the other, and the script had a greater slant, suggesting it was written quickly. It read:

Dear Mrs. Watson,

I received your letter. You cannot know how happy it made me! I have made my travel plans on the L&N out of Chicago. I will be arriving in Clarksville on September 4 at 2:40. Thank George for the offer to get me at the depot. I will see him then.

With much love,
Anna

Burnetta checked the clock in the sitting room. It was nearly supper time and George was not back with Anna yet. She needed someone to fret to, so she went out in search of her oldest son.

Matt had wandered into the wooded area behind the barn. He knew Burnetta would want to talk to him about Anna and the family tragedy, and he couldn't bear to go through that conversation again today. He sat on a rotting log, tossing tiny pieces of wood at flies flitting around the tall, greenish-yellow flowers that grew along the edge of the stream bank. The flies swooped around each other in large and small arcs. Once, Matt had looked up the name of this giant weed: *filmy angelica*. It was poisonous, but the flies seemed unable to pull themselves away from it. Some dropped to the ground in a stupor, then rose slowly to begin the drunken orgy again. Their intoxicated dance had a hypnotic effect on Matt, too.

All at once, Matt heard a series of sounds that let him know their guest had arrived. Echoes of happy greetings and car doors shutting reached him where he was sitting. He decided to wait until the commotion calmed down before joining the group. On each of her visits with Ernest before his death, Matt had watched Anna closely. He had come to know her better than he knew anyone else outside his immediate family. Now that Ernest was gone, Matt realized he was drawn to Anna like the dim-witted flies swarming around the *filmy angelica*. He didn't know if he could hide his desire to be near her. He was afraid he would tell her all that was in his heart and look like the biggest idiot in Davis County. Matt had thoughts and feelings that needed to be aired out to see if they could withstand the harshness of sunlight but he wasn't sure how to express what he was feeling without making himself too vulnerable.

"Hello, Mrs. Watson!" Anna said.

"Ooo, doll-baby. You gotta call me Momma. You lookin' so pretty. Ain't she, George? Just as pretty as a picture! Are you tired, hon? I bet you'll be wantin' to get fresh'd up after that dusty train ride. I got everythin' set up in your room upstairs. D'you brung a trunk, hon? George, grab them bags. You hungry, too? Supper's jest 'bout done." Burnetta chatted on without letting anyone answer her questions.

"Actually, I'd be glad to help out with supper," Anna said quickly, getting in a few words when Burnetta paused to breathe.

"Nah, hon. I ain't gonna have you git anymore tuckered out today!"

"Well, maybe I'll just walk around a bit and stretch my legs."

"You go on and do that. I'll holler real loud when everybody's here." Burnetta started to walk toward the house, but she stopped and turned to give Anna another enveloping hug. Her large bosom was a safe and comforting place to be. Sniffling, Burnetta wiped her eyes on her apron and shuffled back into the house.

Anna walked slowly under the grape arbor that provided an entrance to Burnetta's neat vegetable garden. Like a child, she tried to step only on the irregular stones evenly placed along the path. She bent to look at the odd-shaped okra pods and the row of cherry tomato plants. Picking off a small one, Anna popped it in her mouth, savoring the juicy tartness.

Eventually, she found her way to the barn. The evening was still warm, and the old building trapped the day's heat within the worn walls and the straw of the animal beds. When Matt entered, carrying a heavy saddle, he was surprised to see her sitting alone on a hay bale.

"Oh, Anna. I'm sorry. I didn't know you was here. That is, I knew you was here but I didn't know you was *here*. That is, I heard you pull up, but I didn't 'spect..." Matt stopped stepping over his words. Anna looked to be on the verge of tears.

"I wanted to go for a walk and ended up here." Anna wiped her eyes and smiled. "I was just thinking about the time you threw hay on me. Do you remember that?"

"Yeah. I felt real bad 'bout it," Matt said as he placed his saddle on the long board mounted on the barn wall.

Anna took a deep breath. "I'm so thankful for your parents letting me come and stay. I don't want to be a bother..."

"A bother?" Matt continued to clean up from his day's work. Avoiding any eye contact with her, he hung and re-hung Son of Sassy's tack on the far wall. "Momma's been tellin' everybody in town her daughter-in-law's comin.' I reckon she even tried to git it in the Davis Gazette. You know, you're just the same as one of her own girls."

"I can't imagine why." Anna looked down at her hands. "She hardly knows me...really."

Oh to Grace

"Well, I reckon she likes what she sees. Momma's always been a pretty good judge of character. She sure was right about some of the girls 'round here. She never liked ones with too much flash. I reckon she likes how you're kinda quiet and respectful."

"If she really knew me, things would be different." Anna felt words and thoughts welling up in her that were trying to escape like hot steam. "I don't deserve her love...or anyone else's..."

Matt paused for a second before answering. "Anna, nobody deserves to be loved. You love others, because...well, they're just put in front of you and that makes 'em yours to love."

Since he was a boy reciting a poem at a pie supper, Matt would often speed up his words when he was nervous. Involuntarily, he employed this method with Anna. "Pastor Cooley preached on love just last Sunday." As he spoke, Matt looked down, roughly unwinding a chain that had become tangled in a bit. "Pastor said just before Jesus was killed, he thanked God for his apostles 'cause God had given 'em to him out of the world and half the time, they didn't seem like they had a grain of sense to split between the twelve of 'em. But Jesus kept on teachin' 'em and lovin' 'em." *Oh, Lord*, thought Matt, *now I'm preaching and it's comin' out like vomit! There's no stoppin' it!*

He continued: "You know if anybody deserves to be loved, it's God on account of He's perfect and made this whole dang universe. But the thing is, the thing is...Ah, I'm talkin' too much..." Matt wanted to run out and throw a bucket of well water on his head.

"No, Matt, go on," Anna said quietly. She was glad to hear someone with equally erratic thought processes babble on. To her surprise, she was able to follow Matt's every word.

Tentatively, he continued, "Well, the thing is: God loves us 'cause He *is* love, not 'cause we deserve it. You gotta forgive yourself if you're gonna feel it, though." Matt abruptly finished his words.

"That sounds nice, Matt, but you don't know. Even Ernest never knew the whole of it."

Matt saw the pain on Anna's face and awkwardly went to sit on the hay bale next to her. Not wanting to push, but seeing her need to unload a burden, he waited, barely breathing. Finally, he spoke, "You know, this reminds me of the day that we went to fetch you after Ernest...after we lost him. All I could do was sit there and pat your hand. I never felt so helpless."

"You were sweet to come...but I can only imagine what you're thinking about me right now, Matt. You probably think I've lost my mind. I don't normally talk about private matters. It's just that Ernest always had such a high opinion of you. He always said how smart and sure you were about everything." Anna looked over at Matt and said, "I guess you're just easy to talk to, and I did a lot of thinking back in Chicago." She looked back down at her hands again.

"Oh, Ernest was always the smart one. He probably shoulda been a lawyer or somethin'. He could talk a train into takin' a dirt road. He could convince himself of just about anything. Not that I'm bein' critical of him! That's just how Ernest was."

"I know what you mean. He was hopeful to the point of lying to himself sometimes. I guess that's why I let Ernest think I went to a fancy boarding school and grew up in a rich family." Anna paused, gathering courage to continue. "But the truth is...after my father died, my mother went crazy and left me at an orphanage. I lived there until they sent me to a woman's house who was a bootlegger." Anna gulped a breath, but didn't raise her eyes.

"Anna, none of that's your fault. You didn't do nothin' wrong..." Matt began.

"You just don't know..."

"Everyone's got a past, Anna..."

"Not everyone—not like mine."

Anna was shaking now. Matt asked, "What in heaven's name could you've done that would make you so sick just from the thought of it?"

"When I first started working...before I ever started going with Ernest...I had an affair with a married man." She blurted out the last part hastily, regretting her confession immediately. She put a trembling hand to her mouth and turned to look, wide-eyed, at Matt, who wore a surprised expression. "It went on for almost three years...then I ended it. Oh, Matt...now you can see why I didn't tell Ernest. You can see why no one will ever want me..."

"I would," Matt said softly, laying his rough hand on her small, trembling one.

Anna looked up to meet his eyes, and at that moment, Frankie and Della burst into the barn. "Anna!" they both squealed with delight. Painfully embarrassed and full of compunction, Matt stood up and re-rearranged the saddles and bridles hanging on the wall.

"It's time for supper," said Della.

Frankie Jane gave them a sideways glance and asked, "What've you two been talkin' 'bout out here?"

"Oh, nothing," said Anna. Matt faced the wall, closed his eyes and held a deep breath. "What's for supper?" Anna asked.

"Momma's cooked up her Sunday best for you, Anna," Della said, smiling. The girls hooked their arms in Anna's and escorted her back to the house, both talking at the same time.

As soon as they were out of earshot, Matt threw the saddle on the floor and stomped on it. "Wanting something unasked for without getting it is bad enough," he muttered under his breath, "but asking for it and being denied is a hundredfold worse." He brushed the dry dust off his shirt and pants, slapping much harder than necessary, and re-hung the saddle for the last time. Then, ever so slowly, Matt made his way up to the house for supper.

Burnetta had laid a table worthy of a holiday. That morning, she had asked Clarence to catch a boatload of catfish that she fried up and served with sweet chow relish. They also ate warm applesauce, pickled beets, creamy corn pudding, buttermilk biscuits, string beans, and fried okra, and topped it off with Burnetta's prize-winning blackberry pie. All through the feast, Matt ate in near silence. A few times, Frank asked him a question about the farm, and he was forced to answer with a "yessir" or "no sir." Matt ate quickly and excused himself from the table.

"Don't go too far, Matt. This is a fine night for some rockin' and we need your gee-tar," said Burnetta. After the dishes had been washed, dried, and put away, the family retired to the back porch. Fireflies darted around the vegetable garden and bullfrogs joined the cicadas in their nighttime chorus.

"Play 'Mama Gets What She Wants,' Matt," said Della.

"Uh-uh. Let's hear 'Oh Baby, You Done Me Wrong' or 'She's Got the Money, Too,'" said Frankie.

"Nah, now girls, you know we always start and finish up with a hymn," Burnetta corrected. "Go on, son."

Matt sat, contemplating his selection, then he began to play. After strumming a few chords, he sang with quiet tenderness.

Come, Thou Fount of every blessing,
Tune my heart to sing Thy grace;
Streams of mercy, never ceasing,
Call for songs of loudest praise.

Everyone joined in. Clarence set his knife to slide along the piece of wood in his hands in time to the song. George tapped his foot on the step as he leaned against the railing, and Homer lay on the ground nearby, staring up at the stars. Frank beat his pipe on the arm of the rocker. Burnetta clapped her hands softly as she swayed in the hanging porch swing with her girls on both sides laying their heads on her soft shoulders. Anna sat motionless in the metal rocker and looked out into the garden, mesmerized by the floating lights.

When Matt came to the next verse, he looked up at Anna

and sang:
> O to grace how great a debtor
> Daily I'm constrained to be!
> Let Thy goodness, like a fetter,
> Bind my wandering heart to Thee.
> Prone to wander, Lord, I feel it,
> Prone to leave the God I love;
> Here's my heart, O take and seal it,
> Seal it for Thy courts above.

Anna met his gaze and her eyes filled with unspilled tears. For the first time in her life, someone looked at her with full knowledge of her past but without a trace of judgment.

After singing several more songs, peppered with laughter at forgotten words, they all began to prepare for the night.

Matt said goodnight to the group and went out to the barn to check on his horse. Burnetta shuffled over to Anna and held her chin in her pudgy hand. "Doll-baby, you okay? You look plum wore out," she said.

"I'm fine, Miss Wat…Momma. I think I'll stay out here for another couple of minutes. It's so peaceful," Anna said as she looked up at Burnetta and smiled.

"Okay, hon. Don't stay out here too late." Burnetta bent down and kissed her forehead.

Frank re-emerged from the house with an afghan and laid it across Anna's shoulders. "Good night, shug," he said with a wink as he tapped the tobacco out of his pipe on the porch railing.

Anna rocked quietly, letting the minutes tick past. She listened to the sound of the cicadas—a buzzing wave that seemed to wash over her and clean her mind of the busy city. To anyone watching her, it would seem that she let the time pass mindlessly, but there was a purpose to her rocking. It was as if each rocking motion was a step forward into something better. She felt an odd expectancy like she was waiting for something monumental to happen, but what was it she was expecting?

She struggled to remember the words to the hymn Matt sang. "Streams of mercy, never ceasing...Here's my heart, O take and seal it, seal it for thy courts above." What would it be like to give your heart away? Had she ever really given it to anyone? If it must be given away, she liked the idea of having it sealed and stored in heaven—what better vault than one behind pearly gates? Suddenly, Anna prayed, "Lord, seal up my heart and if you see where it can be used safely down here, lend it back to me. I'm a terrible judge when it comes to my heart—probably for lack of practice. I need you to guard it for me. I'm afraid it'll crumble to a thousand pieces if it takes much more breaks."

Anna felt a warm relief. She hadn't said a real, original prayer in years. The feelings she had of expectancy increased now, but without the anxiety. The prayer felt like a reasonable request, and all she had to do now was wait for the response. She wrapped the afghan tighter around her shoulders, and went inside, content in knowing that she would be able to sleep well.

Just as the screen door shut behind her, Matt came out of the barn and watched her silhouetted figure enter the house. Sure that he would never be able to face Anna again, Matt walked home to his little bachelor cottage tucked away from the world in a moonlit corner of the woods.

Oh to Grace

Chapter 27

You know, it's not just the bad times I can recall. I can remember good times, too. I can remember plain as anythin' my first dance. I reckon it might not count as my first dance—in a way—on account of I never danced with a boy that night. Jefferson Hollis asked me though, but momma said I was not yet thirteen and wasn't about to have Jeff Hollis holdin' me in front of all of these strangers. What I remember most 'bout that night was the dance team that came and did a hoedown. The ladies on the dance team had the most twirly skirts—they nearly went up to their ears when they took to turnin' real fast. Most of us growin' up Baptist weren't allowed to dance in front of others, but momma wanted to do somethin' fun to celebrate Anna's birthday and her comin' to live in Morgan's Hat. I reckon Momma didn't really know what we'd see at the dance that night. She probably thought there'd be clothes a-fallin' off of all the young folk while they was dancin'. I'm glad we went, 'cause it wasn't 'til I was grown and married before I went to another dancin' party. I reckon what was a good idea for Anna wasn't right for me and Della. More's the pity!

Oh to Grace

Morgan's Hat, Tennessee
September 7, 1940

The Watson family piled into vehicles and headed down the dusty road that led out of town. "Frank, don't go through the square! Somebody might see us and know we're a-goin' to a dancin' party," said Burnetta in horror. Frank was driving his Buick with Burnetta in the center of the front seat and Anna next to her. Burnetta had rarely left Anna's side since she came back a few days before, and she insisted that her delicate daughter-in-law squeeze in next to her. Frankie, Della, George, and Homer piled into the back seat, giddy with excitement.

"Ah, honey, ever'body in town's gonna be there, too," said Frank. "I wouldn't be surprised if we see all of Berea Baptist in the parking lot."

Burnetta waved a paper fan with agitated enthusiasm. "Well, if Pastor Cooley asks 'bout this tomorrow, I don't know what I'll do."

"Ah, hon..." Frank gave Burnetta's knee a squeeze.

"If you don't want to go, I'll be happy to go back home with you," said Anna, hopefully. She didn't like the idea of being the pitiful young widow at any social occasion.

"You're sweet, shug, but it's your birthday and I won't ruin your night on account of my high principles," said Burnetta. "Anyhow, we don't have to do nothin' but watch. I mostly thought you'd like to see the folks who're comin' to do that fancy buckdancin'. They been on my favorite program—National Barn Dance Radio—and since it's done outta Chicago and that bein' your hometown, I thought you might enjoy it."

"Thank you, momma," Anna said. "It does sound like fun."

Anna smiled at Burnetta and spontaneously kissed her soft cheek. Burnetta pulled a faded handkerchief out of her purse and wiped her eyes. She held Anna's hand the rest of the way to Clarksville.

Just behind the Buick was Matt's crew. He drove his pickup truck, with Ida Mae in the passenger seat and three-year old Barney in her lap, pointing at every object that went past their window. Buddy and Clarence sat in the bed of truck. Several times during the two-hour car ride, Ida Mae had to punch Matt's arm to make sure he was listening.

"Matt? Didya hear me?"

"Sorry?" Matt said.

"I was askin' if ya like my dress," Ida fussed. "You ain't hear-ed a word of what I been sayin'. You're worse 'n Buddy!"

"Beg your pardon, Ida Mae. I'm sittin' here thinkin' bout the songs I'm gonna play tonight at the show," Matt lied. He had been asked to play his guitar in the band, but he knew every song in the lineup by heart. His thoughts were actually focused on the red-haired young lady sitting in the car in front of him.

"It's a good thing I got little Barney here or I'd be powerful lonesome!" said Ida. "Tell your Uncle Matt somethin' I done taught you, baby."

"Your ass is gwass and I's the lawn mowah!" recited Barney with pride.

"Barney! That's not what you're supposed to say, you little skunk!" said Ida.

"What'd you want him to say?" asked Matt.

"I taught him summa dat poetry you like. I reckon your ma and pa don't think he's gonna be smart, but I know'd you'd give 'im a chance."

Matt smiled. He normally tired of Ida Mae and her crude ways, but he also felt sorry for her. She truly cared about her son, and Buddy, too. *People could surprise you if you let them,* thought Matt.

"Let's hear it, Barney," said Matt.

"It's called 'The Little Robin's Song' and it's from one o' them McGuffey readers. I stole it off of the teacher's desk when I left school," said Ida by way of introduction.

"Ida..." groaned Matt.

"Don't talk. It messes with Barney's concentratin'." Ida gently slapped the back of Barney's head. "Get goin', son," she said.

"'I know'd the Good Lord made the robin to sing. I know'd He taught her sweet songs,'" quoted Barney, as Ida silently mouthed the words with him. He continued: "'He whispered the tunes and the words in her ear so she could sing along. He told her...'"

"Go on, baby," prompted Ida. "'He told her...' Come on with it. You ain't half done yet. You know the rest."

"Nope. That's all," Barney said with finality.

Ida Mae was about to slap the back of his head again, when Matt said, "That's mighty good, Barney! He's a right sharp little fella, Ida Mae."

Ida inhaled his words and let them fill her up. She was banking all her hopes on Barney. She desired nothing more than for her son to be the smartest and most upstanding citizen in Morgan's Hat—nothing like her own family.

When they finally reached the Second Presbyterian Church in Clarksville, the parking lot was already full. Matt grabbed his guitar and headed into the lecture hall to find the rest of the band. The church had just finished construction of the new hall that summer and this was their first large gathering. The dance was originally scheduled to be in the VFW hall, but when news came that The Tennessee Travelers were coming, they moved to a larger venue. One of the band members was an elder at Second Presbyterian, so it was a logical step.

"There are so many people in here, you couldn't stir 'em with a stick," said Burnetta as she nervously glanced around the crowded room. "Anna, girls, you wanna come with me and get some lem'nade?"

Burnetta took Anna's hand, and Frankie and Della followed them to the punchbowl table. Matt found his place on the stage with another guitar player, two men with fiddles, a banjo player and another man sitting behind the squat upright piano. After all their instruments had been tuned and primed, the band started up with "Sweet Georgia Brown." Everyone visited around the edge of the room. Burnetta began to relax as she saw members of her church in the group.

"There's Deacon Boyd...and there's Pastor Cooley's sister. Hey Charity, honey! Don't you look pretty tonight?" Burnetta turned to Anna and whispered, "What's she thinkin', wearing that dress at her age? She's near naked as a boiled chicken."

After a few more numbers, Eddie Buchanan stepped out from behind the piano and introduced the dancing team. The Tennessee Travelers took their places, grouped by couples in coordinating outfits—the men in gingham shirts with long, full sleeves and the women in their white cotton dresses with layers of gingham ruffles on the skirts. The couples stood with the women in front, holding the right hands of their partners high above their heads—their white leather shoes pointing with precision. The crowd applauded and whistled, and the band started up with an instrumental song called "Uncle Zeke" that showed off the dancers' rapid footwork.

The men promenaded their partners around the room, spinning them at regular intervals. One man would call out a step and the group would obey in unison. "Gather up, gals!" he said, and the women marched out in front of the men, bending their knees and slapping the floor hard. Then they switched places, allowing the men to take center stage. The men were all tall and thin, and their long legs curved slightly like supple willow branches. They slapped their white shoes on the floor so powerfully that some in the crowd wondered if they would snap their ankles with the force.

Everyone in the room was under the spell of the constant, tapping beat of the dancers. Crystal punch glasses shook their contents onto the tablecloths, and framed pictures of flower arrangements bumped against the walls. Seated a few tables away from her mother-in-law, Ida Mae carried Barney to

Burnetta and set him in her lap. "I'll be right back," said Ida. "I shouldn't-a drank all that tea 'fore we left." She hurried to find a bathroom.

Deacon Boyd and his wife, Juniper, walked over to where Burnetta was holding her precocious grandson.

"You must've spit that baby, Burnetta," said Deacon Boyd. "He looks just like you and yours."

"He's a real fine boy, deacon," said Burnetta. She felt more and more at home every minute.

Frank noticed her growing satisfaction and said, "You look as happy as a hog after suppertime, Momma. If you don't watch it, you'll be askin' me to put those metal strips on all our shoes so we can go dancin' every night."

"Ah, hesh, Frank," said Burnetta with a grin.

After several numbers, the dancers left the floor to take a break. Eddie Buchanan stood up again and said, "Folks, it's your turn now. Get up and dance to 'Like Me A Little at Least.'"

Matt, who had been in the back for every song up to this point, walked to the center of the small stage. He lifted his guitar and picked the notes for the chorus, with the rest of the musicians backing him up. Then he began to sing in a clear, rich baritone: *I know we ain't always seen eye to eye. I know I ain't always been fair. But if you'll give me just one more chance I'll show you how much I care.* Matt's family was amazed at his singing, even though they had heard him perform on their front porch for nearly twenty years. Frank and Burnetta knew he had been going over to Eddie's house on the other side of town nearly every other night, but Matt had never mentioned his role in the upcoming performance. The rest of the audience was in a similar state of shock.

Juniper Boyd turned to Burnetta and said, "Why, Burnetta, your boy has got a beautiful voice."

"He ought to help with the youth choir this Christmas," said Deacon Boyd. Burnetta beamed like a lighthouse.

At the age of thirty-three, Matt had finally made his debut.

As the song ended, Matt sang, *I'd climb the highest mountain. I'd slay the fiercest beast. Even if you can't love me right now could you like me a little at least?* Everyone cheered, but no one louder than Burnetta, who almost dropped Barney out of her lap and onto the floor. With his solo over, Matt took his place behind the fiddlers again.

Eddie started a lengthy intro to a bluesy song called "Your Love Makes Me Rich." More couples were forming on the dance floor, and soon there were spinning ladies with unfurled skirts in every direction. Matt strummed his chords and looked back over the audience as Eddie energetically tore into his first verse. Suddenly, Matt saw Hobart Tipler, still pink-faced and towheaded, walking to where Anna was seated next to Burnetta. From his gestures, Matt could discern that Hobart was asking Anna to dance. Anna shook her head, but Hobart seemed determined as he pointed with his thumb to the dance floor with one hand and tugged on Anna's hand with the other. Without a second thought, Matt handed his guitar to the idle banjo player and stepped off the stage. He approached Anna and Hobart and said, "Sorry Hobart, Anna was savin' this one for me. Maybe next time..." He took Anna's hand and escorted her onto the dance floor.

Anna was so struck by what had happened that she couldn't even speak. As the adrenaline leaked out of him, Matt realized what he had done. He rarely made any decision without calculating the outcomes and weighing the risks. This time he had just acted; now he was stuck. It was either fish or cut bait, as Burnetta would have said. Matt put his right hand behind Anna's back, held her right hand in his left, and they began circling the room together.

Eddie was singing, *I'm as poor as a plowboy. I'm lower 'n a cowpea. But with you as my sweetheart, I'll be as rich as any man can be.* Matt knew he wasn't really dancing with Anna. It was more like escorting. He felt like he was a young boy at the fair again, walking his prize goat before the judges.

"Sorry, Anna, I'm not much of a dancer," said Matt. "I just know what kind of a rascal Hobart Tipler is and I couldn't abide seein' him houndin' you."

"I appreciate that, Matt." They danced on in silence. Matt imagined a thick layer of heat surrounding him as he led her around the other couples. His embarrassment was so acute that he couldn't look at Anna's face, which was fine because she was constantly looking over his shoulder. He was reminded of his failed attempt at public poetry recitation at the schoolhouse—only this time he wasn't standing alone in front of the whole town. He was with Anna. He wasn't sure which was worse. The song ended. They stood, finally looking at each other, holding hands for a moment.

"If we could borry you for another song, Matt?" said Eddie from the stage.

Everyone laughed as Matt and Anna blushed. Matt returned to his place on stage to play out the rest of the set, and Anna found her seat next to Burnetta. For the rest of the evening, no one asked her to dance again, which was perfectly fine with her. Burnetta would whisper, "Honey, you oughtta get out there again. You done real good." Anna just smiled and shook her head.

After the band had played every song in their repertoire—some of them two or three times—they told the group good night. As everyone stepped out into the cooling night air, Ida Mae grabbed Anna's arm. "Anna, why don't you ride in the truck with me and Barney? Matt won't hardly talk while he's drivin' and Barney's already asleep." Anna agreed.

Burnetta walked to the Buick with Frank and the kids, and Anna heard her saying to Frank, "I haven't had such fun since the hogs ate grandma." Anna walked on, with Ida Mae carrying her sleeping toddler, to Matt's truck. After shaking hands with most of Morgan's Hat and half of Clarksville, Matt arrived. He was surprised to see Anna sitting in the center seat, with Ida Mae by the window.

He gave Anna a smile and started the truck. All but about half an hour of the drive home was nearly silent. The first fifteen minutes consisted of Ida Mae telling Anna how she could stay awake late into the night. The next fifteen minutes were filled with complaints about Buddy's snoring. For the rest of the drive to Morgan's Hat, Matt and Anna listened to Ida Mae's snoring as she fogged up the passenger side window.

After they dropped Buddy's family at their house, they drove to Frank and Burnetta's place. Matt let Anna off at the back porch and told her goodnight, then he drove the truck back behind the barn near the haystacks.

Anna walked up the steps, but instead of going inside, she stopped on the porch and sat down on the porch swing. Tired enough to drop fully clothed onto the guest room bed, she wasn't sure why she had stopped. Her mind was humming. She heard a small voice encouraging her to sit and wait. Anna sat alone for a few minutes until Matt came out from behind the barn. For the second time that night, her presence surprised him. When he saw her, he stopped and swallowed hard. Hesitantly, he walked away from the path that led to his house and walked up to the porch. He laid his hand on the railing and one foot on the first step. Anna looked at him with a brief smile that developed into a searching stare.

"Will you sit with me for a minute, Matt?" she asked shyly.

Without a word, Matt walked up the steps and sat down in his father's oak plantation porch rocker. It had just the right amount of creak in the curved rockers, but Matt kept the chair from moving so as not to break the perfect silence of the night.

After a few heavy seconds, Anna spoke. "Did you mean what you said in the barn the other day? That is, after all that you know about my past…" She trailed off, losing her nerve.

Matt's heart thundered in his chest. He chose his words carefully. "Anna, there's somethin' 'bout you I saw that day in the barn when you was covered in hay. I'd be lyin' if I told you I wasn't jealous to hear you was married to Ernest, but I just tried to be happy for him 'cause he was my brother." He paused, gathering his strength. "But I knew—then and there—he was the luckiest man in the world."

Anna looked squarely into Matt's eyes, matching his gaze in intensity and hopefulness. The same small voice she had heard before was now whispering that this was a monumental moment, overshadowing the preceding everyday decisions and extraordinary twists and turns that had made up her life so far. Without saying a word, her thoughts composed a melody that praised a God who would arrange and rearrange these details for the children He loved. Anna's mind wanted to turn back toward the familiar paths of pessimism, but she kept her eyes on Matt, continually renewed by hope. She felt God telling her that this man could be trusted with her heart.

They talked through the night. Matt eventually moved to the swing so he could put his arm around Anna. He listened while she told him everything about her life in the orphanage and living with Mrs. Sanders. And Anna cried when Matt described the day they lost Clara.

"You don't remember how you got it?" Matt asked, as he held her hand and traced the faded scar on her palm with his finger.

"All I can remember is having one of the Sisters in the orphanage clean it and bandage it," she answered. "But I've always felt like it happened before I went to live there."

Matt raised her hand and pressed it against his mouth. "It's healed now and it don't hurt. That's what matters."

"Sometimes it feels like my life is like that scar—some kind of reminder, but of what?" Anna felt a restless frustration growing inside her.

"Did you ever hear 'bout Joe and Versa Davis?" Matt asked.

"I don't believe so." Anna loved to hear his stories. She settled into Matt's side to listen.

"Joe lost both legs in the war but you'll never meet a happier fella. Instead of pinin' away for what had been taken from him, Joe let those missin' legs remind him of how much he needed his wife Versa. I'll tell you somethin' Joe once told me. He said 'we don't often get what we deserve—sometimes more and sometimes not all, but we get what we need.' I know I need you, Anna." Anna let the tears fall as she laid her head on Matt's shoulder.

The sun rose imperceptibly in the sky behind them as they tried to contain their happiness in finding each other. Resting his head on the top of Anna's, Matt whispered, "Happy birthday, Anna." She felt reborn.

Oh to Grace

Chapter 28

It weren't too long after the dance in Clarksville that Matt asked Anna to marry him. It was fall—maybe October—and me and Anna was layin' out pattern pieces to make her a new dress. Anna was all thumbs when it came to sewin'. She didn't know her back yoke from her bias ruffle. We had everythin' spread out on the floor in the front room and were about to start pinnin' the fabric to the tissue paper we cut out, when Matt opened the front door. A strong autumn breeze blew in and tossed all them flimsy pieces o' paper everywhere. I started to fuss at Matt, but then I caught the wild look in his eyes. Without a word, he swooped over to Anna, lifted her up, and kissed her. "Marry me, please, ma'am, will you?" he asked her. Anna hugged him and choked out a little 'yes.' The family was mighty surprised by their engagement—not a one of us saw it comin'—but once we saw the happy couple together, everyone knew it was a perfect match. Anna and Matt had a Christmas weddin' at Berea Baptist. Pastor Cooley officiated it, and me and Della were the bridesmaids. I reckon we was all mighty encouraged to see somethin' good happen to them. They just set their minds to find happiness no matter what. It's like FDR said, "Men are not prisoners of fate, but only prisoners of their own minds." We can't pick the cards that are dealt to us but we can decide on how to play 'em.

MORGAN'S HAT, TENNESSEE
OCTOBER 22, 1940

Anna stood at the kitchen sink with both hands in dirty dishwater. Her eyes seemed intensely fixed on the text of an old stitched sampler that Burnetta had hung on the wall behind the sink. It read: "Whatsoever thy hand findeth to do, do it with thy might. Ecclesiastes 9:10." The verse was embellished with a simple and repetitive pattern of flowers and geometric shapes. Near the bottom was the date of Frank and Burnetta's wedding day, May 6, 1906, and there was a picture of a tall house stitched just below it.

In reality, Anna wasn't reading the sampler at all. Her eyes had the glazed look of someone whose mind was in an entirely different place. She chewed the inside of her lip, a habit she had claimed early on during moments of nervous reflection.

Burnetta entered the kitchen, pausing in the doorway to watch her daughter-in-law. Realizing that Anna was neither washing dishes nor making any kind of movement, Burnetta asked, "Hon, you doin' all right?"

The question startled Anna. She was still getting used to not living alone, and the presence of others often surprised her. "Yes, ma'am. I'm finishing these breakfast dishes."

"Where's Matt?" Burnetta asked. "Is he fetchin' me them acorn squash?" She looked out the window toward the vegetable patch.

"No. He went to Clarksville to sign on at the draft board."

"What? Now why would he go and do somethin' foolish like that?"

"He read in the paper that President Roosevelt wants every man age twenty-one to thirty-five to register." Anna sniffed quietly.

"Don't you fret, Hon. He's nearly thirty-four. He's too old to do any fightin.' Anyhow all that mess with the Germans will stay on that side of the world. It won't bother us none over here."

Burnetta silently fumed at her oldest son as she dusted her way into the parlor. Frank was reading the newspaper in his favorite chair. "Do you know where your son is right now?" she asked him.

"Which one?"

"Why, Matt, 'o course. He's gone into town to sign up at the draft board."

Frank folded his newspaper to hide the article he had been reading about Canadian ships recently destroyed by German U-boats. "Ah, hon, he's just doin' his duty by his country."

"His duty?" she said, loudly. Frank shushed her, pointing to the kitchen where Anna still stood. Burnetta continued in a loud whisper. "What is Matt thinkin' worrying his pretty wife-to-be like this? Haven't we all suffered enough? I'm gonna give him a piece of my mind when he gets home. I will." She left in a huff.

Matt returned in the afternoon and found Anna waiting for him on the back porch. Walking up the steps to where she sat in the porch swing reminded him of the night he learned that Anna held feelings for him. It had only been a month and a half since that extraordinary night, but he already felt a remarkable comfort and ease in her presence. Reliving the memory pleased Matt until he saw how Anna bowed her head, covering her eyes. "What's the matter, honey?"

Matt came closer to her and Anna raised her face to look at him. He was struck full-force by her expression. It was a version of the way she used to look at Ernest, but with added despair. In her eyes he saw a kind of pleading that made the hair on his forearms stand up.

"Matt, I don't know what I'll do if something happens to you..." She broke down and sobbed.

"Anna, I'm not leavin.' I'm just doin' my duty as a citizen—just like the president said."

"But what if you have to fight?"

"Well, we'll just cross that bridge if we come to it."

"What if I lose you, too?"

"Don't talk like that..."

"It'd be all my fault if you got killed," Anna said between sobs.

"All your fault? Now why would you say that?"

Anna looked up. "Sometimes I think God is punishing me with misfortune because of what I've done," she said quietly.

"Maybe it's not punishment so much as it's God allowin' you to learn somethin' valuable."

"That's not what it feels like. It feels like God's never going to let me alone."

"Is that what you want—to be left alone?"

"No. Not really. It's just that everything's falling right into place with me and you—but I know it won't last." Anna's eyes pleaded with him again.

"Anna, I'm awful glad you're so attached to me—you don't know how glad—but you can't go on livin' like this. It's just not right."

Anna stopped crying and looked up at him with questioning eyes. Matt sat next to her and took her hand.

"Don't be angry with me, Honey. It's just that I saw you look at Ernest like this—like he was all you could count on—all that was worth livin' for. It wasn't fair to him and it ain't fair to me."

"What do you mean? How can you say that?" she said with hurt in her voice.

"Right now you think I'm just what you been searchin' for. But what's gonna happen the first time I lose my temper or say a curse word or snore all night or get old and half my teeth fall out? What's gonna happen when you see I'm not perfect? I'm gonna do everythin' in my power to make sure you feel happy and safe and loved, but some days I'm gonna slip up, then what?"

"Well, I'll still love you, of course."

"I know, but what'll it do to your spirit? It just makes me wonder..."

"Matt, I don't understand. Don't you want to marry me?"

"More than anythin'! But I wanna play straight with you, that's all. Just like you can't put all your eggs in one basket, you can't put all your faith in one person. A person is liable to let you down."

Anna furrowed her brow in confusion. "So what are you saying?"

Matt looked at her and made up his mind. "Let's go talk to Pastor Cooley. It'll sound better comin' from him."

"Oh, I'm not sure, Matt..."

"He won't make you do nothin' you don't wanna do. He just has a way of talkin' to people. I'll stay with you the whole time. I promise."

Anna reluctantly agreed and they drove to the church. They made their way past the pews in the sanctuary and Matt knocked on the office door. When they entered, they found Pastor Cooley with his entirely bald head bent over a book, reading intently. Little had changed over the years concerning this bachelor preacher, except that he now had a mottled design of liver spots covering his hands and the top of his head.

"Come on in, children!" Pastor Cooley hopped up to remove books stacked on the two chairs facing his desk. "I heard the blissful news from your Momma, Matt! I reckon you've come in to talk about the wedding. I'm sure glad you're here, 'cause

I got some new ideas about my homily that I wanted to run past you…"

"Well, pastor," Matt interrupted. "We're not here to talk 'bout the wedding. We're actually wantin' some counsel on spiritual matters."

Anna's eyes were huge. She had no idea what would happen next. She almost crossed herself in the way the sisters at Saint Regina had taught her, but she thought better of it and kept her hands folded in her lap.

"What seems to be the trouble?" the pastor asked.

Matt cleared his throat. "Anna has had many trials and tribulations in her past and it's due to her past troubles that she can't quite find her footin' now. I brung her in for you to speak some comfortin' words over her."

Pastor Cooley wore a severe look of gravity. "Have you been studying the scriptures, Anna?"

Anna looked at Matt before speaking. She had been reading the Bible again, for the first time since her childhood. Burnetta had laid a worn copy of the New Testament on the bedside table of the tiny guest room where Anna slept. She had picked it up on her first night back in Morgan's Hat to help her sleep. Seven weeks later, she had read all four gospels, the book of Acts, and the letter to the Romans. "Yes sir," she squeaked out.

"That's good. That's real good. Has there been anything in it that has struck you in a particular way?"

"Well, I was reading in the book of Romans the other day…" she began. Pastor Cooley opened a Bible sitting on his desk to Romans and handed it to her. Anna thanked him and flipped through the pages until she found chapter eight. "Here…it says: 'For ye have not received the spirit of bondage again to fear; but ye have received the Spirit of adoption, whereby we cry, Abba, Father.'" Anna sat, looking at the words.

"And that passage held a special meaning for you, Anna?"

"Yes, sir."

"Why is that, do you think?"

"I suppose I can understand what a 'bondage to fear' is," she said, as Matt squeezed her hand.

"Is that so?" asked Pastor Cooley.

"Pastor, I have no parents. People in town don't know this, but I grew up an orphan, so when I read that I could..." she looked down to find the verse again and read: "'...receive the Spirit of adoption, whereby we cry, Abba, Father'...um, what does 'Abba' mean, pastor?"

"Well, it's kinda like saying 'daddy' I reckon," he answered. Anna tried to remember if she had ever said the word 'daddy' before. Pastor Cooley continued: "God's saying that when you become his son or daughter, you're given the Spirit and your sin won't condemn you."

"When I lived in the orphanage, no one talked about being adopted but it was on my mind every day. I didn't really know what it would be like, but I knew that having a family was something I was missing."

"We all want to belong to somebody, whether we admit it or not. The thing about belonging to God is that nothing can take it away. Read down a little further to verse thirty-eight and thirty-nine." Pastor Cooley quoted from memory: "'For I am persuaded, that neither death, nor life, nor angels, nor principalities, nor powers, nor things present, nor things to come, nor height, nor depth, nor any other creature, shall be able to separate us from the love of God, which is in Christ Jesus our Lord.'"

"Love like that, and grace and mercy. It just doesn't sound...well, possible," said Anna.

"That's why the song is called 'Amazing Grace' instead of 'Plain and Ordinary Grace,' Anna. There's gotta be something mighty amazing about it and the amazing part is that it's free. But you gotta stop holding on to that stinking, rotten sin. It's weighing you down. Set down that load and put your faith in Christ."

Anna considered this for a moment. "Matt said I'm putting all my faith in him, and he thinks that's wrong." Matt started to interrupt, but Anna waved him off. "I think maybe I understand now what he means."

"Jesus isn't gonna let you down, Anna. Now that doesn't mean he's always gonna do everything just like you want him to, but he promises us that he'll never leave us. In the book of Deuteronomy it says: 'For the Lord thy God, it is he that doth go with thee; he will not fail thee, nor forsake thee.' Do you believe that, Anna?"

"Yes. I want to. But how can I...really?"

"Look there in Romans again, verse 24. Read where it says 'For we are saved by hope: but hope that is seen is not hope: for what a man seeth, why doth he yet hope for. But if we hope for that we see not, then we with patience wait for it.' Hope stands hand-in-hand with faith, Anna. And they're both just waiting at the front door of grace. They're all working together for our salvation."

"I want all of that, pastor."

"More than you want a husband or a family or a nice house in town?"

Anna searched her heart for the answer. She looked at Matt and said, "Yes."

"Then you're ready," said Pastor Cooley.

"Ready? For what?" she gulped.

"Ready to be buried with Christ in baptism..."

"Pastor," Matt said, "Maybe Anna should go on home and think it over."

"Think what over? You heard her confession, Matt. What did they tell the Apostle Paul after his sight was restored? They said, 'Why tarriest thou? Arise, and be baptized, and wash away thy sins, calling on the name of the Lord.'" Pastor Cooley's eyes were blazing. Nothing fired him up like lost souls and dunking new believers.

"No, Matt," Anna said meekly, patting his hand. "Pastor

Cooley's right." She turned back a few chapters in her Bible and read: "'Therefore we are buried with him by baptism into death: as Christ was raised up from the dead by the glory of the Father, even so we also should walk in newness of life.'" She turned to face Matt. "That's what I want."

"But, Pastor, it's October and it's turnin' chilly. Where will we do it?" Matt asked.

"The river's the best place to go," said Pastor Cooley. "Anna, you'll carry this day with you all your life."

They made plans with Pastor Cooley to have the baptism on the following day. They'd wait until early afternoon—the warmest time of the day, meeting at the church building before walking down to the river.

After supper, Matt and Anna discussed the next day's events as they drank coffee in Burnetta's kitchen.

"Momma's gonna wear me out if you get sick gettin' baptized in the river. Are you sure you wanna do it there? J.T. Fuller's got a big ole rain barrel on his farm where I'd bet the water would be warmer..."

"I'll be alright. And I know just where we'll go—that spot where it's deep in the middle but the bank is shallow...by that crooked tree."

"But that's where Clara..." Matt began.

"It'll be good for both of us—a new start."

"I reckon so," he said, looking down.

"You need to unload guilt about Clara and I need to stop worrying over everything I've done or had done to me." Anna's face held a confidence she'd never felt before. They sipped their coffee silently for several minutes, then Matt stood to leave.

"I'll see you in the morning, Anna." He bent down and kissed her hair.

Anna stood up and hugged him. As she buried her face in his chest, she said, "Thank you for taking me to see Pastor Cooley today."

"I'm glad it helped." He continued to hold her tightly.

Anna sighed. "Soon we won't have to say good night in your mother's kitchen."

Matt pulled her away to look at her face. "I believe findin' religion agrees with you, Anna. I never seen you look more pretty. Good night," he said, grudgingly, hating to leave her side.

"Good night, Matt." She raised herself up on tiptoes and kissed him. Then she watched him walk down the back porch steps and disappear into the cooling night.

Chapter 29

Pardon me, honey. I need a minute to blow my nose from all these tears. Thinkin' back on those olden times taxes my heart just a little. When you've lived as long as I have, there's just so many memories. Some are good memories and some are bad but I reckon there's a plan for it all. Take Anna gettin' baptized, for instance. She had to get to a mighty low point 'fore she could own up to the fact that she needed anything at all. I thought Momma was gonna blow a gasket when she heard what they was plannin' but it turned out to be a meaningful thing for all of us. After Anna come up outta the water, Momma and Matt covered her up with blankets and old quilts. Then Momma told Matt, "It's a blessed day, son." And she hugged him like I'd never seen her do before. It was like something painful between the two of them just melted away. It's too bad we have to get so low oft-times but there's some comfort in knowin' the pain is worth the prize. It's like havin' babies. After all that strugglin' it's worth it if you get a precious bundle of joy at the end. The day my youngest son was born, I thought I'd never get to the hospital in time. I had the twins and Dwayne with time to spare, but little Matty was itchin' to get out, I reckon. I just remember my Ronnie drivin' us to the hospital *early in the morning.* We passed a little church with one of them marquee signs. I still recall what it said: "First Corinthians 15:58. Fear not! Thy labor is not in vain." That was some comfort, I reckon. They knocked me out for my first babies, but I got there too late to get knocked out with Little Matty—that's what we called him 'til he was 'bout forty. They was wheelin' me into an elevator to get me to the delivery room, when he made his appearance in the world. It was an awful mess, but it was still kinda sweet. I wish you could've seen the look on the faces of the people tryin' to get on the elevator. Whoo-hoo!

MORGAN'S HAT, TENNESSEE
OCTOBER 31, 1941

"You can go in now, Matt," said Dr. Jameson as he rolled down his sleeves and walked out of the room. It had been a long night for everyone and the aging doctor looked ragged. Burnetta followed the doctor out, with tears trickling down her wrinkled cheeks. She stopped and looked at Matt. Then standing on tiptoes to reach her tall son, she kissed his cheek.

"I love you, Matt," she said as she squeezed his hand.

Matt paused before entering the bedroom he had shared with Anna for almost a year. It was a sacred place for him; a place where he could wholly cherish the woman he adored; a place where he first understood God's plan in creating man and woman; a place where he could lie close to his wife—face-to-face—holding right hands until they both fell asleep.

As he crossed the threshold, Anna held out her brand new baby girl for the happy father. He let out a long breath—without realizing he had been holding it—and rushed to the side of the bed.

"Isn't she beautiful, Matt?"

"She looks just like you, honey," Matt said as he kissed Anna on the lips. It was true. The tiny baby already had the beginings of a head full of curly, red hair. Anna handed her to Matt. The baby opened her gray-blue eyes and looked up at him with wonder.

"What'll we call her?" he asked. He spoke softly, without taking his eyes off his baby girl.

"Well, I was thinking about Genevieve but we could call her Genny, for short. I can't decide on a middle name, though."

Matt hummed to Genny as he carried her around their room. Anna lay back on the pillow, wishing she could freeze the three of them in this moment. To think that a year and a half ago she was mourning a lost husband and still living alone in Chicago, at her most miserable. She had been overwhelmed with guilt and overcome by life's pitfalls. Each day she had spent alone in the apartment she had shared with Ernest had seemed endless.

Then she had come back to Morgan's Hat and time had taken on a new pace—one that sped up her days, making her allotment of hours insufficient for all of her emotions and plans. Now watching Matt and their baby, Anna's heart couldn't contain the happiness she felt. In wonder, she asked, "Are we really supposed to be this happy?"

Matt was becoming accustomed to Anna's ability to read his thoughts, for he was thinking the same thing. "It's hard to believe that anyone in all of history was this blessed, but I reckon some man and some woman at some time was this full of joy. I feel like I oughtta be shinin' or somethin' just to give this feeling a place to vent." He ran a finger down baby Genny's forehead and the bridge of her nose, causing her to close her tiny eyelids. "In stories, there's most times a happy endin'. We're 'specially blessed that we get one in real life."

"I never knew this feeling could be possible...growing up like I did. Do you really think other people have felt it?" she asked.

"All through the ages there's been bliss like this, I reckon. Sometimes it lasts a short while due to some tragedy or dreadful circumstances..."

"Oh, Matt, don't say it like that..."

"Honey, I'm not tryin' to be discouragin'. God's timin' is always best. Most times, the pair'll get years and years to stretch out in it and soak it all up. I'm just grateful He gives us these happy times at all. I don't know—maybe He gives 'em to us so we'll know what heaven'll be like."

Anna tried to fight sleep. She just wanted to gaze at this perfect picture and listen to her wise husband's profound thoughts. Matt stood and began humming again as he walked around the room. After a moment, Anna realized what Matt was humming. It was one of his favorite hymns, the one he had chosen that night on the back porch when she had returned to Morgan's Hat. In a drowsy fog, she sang softly to herself: "O to grace, how great a debtor..." She smiled. "It's Grace," she said. "Let's call her Genny Grace Watson."

Chapter 30

Skunk Pelt Cove
1864

I'm mighty glad you had me sit here and say all these things in that there tape recorder today. When you called me up and said you wanted to know about your Grandma Genny and her people I was so pleased. I wasn't so sure I could recall much when we got started, but I done pretty well, wouldn't you say? Matt would've sat proud—him being the great storyteller of the family. He would've got all the details in the right order, though. I'm a-feared I been jumpin' all over God's time recountin' my youth. Of course, what I told you today has been just a drop in the bucket to all I seen and done. And it's nothing to the things I was never 'round to see. There was deep love and terrible loneliness happenin' when I was off doin' somethin' else, I 'spect. When you're young, you think the time you're livin' in is the most important time of all, but when you get older you see that everythin' works in a circle: getting' born, havin' babies, dyin'... it just keeps goin' round and round. I reckon that's why I like talkin' 'bout them old times. There's somethin' there that other folks can understand from their own lives. I also like hearin' other peoples' stories 'round here at the old folks' home and readin' old letters and newspapers. One of my favorites was a letter my daddy found out in a field near our house. It was in a leather sack at the root of a big ole walnut tree. The letter was yellow and torn up a bit, but you could make out most of the words. It was from a Union soldier to his gal back home, though I reckon it never got mailed. I think I got it here somewhere...ah, here we go. Read it for yourself.

September 7, 1864
Skunk Pelt Cove, Tennessee

Dear Miss Marie Tilden,

    I write these words to you by the light of a dim campfire, so I beg your indulgence of my ink spots. It seems I am always begging something of you and somehow you always yield to me. My mind wanders back to the last night I saw you in Columbus. Your dress was the exact shade of the lilacs you wore in your hair. As I recall, I begged a waltz of you that night and you, most generous of creatures, gave me three! I can speak no more of that night now. Seeing the dirty, hungry faces gathered round this fire and hearing the moaning of my suffering men, it seems that night was but a dream. And you were a vision of misty black curls and purple satin.

    We have staged raid after raid in this countryside and there is little food left for my men. At present, my unit is sheltered in a tiny town with the unfortunate name of Skunk Pelt Cove. Rumor has it that the townspeople will rename it after a fallen Reb who died east of here—a hotheaded general named Morgan. Well, any name would be better than Skunk Pelt Cove.

    I received your letters and have been cheered daily by them.

They stay in my sack with the pocket watch for your brother Randall.

I will find him, sweet Marie. His homecoming has consumed my every thought since you gave me your charge. Perhaps you envisioned yourself Guinevere handing down a quest to one of King Arthur's knights. (Yes, I did read Tennyson's Idylls of the King, as you requested.) And just as Tennyson described Arthur's knights, my men are equally hardy and valiant. If we must scale the walls of the prison in Selma, we will bring Randall home to Columbus. Randall is also most brave and heroic. He survived Shiloh; he can withstand the evils of prison life.

Randall will be so pleased with the watch you bought for him last spring. I know he will treasure it with the engraving of the deer and her fawn. How tranquil is the scene. I pray that we will all feel that tranquility again. And my greatest prayer is that you will find it in my arms. Dearest Marie, I beg of you once again, and this will be your most merciful indulgence to me on this earth: when I return, I plead for your hand. I now know what it is to be stripped of everything in this world—food, shelter, warmth—the one solace I have is you. You are better than I deserve, but all that I require. Be my wife. Be my breath. Be my life.

Yours with utmost affection and devotion,
Corporal James Bennington
United States Army

(If, by some unfortunate circumstance, I do not return, I am writing a note of explanation with the watch so that it will make it back to you. Whatever happens, do not sell it or in any way transfer its ownership to another. It is meant for Randall only. Hold it until you see him. Do not lose hope.)

Oh to Grace

Epilogue

Journey of a Pocket Watch

CREATIVE WRITING 101

NOVEMBER 15, 2012

We make insignificant decisions everyday: Stay for another cup of coffee or go ahead and leave for work? Liquid fabric softener or dryer sheets? Chicken salad or tuna? It may seem immaterial but sometimes the things that seem insignificant and irrelevant hold the greatest time-spent-deciding/weight-of-consequence ratio. We often toss and turn over life's biggest decisions but give little foresight to the small ones.

When I entered the Dogwood Meadows Nursing Home to interview my great-great aunt I assumed I would hear personally significant stories about her life with details about a few other family members and friends thrown in. Instead, she told me stories that directly and indirectly affected her. She told me about world wars and gang wars, famous singers and an ordinary man who repaired shoes.

One item that caught my attention was a gold pocket watch owned by her brother in the 1930's. After diligent research and creative detective skills, I have tracked down the tumultuous journey of the gold pocket watch in question. It changed hands so many times but the tale weaves an invisible thread through the lives of four families.

• Marie Tilden buys the watch in the spring of 1864. She asks James Bennington to give it to her brother Randall. It is returned to Marie at the end of the Civil War.

• Marie Tilden sells the watch to Schmidt's Pawn Shop December 18, 1916. Emma Simmons buys it that same day to give to her husband Thomas for Christmas.

• Thomas Simmons trades the watch for a pocketknife from Bo Dickson during World War One in 1919.

• Bo Dickson gives the watch to his son Harley just before he dies in 1925.

• Harley loses the watch during a Civil War re-enactment on July 13, 1926.

• George and Homer find the watch and give it to Ernest as a going-away present: March 30, 1931.

• Harley shoots Ernest after seeing him with the watch on July 14, 1939.

• The Watson family gives the watch to Harley after the murder trial. Harley enters Buford County Prison in 1940 and dies in 1949 at the age of forty-seven. Just before they close the lid on the coffin, Harley's son Bo Jr., slips the watch in the inside breast pocket of Harley's burial suit coat.

So often in my own life, I've wondered why things happen. I've questioned the bad circumstances and the good that might come of them. I've struggled with what I see as inconsistencies in the storyline that is my—or anyone else's—life. But mine is the perspective of youth. It is in old age that we can see the times that we were prodded or even shoved aside from catastrophe. Sitting with my aunt and hearing her stories of tragedy and triumph, I understand more fully what it is to rely on Forces greater than myself. I see a resignation in her to live a contented life. It is not of weakness that she resigns her will. It is of faith in a Power that rebukes and redirects but also yearns to show us grace unimaginable.

——— ABOUT THE AUTHOR OF ———

Oh to Grace

ABBY ROSSER is a former kindergarten teacher and mother of three living with her husband and kids in Murfreesboro, Tennessee. She enjoys writing on her blog—blessedintheboro.blogspot.com—and developing children's Bible curriculum for her congregation, North Boulevard Church of Christ.

    Considering that she is the daughter of a college professor and a school librarian, one would assume this collaboration would create offspring abounding in love for the written word. It did: her older sister, the English major. It wasn't until the birth of her twin daughters, when she was locked into a nursing schedule that would make a dairy cow put in her two-week's notice that she picked up reading. Eleven years later, she doesn't feel balanced unless there's a good book or two waiting for her on her bedside table. She hopes that OH TO GRACE will entertain its readers while conveying the blessings of living with an understanding of God's freely given grace.

FOR MORE GOOD READS,

VISIT WWW.WOMENINJOURNEY.COM.

CPSIA information can be obtained at www.ICGtesting.com
Printed in the USA
BVOW031314100613

322909BV00002B/15/P